T BELL

Letters of Faith

Parts of this book were originally published on Kindle Vella.

Cover: Ya'll That Graphic

First edition

This book was professionally typeset on Reedsy.
Find out more at reedsy.com

To Brynn for always being my sounding board—I think I owe you a hundred boxes of Kleenex at this point.

Contents

Chapter 1	1
Chapter 2	9
Chapter 3	14
Chapter 4	24
Chapter 5	32
Chapter 6	34
Chapter 7	41
Chapter 8	47
Chapter 9	57
Chapter 10	60
Chapter 11	69
Chapter 12	76
Chapter 13	82
Chapter 14	93
Chapter 15	101
Chapter 16	106
Chapter 17	108
Chapter 18	117
Chapter 19	127
Chapter 20	141
Chapter 21	147
Chapter 22	155
Chapter 23	161
Chapter 24	169

Chapter 25	171
Chapter 26	176
Chapter 27	182
Chapter 28	189
Chapter 29	197
Chapter 30	204
Chapter 31	210
Chapter 32	219
Chapter 33	226
Chapter 34	228
Chapter 35	235
Chapter 36	238
Epilogue	241
About the Author	244
Also by T Bell	245

Chapter 1

Georgia
14 Months Ago

My heart thunders in my ears. There's noise around me, but it's muffled like I'm underwater. Someone is trying to talk to me, but I can't focus on processing the words when five are already stuck in my brain, refusing to move.

"There's nothing we can do."

Those words keep bouncing around in my mind, inflicting pain each time they hit. I need to process them because once I do, we can devise a plan.

Yeah, that's what I need—a plan. A plan can fix anything because I refuse to accept that nothing is left. There has to be something. God works miracles all the time. He can do that here, too.

"I'm sorry, ma'am. There's nothing more we can do for your husband." The doctor's voice is raw, laden with the emotion he's trying to hold back. It's a good thing, too, because there isn't room for another person's breakdown here.

I'm losing my mind—that has to be what's happening. I've gone too many nights without sleep, and now I'm hallucinating, living my worst nightmare.

Looking up, I see the doctor's face filled with the same emotion as his voice, and I know I'm not hallucinating. This is my real-life nightmare.

Pity sparkles in his eyes as concern wrinkles his brow.

I can handle a lot of emotions, but pity and hopelessness are not two of them.

Fire burns through my veins.

I don't want his pity. I want him to help my husband. I want him to take away the cancer that's ravaging the fit and healthy man I love. I want a lot of things. I don't want pity. Pity is for those who have given up, and I refuse to give up. If this man won't help, I will find another doctor who will.

Nate is too good of a man to be gone from this world. He has to stay.

I *need* him to stay.

Sitting on the edge of the hospital bed, my hands shake as I pick up my phone, intent on finding another oncologist within this city…or country…or world, for that matter. This time, it will be someone who won't give up on us so easily.

Before my thumb can make it across my screen to unlock my phone, fragile fingers circle my wrist.

I stare at them a moment, remembering how they used to look so muscular and defined from years of physical labor. Now, the skin sags from radiation and chemotherapy. The bones beneath are visible, moving as the grip on my wrist tightens a little more and squeezes just enough that I know he is trying to comfort me.

Guilt hits me square in the chest.

I should be comforting him, not the other way around.

The pressure of his hand stays, and I know he wants me to look up. If I do, though, I will lose it. I'm barely holding on.

His hand travels down to my fingers, and a light tug is all it takes for me to relent. I drag my eyes up from his hands to his forearms and over his bicep, taking my time as I make my way up to his face. Every time I look at him now, I have to steel myself. Fear takes over whenever I see his sunken cheeks and the blackness beneath his eyes.

Nate's always been able to read me, but I don't want him to take on the burden of my fear.

I need him to focus on getting better.

One more inch and our eyes meet. The steely gray of his is enough to break me. They used to be so vibrant and full of life, but now they are dull and tired.

I lay my head on his chest, hiding the shimmer in my eyes from him, but he sees me. He wraps his arms around me and holds me when I should be holding him.

"Georgia, I'm tired."

The tears slip from my eyes, down my cheeks, and soak into his t-shirt, making it impossible to hide now. A sob croaks out of my throat—raw and unbidden.

I know what he's trying to tell me, but I can't accept it. I don't know how to live life without him. We had so many plans. We were going to buy a farm and start a family. He's only thirty. He can't leave me.

I don't understand what God's doing here. Why would he let me love this man and take him away?

"You...You can't...You can't leave me. Please don't leave me."

His coarse fingers run over the silk of my hair in tender strokes meant to soothe me. My breaths come in shallow gasps, a crushing weight on my chest. It's a pain that will be there long after he is gone.

"Georgia, I promise I will always be with you even after I close my eyes. I need you to promise me something, though." He pinches my chin and tilts it up so I'm looking at him again before he continues, "I need you to promise you won't be mad at God for this. I can't leave here knowing that will happen. So, I need you to promise me that no matter what, you won't think that this is a punishment for something you've done wrong. I know you, and I know that at some point, you will question that."

The air in the room is non-existent. My lungs squeeze as I try to drag in a breath. Nate is asking for something I'm not sure I can promise. Mainly because it already feels like a punishment.

My heart throbs with each beat, and the underside of my jaw goes numb. I have to get out of this room soon.

I thought I was having a stroke the first time my face went numb. It was the day I found out about Nate's cancer. I was at work when Nate called me. It was supposed to be a regular follow-up. It wasn't supposed to be this.

After I got the call, I hid in the bathroom stall while I cried. When my face started to go numb, I called my family doctor, and she examined me. She explained that it was a panic attack, not a stroke. They've happened often since then, but I've never let Nate see them. My poor husband has enough worries. I don't want this to be another one.

So, with a panic attack filling my chest with pressure, I do the only thing I can to escape—I lie.

"Okay, Nate. I promise. If that's what you need from me, I promise."

It's a promise I won't be able to keep in two months when my husband is gone, and burning anger eats at my soul, but it's one I make now to keep at least one thing easy for him.

Two hours later, all remnants of the panic attack are gone, and I'm walking back to Nate's room in the hospital—composed, ready to pretend I'm not breaking.

Earlier, the doctor said Nate would go home on hospice because there's nothing left for us to do except make him comfortable. We'll spend one more night here and go home tomorrow to face this.

The thought makes my throat ache.

I don't want to do this—none of it is fair.

Why Nate? Why the best man I know?

If I sit in those thoughts too long, though, I start to get angry—at the world and God—and that's not a place I can let myself go.

Standing outside the doorway of Nate's room, I steel my expression before stepping through the door. When I hear his voice floating through the room, I pause, staying behind the curtain separating the hospital bed from the door, adding an extra layer of privacy for families.

"I'm worried about her, Gray," Nate says, lowering his voice as if speaking those words aloud pains him.

They hurt me, too, because I thought I was doing a good job of hiding the weight on my shoulders, but I failed if he's calling Grayson instead of talking to me.

Grayson, Nate, and I met in elementary school, and there was a time in my life when I thought I would marry Grayson instead of Nate. We were ten the first time I noticed how handsome Grayson was. He was my first crush.

Then high school came, and I realized that Nate was the guy you relied on, the one who took you on dates and made you feel special, while Grayson was the kind of guy who broke your heart because he was broken himself.

Nate and I started dating my senior year of high school, and I never looked back. It was the best choice I ever made, and even if someone had told me then that I would be facing losing him ten years down the road, I would still choose this life with him again.

He must have Grayson on speaker because I hear his strong voice come across the phone and say, "She loves you, Nate, and she's worried about you. It's hard to think you have your whole life ahead with someone, only to be told you have months instead of years. Man—you're my best friend, and I'm not dealing with it well. She's your wife. Let her cope the way she needs to."

"It isn't coping when she refuses to face reality."

My stomach churns. Is that what Nate thinks I'm doing? Doesn't he realize I spend every day thinking about what comes after him—

planning ways to convince myself to keep breathing without him?

Reality is all I'm thinking about, but reality sucks.

"She has the town. They all love her. She won't have to go through this alone."

"Listen, I need to tell you something before—well, you know," Nate says.

Guilt eats at my stomach for listening—invading Nate's privacy. It's something he hasn't had a lot of in recent months. I step back to retreat out of the room but run straight into the nurse coming in to check vitals. She squeals as I squish at least three of her toes. I'm busy apologizing when I hear Nate tell Grayson he will call him back later, and then he's calling my name.

With heat flooding my cheeks and the nurse beside me, I pull the curtain back for my husband to see me.

There's a grin on his face—just like there always is when he looks at me. I want to bottle the memory of that smile up and keep it forever so I never lose it. That's what I'm afraid of the most—forgetting things about him. What if I wake up one day and forget how he smells or how it feels when his lips press against mine?

Placing my hands behind my back, I try not to look guilty.

"Where have you been?" Nate asks as the nurse pokes around him, checking his blood pressure and listening to his lungs.

"I needed some air, so I went for a walk outside of the hospital."

His smile drops, and he lowers his brows, glowering at me—it's a new look for him. "Georgia—you've got to have some self-preservation. This isn't Middle Creek, where you can wander at all times of night, and no one will look twice at you. I can't come to your rescue right now—and that kills me—so can you just use some common sense here?"

My head jerks back as if he slapped me. Nate has never talked to me that way. Even when we've argued, he's always been the calm to my storm, but this is anything but calm. His jaw is clenched, and when I look up at his eyes, there's life there in the form of anger.

I step aside as the nurse speeds out of the room, quick to no longer be a part of this conversation. My bottom lip trembles, but I tuck it between my teeth, refusing to let him see it.

"Nate," I start, but my voice wavers, a mixture of anger and sadness. I clear my throat and try again. "I heard you talk to Grayson, and I know you think you have to worry about me, but you don't. I'm fine."

The lie is bitter on my tongue because I'm the furthest thing from fine, but, like he always has, Nate sees right through me.

A heavy sigh leaves my husband's chest, then he scoots over in his bed and pulls the blankets back.

"Come here, Georgia," he says, crooking his finger and calling me to him.

My stubborn streak is tempted to hold out for a second just for spite. Then I remember that we are living on borrowed time, and it has me rushing over to crawl under the blanket with him—needing to memorize how it feels to have his chest pressed against my back and his arms wrapped around me.

His hands smooth down the length of my hair, and I close my eyes, cataloging this moment.

"You don't have to lie to me, pretty girl," Nate whispers against my head, "You're not fine, and I know that because if the situation were reversed, I wouldn't be fine either. You're going to have to let it out sooner or later."

Shaking my head, I squeeze my eyes tighter.

Denial—that's the first stage, right?

"When I'm gone—"

"Don't—don't say that," I interrupt.

"Listen to me," he says, tugging my shoulder until I turn so that I'm facing him.

There was a time when he would have simply lifted me, but these days, he can hardly walk alone, let alone pull me to him.

When I'm facing him, and we are chest to chest, he begins again, "When I'm gone, I want you to keep living. You're not dying with me—even if it might feel like it for a while."

"You're asking for a lot today," I say, burying my head into his chest.

He drops a kiss on my forehead, his lips paper dry against my skin. "I know I am—but you can do it, Georgia. Life will go on even when I'm gone. Don't be afraid to live that life."

"I am afraid."

It's the first time I've admitted it aloud. I had hoped by doing so, some of the weight would finally lift off my chest, but it's still there, digging in and making it hard to breathe.

"It's okay to be afraid, pretty girl. I'm afraid, too, but you have people on your side. Let them in, okay?"

"Any other requests?" I ask, sarcasm oozing out of my voice.

Nate chuckles, shooting me a grin that makes my heart flutter. "Maybe, but I can't tell you about them yet."

A smile creeps onto my face for the first time all day, and I pat my hand against his chest. "Just make this one easy, okay?"

Nate's grin is sneaky as he says, "Love is always easy."

Chapter 2

Georgia
12 Months Ago

The phone in my hand rings once, twice, maybe more—I've lost count.

There are people in front of me, all vying for my attention, needing me to make decisions, but I can't—not without him. Why can't they all leave me alone? Shouldn't my heartbreak warrant me some semblance of privacy?

It wasn't supposed to be this way. I shouldn't have to do this.

Over the last year, people kept telling me to have a little faith—everything would work out if I had a little faith—and I did, but what about now? What do I do now?

I want to rage and scream and throw things—demand someone, anyone, fix this, but I can't because I'm supposed to be the strong one—the one that people are looking at to hold myself together.

Strong.

I hate that word. I don't want to be strong. I want to lay in bed and not move until I can breathe again because right now, there's a crushing weight sitting on my shoulders that I'm going to crumble under. What I don't want to do is make this phone call.

"Hello." The voice comes across the phone, gruff and familiar, and I'm grasping onto that familiarity with both hands, like a lifeline pulling me back from the sea, even as I protest at the idea of having to say it—to be the one to tell him.

A sob wracks my shoulders as I open my mouth to say the words.

Two words.

That's all I need to say before someone else can shoulder this burden with me, but once those words are out, there's no taking them back.

It will be real, and I'll break someone else with them.

I can't—I can't do this.

"Georgia, are you there?"

I'm paralyzed. My mouth disconnected from the part of my brain that tells it to speak.

Tears run down my neck, soaking into my shirt. I need a breath—one breath, and then I'll be able to say it. I try sitting up straighter to pull air deep into my lungs, but nothing happens.

I try again, a squeak slipping out between my lips, but the air still won't reach my lungs. Black dots swim in front of my eyes, and fear starts to replace the paralysis. My fingers ache from clutching the phone to my ear, but I might throw it against the wall if I don't.

A man's voice calls my name over and over again from the phone, begging me to respond.

Someone needs to take the phone from me and just tell him.

Can they not see me struggling?

The person on the other line is yelling now, but I don't care. I'm past the point of caring because all I can think about is how I lied to my husband.

He asked too much.

I can't keep the promise he asked me to because I can't even make a stupid phone call. How am I supposed to not be angry when that feeling claws at my chest, ready to burst out?

Anger replaces the fear, and enough air enters my lungs for my vision to clear just a little.

Nurses look back at me, concern flicking across their faces, but I ignore them, turning my full attention to the man who is now frantically yelling at me.

I need him to stop. I need this all to stop.

"He's gone."

The words are out, ripping from my throat and delivering a punch to my sternum, taking all the air I had left.

As the edges of my vision fade to black, I hear Grayson say, "I'm coming, Georgia. I'm coming."

"Georgia, we need you to make a decision," the funeral director says kindly.

That's all I've been doing—making decisions. What should he wear? What flowers for the coffin? Speaking of—is this coffin okay? Nate wanted to talk about these decisions before he passed, but I couldn't stand the thought of it. We put it off, always waiting for a better time, and now I'm out of time.

Question after question—thrown at me so fast that it makes my head spin, and that's not even the worst part. No, the worst part is that I have to consider everyone's opinion when deciding.

Nate was loved—is still loved—and because of that, people have opinions, but I can't please everyone, specifically his younger sister. I've never been able to please her.

If I like pink, she likes purple. If I say yes, she says no.

Right now, just once, I wish we could be on the same page.

"What am I deciding again?" I ask.

Harper's laugh is sardonic as she crosses her arms across her chest and rolls her eyes to the ceiling.

I've been in a haze since Nate died—unable to concentrate on anything, and her attitude doesn't help. I want to lie in bed, curl into a ball, and cry, not put up with her snarky remarks. Losing my temper won't benefit anyone, though, and she's hurting just as much as I am. We're just dealing with it in different ways.

She's mean, and I'm—checked out.

Grayson, who is sitting beside me, narrows his eyes at Harper, and I give a subtle shake of my head. He hasn't left my side since I called him with the news. He's slept on the couch at my house every night, sending my mom and dad home to rest until they return the next morning. Everyone's waiting for me to break, and the truth is, I am too.

The funeral director looks between Harper and me, his eyes tightening as he tries to navigate the awkwardness.

"You—uh—I mean, we were deciding the speakers for the visitation and burial," he says, eyes continuing to bounce between us.

Harper's husband, Cole, sits beside her, arms crossed over his chest, looking angry at the world. Though, I'm not sure what he has to be angry at. He and Nate weren't even close. Nate expressed his opinion of the man many times to Harper before they got married, and none of what he had to say was good. It's likely that Cole's angry that he has to be here in the first place—despite the fact that his wife's brother just passed away. He's not a fan of anything that puts him out.

Nate's mom sits on the other side of Cole, but unlike her daughter, she has no opinions.

I lean forward so I can speak to her. She's staring at the wall directly in front of her, her face blank.

"Ellie," I say, calling her attention to me. "Who do you think should speak?"

I love Ellie, and while Nate was my husband, he was her son first.

"We should ask Coach Jones. He's always said Nate was his favorite player," Harper pipes up.

I see the muscle in Grayson's jaw tick out of the corner of my eye.

"She didn't ask you, Harper," he says through clenched teeth. "She asked your mom."

If Harper dislikes me, she despises Grayson for reasons I can't comprehend. The two are more alike than they like to think. Nate and Harper's dad left when they were in high school. Nate was quiet about it. He dealt with it and moved on, but Harper was like Grayson. She held on to that pain, letting it fester. The difference is Harper didn't let anyone in, while Grayson had me and Nate. Nate tried to be there for Harper, too, but she was too lost in her anger.

"Why are you even here, Grayson," Harper throws back. "It's not like you're family."

Wincing, I turn to Grayson, ready to throw myself between them if he decides to throttle her, but when my eyes land on him, he's stone-cold, hands clenched in his lap. The only inclination that he heard her is the way his icy blue eyes narrow by just a hair.

I turn back to Harper and hear Grayson say, "Say what you will, Harper. I'm here for Georgia."

"I bet you are," Harper coughs under her breath.

"Enough," Ellie's voice bounces off the walls, ricocheting until they hit their intended targets.

In all the years I've known her, I've never heard Ellie raise her voice. I squeeze the tissue in my hand, my veneer cracking. We haven't even made it to the funeral yet. How will we survive that if we can't handle planning it?

"Georgia," Ellie says, her voice calmer now. "The speaker seems like it's important to Harper. Can we let her decide this one?"

"Yeah, Ellie. That's fine."

When I answer, I avoid Grayson's eyes. I know what I'll find there—disappointment.

Chapter 3

Grayson

12 months ago

Spots swim in front of my eyes as I step out of the dimly lit church. The tie around my neck is suffocating, and it's only marginally better when I pull at the knot pushing into my Adam's apple. Unbuttoning the cuffs of my sleeves, I roll the material over my forearms, revealing the tattoos that wrap around them. A fresh one stings at the base of my wrist where my shirt has rubbed over it the past two hours. It's an orchid, small and unnoticeable—a promise. Compared to the others surrounding it, it's feminine but fitting all the same.

Taking the steps two at a time, I descend into the crowd of people milling about in the parking lot—neighbors talking among neighbors—but as I walk through them, their voices become hushed, eyes turning judgmental.

I don't lower my eyes, making direct eye contact with each person I pass. If the townspeople had their way, they would have run me out years ago, specifically when I was a teenage menace, drinking too much for my own good and wreaking havoc. But I'm not that kid anymore, and I'm not easily pushed around. It's what makes me a good businessman, and my business has brought them a lot of job opportunities over the last couple of years—not that they will ever acknowledge that. They can ask me for donations for their kid's softball team, but heaven forbid they appreciate the boost in the local economy.

The feeling is mutual, though. I despise this town, yet I willingly choose to be here for two reasons—and two reasons only. Well, one reason now, I guess.

Pain stabs my gut as I let my eyes wander, searching for the sole reason I will continue to stay. After several seconds, I find her standing at the edge of the parking lot, politely smiling and greeting people as they walk by her.

Georgia, the town's sweetheart, their darling girl, and my best friend's wife is putting on a brave face so no one worries, but just one glance should tell these intentionally blind idiots that she's hurting underneath that polite smile.

Her eyes land on me, and a plea for help burns in those green irises.

For one minute, I pause, considering the weight of the letter burning a hole in my pocket—a letter that, if anything, will only add to her heartache today. Guilt eats at my insides when I think about what it means for me—for Georgia—but now's not the time to think about it. I place my guilt back in the nicely wrapped box it came from, intending to leave it there forever.

Dropping my shoulder, I push through the people waiting to talk to Georgia, not bothering to apologize or listen to the protests behind my back.

When she called to tell me Nate was gone, I was sad—of course, I was sad. The man was my best friend, my only friend, but my sadness was overpowered by the fact that the strongest woman I knew was breaking—and if she broke, so would I.

I promised myself that day I would do anything to protect her—even if it meant protecting her from herself.

Georgia is a perpetual people pleaser, and I can see that coming out in her today. She refuses to tell anyone she needs space because she doesn't want to hurt their feelings. Standing by the coffin before the service, she flinched whenever someone touched her. It took everything I had not to intervene—it wasn't the time. She needed to feel like she was giving to someone else so she wouldn't fall apart—but now it's time she let it happen.

Stepping in front of her, I block the path of the crowd that continues to smother her and place my hands on either side of her face, lifting it so she's looking at me. I notice Harper shaking her head out of the corner of my eye. Her husband stands by her side, glaring at everyone around him. I ignore them both. Harper has a lot of opinions, but none that matter to me.

"What do you need me to do?" I ask. My voice is low, so no one else can hear. I might not be afraid of offending the people here, but Georgia is. She hates upsetting anyone—hates confrontation—but if she needs me to take the fall and get her out of here, I will because she deserves as much peace as she can get today.

"I'm fine," she says, but it's a lie. Her breathing is becoming shallow, and I know if I don't get her out of here soon, we will have a repeat of what happened a week ago.

"You're not. You don't have to pretend with me. I'm not one of them," I say, jerking my head to the people behind us.

She starts to protest, reaching to push my hands off her face, but instead, her fingernails dig into my skin, holding on for dear life as her breathing quickens.

That alone makes my decision for me.

I gently pull my hands away from her face and grab both her hands in one of mine. Then I turn so she's behind me—hidden from all the vultures who can't seem to understand that this is not how she needs to grieve. Lowering my eyebrows, I glare—making eye contact with each of them until a chorus of "hmphs" resounds through the crowd, but I'm not here to be liked.

I'm here for Georgia.

"That will be all," I say, my voice low and menacing—leaving no room for argument.

I don't wait for them to respond to my threat. With Georgia's hand still in mine, I pull her along so that she stays behind me, away from the crowd, and when we reach my truck, I open the door, pull her in front of me, and lift her by her waist into the passenger seat. Tears swim in her eyes, waiting to spill over her long eyelashes as her chin wobbles.

"Let it out, Georgia," I say, my thumb rubbing gently across her wrist. "You don't have to be strong—not today."

As the tears start falling onto her cheeks, her emerald eyes lift so I can see all the pain she's hidden over the last year. It's enough to bring me to my knees.

"Thank you," she whispers, and those two words finally drive home the trouble I'm in.

The road in front of Georgia and Nate's house is packed with cars. I let out a curse that has Georgia throwing me a glare. It's a sign of life, and I'm tempted to let another drop just to see it again.

"Do you want to decide what to do, or do you want me to?" I ask, throwing her another glance.

She looks so small in the front seat of my truck, her black dress swallowing her frame. She's lost weight in the two months since she found out that Nate was terminal. Dark circles line the undersides of her eyes, making her look sick.

"I should probably go in since everyone is here," she says, avoiding eye contact.

Slamming on my breaks, we stop in the middle of the subdivision road.

"Georgia," I say, leaving one hand on the steering wheel and the other gripping the center console. "I didn't ask what you think those people expect you to do. I asked what *you* wanted to do. You don't owe anybody anything. I know it's not in your nature, but today, it's okay for you to be selfish."

Her brows knit together as if she can't fathom the thought, and the truth is, she probably can't. "They're waiting on me. It would be rude not to show up. Besides, where would I go?"

My knuckles are starting to turn white on the steering wheel. Everything in me is screaming at me to pull my truck into her driveway and kick every one of these overbearing busybodies out, but I won't, at least not until she tells me that's what she needs.

"Let's pretend it wouldn't be rude to leave. Would you want to stay then?" I ask.

"No," she whispers.

"Why not?" I prompt.

She's folding the hem of her dress between her hands over and over again, worrying it and creating wrinkles. Her eyes stay on her hands as she says, "It hurts to be in that house."

It's answer enough for me.

Throwing my truck in reverse, I place my hand on the back of her headrest as I watch behind me, avoiding cars until I can turn around.

"What are you doing?"

Coming to a stop in a driveway down the street, I turn back around and throw the gearshift into drive.

"I'm doing what you asked."

She looks at me, confused. "I just said that I wanted to go in there."

"No. You said that you should probably go in there. Then we played pretend, and you said it hurts you—so I made an executive decision."

"An executive decision," she questions.

"Yeah. We're leaving."

"And going where?"

"My house."

Her mouth falls open, and she stares at me, bewildered. Color fills her cheeks for the first time in months. Before he died, I went to visit Nate every day, and each time, I would find the same picture when I walked in—Nate asleep in the hospital bed they had brought into the living room and Georgia sitting beside him, watching him as if he might take his last breath if she looked away. Loving Nate through his death took a toll on her.

"Grayson," she chides.

"Georgia."

"We have to go back."

I shake my head. "We don't have to do anything. Besides, I need to talk to you about something—alone."

This piques her interest, and she finally lets go of the hem of her dress, turning her body towards me.

"About what?" She eyes me warily. The woman has been dealt a bad hand here lately, and I don't blame her for being suspicious.

"Your plans now that—well, you know."

"Didn't you just tell me I didn't have to make any decisions?" she asks, anger lacing her voice. "I don't know, Grayson. I don't know what I'm doing because all I can think about is that my husband is no longer here. How am I supposed to make any decisions when that's all I can think about?"

She's worked herself up to where she's practically yelling. Sadness shutters over her eyes. When I brought it up, I knew this would be a topic she wouldn't want to discuss, and she's right—she shouldn't have to make any big decisions right now. But eventually, she will have to, and when that time comes, I want to make sure she's taken care of. Nate was my best friend, and I owe it to him to take care of his girl.

I've never been one to talk about feelings or share my emotions—life never cared if I was sad, but I'm trying for Georgia—for Nate. So that's why I say, "Look, you don't have to make any decisions yet, and I know how you're going to react to this—but before you react, hear me out, okay?"

"No." Her answer is firm, immovable, like a brick wall, but she doesn't realize I learned to be a wrecking ball a long time ago.

"You haven't heard the question yet," I say.

"I don't need to. I know you. You're going to offer to take care of something that isn't your place to take care of. It's what you've always done—for both Nate and me—and while I love you for it, I can't let you."

Love me—I'm a traitor for how those words make the hairs on my neck stand up. There was a time, before she was Nate's girl, when I thought one day I would deserve a girl like Georgia, but then I realized that girls like her are always meant to end up with men like Nate. So—I stepped aside and cheered my best friend on as he got his girl.

"Then you should also know that I'm not one to give up easily," I deadpan. "Anyway, this would be as much for you as it would be for me."

"How so?" she asks, wary once again.

"As you know, I'm not much of a people person—" I start.

Georgia coughs, "Understatement."

Shooting her a look, I shake my head. It's another sign of life.

"As I was saying, I'm not much of a people person, and my assistant retired last month. I haven't gotten around to interviewing anyone. I don't know what your plans are for going back to work, but maybe you could take the job and save me the hassle. It doesn't have to be permanent—just until you're ready to find something else."

I don't look at her, afraid she will see right through me if I do. The moment stretches to a minute, the silence stomping on each one of my nerves.

"I don't know, Gray."

"Today has been a lot for you, and I wasn't planning on throwing this at you. Take your time. I don't need an answer right away. You and Nate are two of my best friends. This isn't a pity offer. This is me wanting to help my friend. Plus, I may not be a people person, but I'm not as grumpy with you. Working with someone who doesn't constantly get on my nerves would be nice."

A smile wavers on her lips—brief, and then it's gone—but it was a smile all the same.

"How do you know I won't get on your nerves? Nate says I'm a handful. Said—Nate said."

The mood, while not exactly happy before, plummets into despair.

"It's okay, Georgia Peach. You won't get on my nerves, but I promise I'll continue to remind you how much of a handful you are," I say, throwing her a sad smile.

She doesn't answer, but she doesn't have to because I'm telling her the truth. I'll make sure that all the good parts of Nate live on in her memory.

My house comes into view as I take the curve that leads to my driveway. When I bought the place, it was a dump. I converted the detached garage into an apartment until I could fix the main house. It took me several years, but it was worth it. It's the first house I've ever lived in that I didn't have to worry about mice crawling across me at night or food being overrun with roaches. My mom tried—she really did—but she was a single mom, raising a kid that didn't give her a lot of breaks. I was angry—at her and the world—and made a lot of bad decisions. Nate and Georgia were my saving grace. They will never know just how much they saved me. I owe them everything. It's why, when I tell Georgia that offering her this job is doing me a favor, I'm telling her the truth. It's a way for me to save her like she did me.

"Stay tight," I say, opening my truck door and stepping out.

I round the front of the truck until I'm standing on her side and opening the door. Placing my hand out, she takes it, and I help her out of the truck.

"Main house or the guest house?" I ask.

"I think I just need to sleep," she says.

I nod, close the door, and place my hand on her lower back, guiding her to the detached garage. Unlocking it, I switch on the light switch as we walk in. It's a bachelor pad—there's no denying that, but right now, it's a place where Georgia won't be bombarded with nosy well-doers.

As I flip on the rest of the lights, she walks over to the kitchen and grabs a water bottle out of the refrigerator. Sometimes, I have business meetings in the office here, so my assistant always keeps it clean and stocked. I turn my back to her to flip on the heat to take some of the chill out of the air. Fall is slipping into winter, so we still have bitter days to come.

When I turn back, she's standing in front of the counter, staring into the living room. Her eyes are vacant—void of emotion—as if she's bottled them up so much the last few months that they finally combusted and left her empty.

"Georgia," I say, approaching her slowly, not wanting to spook her.

Her eyes turn to me and find mine, and the emptiness there is soul-shattering. She's lost, and I don't know how to help her find her way because I'm lost with her.

"Why, Gray? Why did God need Nate? Why my husband?"

"I don't know, Georgia, I can't answer that. I wish I could. I wish I could take his place so you could still have him here, but I can't."

"I'm so angry. It's like a fire burning through my veins and leaving bitterness behind in its ashes. I want it to stop. I just want it all to stop."

One more step, and I'm standing next to her. I open my arms, letting her fall into them. Her small frame shutters as sobs overtake her. It's another crack in a piece of my soul that is long past healing.

"I know Georgia. I know," I say, stroking her hair. It's the only comfort I can offer her because nothing I say will bring Nate back.

We stand there, letting the minutes fade into some infinite number. Until her sobs begin to fade, and all that's left is exhaustion.

"Let's get you to bed, okay?" I prod.

She doesn't put up a fight, merely nodding and closing her eyes. Fatigue drags her long lashes against her ivory skin, causing them to open slowly. Her body sags against me, and without warning, I'm lifting her in my arms and carrying her to the single bedroom.

I'll sleep on the couch so she isn't alone tonight. Maybe in a few weeks—or months—she'll be okay, and I'll be able to go to my own bed. Until that day, though, wherever she is, I am too—keeping a promise I made to a man that I owe my life to.

As I place her on the bed, her sobs start to subside, her breathing evening out. Before she's asleep, I need her to know one more thing.

"Georgia," I whisper her name.

"Hmm?" she hums.

"No one is forcing you to go back home. You have to find a way to heal, and if you can't do that at your house right now, then it's something you face later. Don't force it all at once. Stay as long as you want, okay?"

She doesn't respond, her consciousness long overtaken by sleep. Sighing, I run my calloused hands over her hair, careful not to wake her. The tattoos on my knuckles are a juxtaposition to the softness of her features, once again reminding me that the girl I've loved half my life was always supposed to be with someone better.

Chapter 4

Georgia
Present Day

Three hundred and sixty-five days.

That's how long it's been since I've heard my husband's voice—felt his hand in my hand. Somehow, I've managed to keep breathing—filling my lungs with air—but the days bleed together, monotonous.

Grayson told me to take the day off, but I couldn't. I didn't want to be alone—not today.

The phone rings for the hundredth time this morning, slicing into my thoughts.

"G.L. Inspection. This is Georgia. How may I help you?"

"Georgia, it's your mother."

I roll my eyes, thankful she can't see me. She acts like I haven't been avoiding her, and the rest of the town for that matter, all day. They mean well, but I'm stuck under their microscope as they all wait for me to break.

"Hi, Mom," I say, controlling my tone to hide the irritation.

"Darling, I've been calling you all morning."

"It's been a busy morning." I hate lying to her. She's a good mom—just smothering and blunt. I've been dreading this day for weeks, partly because with each day that passes, I seem to lose another memory of

Nate—the way he smelled, the timbre of his voice—but also because I knew it wouldn't pass without phone calls and visits from the entire town. Their intentions are good—they have been since Nate died—but they all have advice for something they haven't experienced. I've taken that advice and smiled each time it was offered, but today, I can't. Instead, I've avoided them.

"You work too hard. You really should slow down."

"I'm fine, Mom. Did you need something?"

The door to my right opens as I wait for my mom to respond. Grayson steps out, dressed immaculately in a suit and handsome as ever—impartially speaking, of course. With a clean-cut beard accentuating the line of his jaw and blue eyes that stare into a girl's soul, the man could have any girl he wanted.

He walks towards me, pulling on the edges of his sleeve. Tattoos peek out from below his cuff link, and one, in particular, draws my attention—the orchid he got the week after Nate died. Each of his tattoos has a story—a reason behind why he got it. Whenever he would get a new one, he would regale Nate and me with the story behind it, but he refuses to tell me anything about this one. At first, I was worried it was because Nate was the buffer for our friendship, and with him gone, Grayson would slip away, too. But a year later, Grayson's still around, and our friendship has changed—grown. I just wish it hadn't taken Nate dying for it to happen.

"Georgia, are you listening to me?" Mom says, pulling my attention back to her.

"Sorry. What were you saying?" I ask.

"I'm worried about you. Nate wouldn't want this for you. He would want you to live."

I shake my head, knowing that she can't see me. Grayson, now standing beside me, arches a brow in silent question. His presence is distracting, pulling my attention away from everything else until he's all I can focus on. I've chalked it up to the fact that we've been each other's stronghold the last year, making us in tune.

"I am living, Mom."

"No, honey, you aren't. When you aren't at work, you're at home—and not even your own home. You haven't gone back. You've been staying in Grayson's guest house, and while I'm thankful he has been there for you, you're hiding behind him so you don't have to face your reality."

An audible gasp slips past my lips, drawing Grayson's brow higher. Anger burrows deep inside my chest. She doesn't know what it feels like to have the other half of your heart buried in the ground.

"I'm trying—surviving the only way I know how."

Her sigh sends static through the phone. I pull it away from my face, just enough that it doesn't crackle in my ear.

"I know you are. Maybe you can start with small steps. There's a function at the church this weekend. You haven't been for a while—"

Blinking, I bite my lip so I don't tell her that it is intentional—that I feel like God let me down. I try to keep the angry tears at bay, but a single one slips out. I dash it away with the back of my hand, hoping that Grayson doesn't see.

When I glance his way, though, I know he has.

He's become protective since Nate died, and I've let him because he's the only person who really understands what it feels like. Nate was his best friend, too—the other half of his soul. It's hard for Grayson to let people in, but he let Nate and me in. I've clung to his strength this past year, but that's only part of the truth. I've been afraid that with Nate gone, Grayson would lose the man he's fought hard to become. He did okay for a while, but then he found out about his dad and brother a few months back. Kip, his dad, had come around claiming that he never knew about Grayson, which was like a shot in the heart for Gray. His mom had died a few years back, and I know he wonders why she never told him. Gray loved his mom, but their relationship was tough. She was a single mom trying to take care of her kid, and he was a rough teenager with a mom who was always busy and a dad who was not around. He will never admit it, but I think he wonders if it would be different if he had known. Plus, when Kip crashed into Grayson's life, so did his brother, Brooks. I had hoped that maybe a relationship would bloom between them, but then Kip asked Grayson to give Brooks a job. We didn't talk about it, but I was angry for him. This new family didn't want to get to know Grayson, one of the greatest men I know. They wanted something that would benefit them.

Gray hasn't told me what happened in the interview with Brooks, but I can see him slipping, slowly losing control of his anger he's worked hard to keep in check.

Grayson's eyes bore into the side of my face, and for both our sake, I need to get off the phone with my mom.

"I'll think about it, Mom—that's all I can promise you."

There's a beat of silence, and then she says, "I guess that's all I can ask for. Take care of yourself today, honey."

Hanging up, I turn to face Grayson.

"Well—that went as expected," I say, trying to lighten the mood.

His features remain stern as he takes me in, looking for a chink in the armor I've put on today. I steel my spine under his scrutiny.

"How are you *really* doing today, Peach?"

A small smile slips onto my lips. Grayson's always called me that. When I asked him about it in middle school, he said it was because I was as sweet as his mom's peach cobbler. This was around the time my crush was at an all-time high, so my heart nearly beat out of my preteen chest because I felt like he saw me. Then, the next week, I saw him holding hands with Molly Jenkins. She was the cheer captain—the type of girl that fit Grayson—and I was a book nerd. It was then I decided it was best for Grayson and me to be friends, realizing he would never see me that way. When Nate asked me out in high school, I was glad I never told Grayson how I felt. Nate was the guy for me—we made sense because while he was popular and played football just like Grayson, he was safe, and I thrived in safe.

"I'm as okay as I can be. I needed to be here today. I'm going to visit him after work."

He nods, still studying me.

"Do you want company?"

Guilt prickles my stomach because I know he misses Nate too, but I need a minute alone with my husband.

"I kind of need to do this alone. I hope that's okay."

"Of course, it's okay. You don't have to ask for my permission."

Shrugging, I say, "I know, but I don't want you to think I'm ungrateful for everything you've done for me this year."

A rumble emanates from his chest. He takes one long stride forward, and then he's spinning my chair so I'm facing him. Kneeling in front of me, he rests his calloused hands against my legs, the heat searing through my dress pants and making it a little hard to focus.

"Georgia, never—and I do mean never—feel bad for taking the things you need, not with me."

My eyes track his as he studies my face, waiting for what he said to sink in. There's a thundering in my ears that I don't understand. I wheel my chair back so I'm just out of reach, putting space between us so I can think. Lately, my emotions are a jumbled mess when I'm around Grayson. When he's around, my heart doesn't hurt as much, and then when he's gone, guilt eats at the pit of my stomach because those fleeting moments when it doesn't hurt feel like a betrayal to Nate.

"Thanks, Gray. You're a good friend," I say, a reminder to myself of the roles we play in each other's lives.

The corner of his lip tips up. It's not a smile but an acquisition—an acceptance of what I'm not sure. Then he's standing and backing away. When he reaches his door, he pauses one last time before shaking his head and disappearing into his office.

The drive from Grayson's office to the cemetery takes fifteen minutes, but today, it might as well take hours. I usually come out here every Saturday to refresh the flowers and sit awhile, but today hurts a little more than all the others.

Maybe it's self-induced guilt because I haven't stuck to the promises I made Nate—or perhaps it's because I can't quit picturing how Grayson looked betrayed, just for a moment, when I told him I needed to come here alone.

The panic attacks have slowed down. The doctors prescribed me medication after Nate died. Things got dark for a while, but then Grayson stepped in and made me go to the doctor. The medicine helps, but sometimes, when I'm stressed, like today, that feeling of hopelessness starts to creep in, causing anxiety to weigh on my chest. I've come to accept that some days will be better than others.

Pulling the keys from my ignition, I grab the flowers from my seat. Nate would think they are girly. He'd want me to bring something more manly—like rocks or sticks, but the groundskeepers would throw a fit. So—flowers it is.

Nate's plot is halfway down a long row, and while I walk, I work on the breathing technique my therapist taught me.

One breath in—four seconds.

Hold—seven seconds.

Breathe out—eight seconds.

I repeat the process until my heart rate starts to slow, and then I'm standing in front of Nate's grave.

Falling to my knees, I remove the flowers from last week and replace them with new ones.

"Hi, Nate. Long time no see."

The dark humor slips out before I can stop it, and I look around to make sure no one is around. It's how I cope, but if anyone heard it, they would think I'm more unhinged than they already do.

"Sorry, I know you're probably rolling your eyes right now at that lame attempt at a joke. I just—I miss you, that's all."

The breeze blows through my hair, and I imagine that's Nate's way of responding to me—telling me he's here, listening. The cold air fills my lungs, and I breathe it in, savoring the smell of the start of winter. It reminds me that I'm still alive—still here breathing, even if that's felt impossible most days.

The first few times I came out here, I sat in silence, unsure of what I was supposed to be doing. Then, when I started to go to therapy, she suggested that I talk to Nate. I thought she was crazy at first, but strangely, it wasn't as hard as I thought. Now I come out here and tell him about my life—the good and bad—and in a way, it's like he still gets to be a part of it.

"I wonder if you would be disappointed in me? I haven't lived up to my promises. I'm sorry for that. It's harder than I thought. Don't get me wrong—I knew I would miss you, but sometimes it's almost debilitating."

While the panic attacks have subsided, I don't know how to live my life without Nate. There have been days when Grayson's found me still in bed with the lights off at five in the afternoon and others when I forget to eat. Something needs to change—I know it needs to change, but I don't know how to break out of this rut.

"What should I do, Nate?"

Silence. Not that I expected an answer, but I would do anything to have one.

"God, I know it's been a while, but if you're listening, can you send me a sign? What am I supposed to be doing here? Because I have to admit, I'm lost."

I wait for something to happen—anything really—but like before, I'm met with silence. This time, I expected it.

Chapter 5

Georgia,

I'm writing this letter as you sleep on the couch beside me. Your dark hair is spread out around you, and I want to reach over and run my fingers through it—anchoring me to you, letting me know that I'm not gone yet.

You look peaceful with your eyes closed and face relaxed—no worries lining it. It's taking everything in me not to lean over and place a kiss on your forehead, right in the spot where those lines usually appear, but I want you to have your moment of peace because soon, those moments will be harder to hold on to.

We found out I have cancer today. The doctors say they will do everything possible, but they aren't confident it will be enough. When they told me about the cancer, I think, in a way, I became numb. Then I started thinking—what about my wife? I can't leave my wife.

I promise, Georgia, I will fight to stay with you, but if I can't, I need you to know I love you. I love you so much.

I hope you never receive this letter. I'm writing it as my contingency plan because if I'm gone, there are some things I want you to know.

You are strong. I know you don't believe that, but you are. And, baby, I need you to show that strength now. If I'm gone, that probably means you're struggling. I would be if I were you, but my death can't define the rest of your life—or your faith. Don't let it define your faith.

At first, I was scared—but I know where I'm going, Georgia. I'm going home. The only thing that scares me now is leaving you alone. When I leave, will you hide yourself away? The town loves you, but will you allow them to smother you?

I don't want those things for you. I want you to thrive, and live, and love, and most of all, I want you to hold onto your faith.

There are moments in our life that are going to test us. This is one of them. Whether it ends in our happily ever after or you finding your own way, this journey is a moment to test us—to test what we are made of.

I wanted life with you, but if I can't have it, live for me. Don't hide from the pain. Let people love you, but also set boundaries. You struggle with both of those—finding the balance between them.

Find your strength, Georgia. Find who you are without me—go on adventures and find love again. I can picture you rolling your eyes at that last part, but I'm serious. Life is about love and finding someone to spend it with. You've only known our love, but if you're getting this letter, that means I'm gone. And—that's a shame, baby, because you were made to be loved. You pour all you love into everyone else—filling their cup—but you deserve to have your cup filled, too. Don't stay lonely out of loyalty to me. I know you love me, but your love doesn't start and end with me.

PS This letter is only meant for when I'm gone. You don't get to leave me if I'm still here because I love you with my whole heart, and I won't share. I'm not selfish enough to make you miss the chance at love if I'm gone, though.

One more thing—I know you feel lost right now. We talked about forever only to have it ripped away from us, but you'll find yourself, Georgia. I promise—just don't be too afraid to take chances when they arise. Sometimes, our best opportunities are right in front of our faces. We just have to look.

Love,

Nate

Chapter 6

Georgia

A sheen of sweat glistens on my forehead as my stomach churns.

I'm going to puke.

Rushing to the bathroom with the letter still in hand, I place it on the sink before dry-heaving into the toilet. Between the phone call with my mom, the talk with Grayson, and the visit with Nate tonight, I haven't eaten since this morning, and I'm counting my blessings.

When I got home from the cemetery, the letter was sitting in the mailbox on top of all my other mail. My heart stopped when I saw my name written in Nate's clean handwriting. If it weren't for that one detail, I would have thought someone was pranking me—a cruel prank, but a prank all the same. But there's no denying that smooth handwriting.

Grayson used to make fun of Nate for it, telling him it looked like a girl's. Nate took it all in stride, never letting Gray ruffle his feathers. His ability to take a joke and give it back was just one of the many things I loved about him. He was one of the happiest people I knew.

Once I convinced myself to pick the envelope up from the mailbox, I wasted no time slinging open the guest house door and ripping into it, careful not to get the letter in my haste. Fear, anxiety, and a little bit of hope—for what I'm not sure—ran through my veins as I began to read over the words, but I didn't make it more than the first line before running in here.

With my nerves under control, I stand, wipe the back of my hand across my mouth, and pick up the letter from where I laid it. My hands tremble as I read the first words my husband has said to me in over a year.

The words sink into my veins like a drug. One hit, and I'm addicted to how Nate's voice flits across the edges of my mind as I read each word. But when I get to the end of this letter, it will be over, and there are no more hits for me to take. So I take my time, savoring each word one by one, and when it's over, I crumble to the ground, exhausted.

My heart cracks as I think about the person Nate thought I was and who I actually am.

He thought I was brave and strong, but I'm neither. Without him, I'm a coward—going through the motions, not really living.

What would he say if he could see me now?

I haven't stepped foot in a church in a year. At the funeral, I sat in a pew while the pastor spoke, but I couldn't hear a word he said because anger bubbled up in my chest, threatening to strangle me. I made Nate a promise that day we found out he was terminal, but I knew I wouldn't be able to keep it. On the day of his funeral, anger over his death simmered through my blood, and that feeling hasn't left—pushing me further and further away from God.

And moving on?

A maniacal laugh slips out—wild and uncontrolled.

This must be what it feels like to be on the edge of insanity.

What was Nate thinking? Move on?

There's him—only him.

Life might be about love, but so is death. I counted every breath he took, praying it wouldn't be his last. Then I watched as those prayers didn't work, and he withered away. I lost pieces of myself I will never get back.

So, even if I wanted to move on and find love again, I'm broken, and that wouldn't be fair to anyone else.

They say there are five stages of grief, but that's a lie. There's only one—emptiness.

There's no guide—just the raw and jagged emptiness that can only be filled with the person who's gone.

After an hour of lying on the bathroom floor, my neck aches.

I should get up.

I've told myself that a thousand times in the last hour, but it's not until I hear the doorbell ring that I can finally do it.

Rising slowly, I shake my legs out. They went to sleep thirty minutes ago, and as much as I despise that feeling, I haven't moved.

The tingling stabs up my legs as I drag my eyes to the mirror above the sink and wince at my reflection.

Dull, lifeless eyes stare back at me. Frizzy hair falls out of my ponytail. My eye bags are turning purple from the tears I've shed today. Overall, it's a scary sight.

Pulling the ponytail holder from my hair, I run a brush through it as the doorbell rings again.

A loud knock follows the ring, and I throw the brush down on the counter before grabbing the letter off the floor where I was lying.

Squaring my shoulders, I ready myself to face the firing squad as I slip into the hall.

There's a bookcase in the living room next to the front door. Slipping a book off the shelf, I drop the letter between the pages.

I don't know who delivered it, but I don't want to share it with anyone else yet—not until I have more time to process the words.

The doorbell rings again, and I reach for the handle, having left the person on the other side waiting long enough. When I open the door, though, I wish I had pretended I wasn't home. Harper stands on the other side, a sour look on her face.

She looks me up and down, her nose snarled in disgust, before looking past me into the apartment.

"What are you doing here?" I ask.

She doesn't look at me when she answers, instead letting her gaze sweep the room behind me. "Mom's on her way. She wanted to have dinner here. Are you going to let me in?"

I sweep my arm out in front of me, gesturing for her to come in, all while praying for the patience of Job.

In the year that I've been living here, Harper hasn't been here once. Ellie has, but never Harper—not that I expected anything different.

"Where's Cole?" I ask, closing the door behind her.

A flash sparks through her eyes at the question, and it takes me a minute to recognize that it's pain. By the time I realize, though, Harper already has her face twisted into a mask of indifference.

"He's visiting a friend out of town," she says, distaste clear in how she says the word friend.

If we had a better relationship, I wouldn't hesitate to ask what's happening between her and Cole, but Harper's dislike for me doesn't allow for that type of relationship. She doesn't let anyone behind those steel walls of hers, and if I were to ask, she'd likely bite my head off.

Instead, I extend the olive branch with a simple, "If you need anything while he's gone, let me know."

Her only answer is a sharp "humph" as I walk to the kitchen. Standing by the refrigerator, I turn to offer her a drink, but before I can, she says, "You're awfully cozy here, aren't you? Are you ever planning on returning to the house you bought with my brother? You do remember him, right?"

And that right there is the problem. I offer an olive branch, and she snaps it in two.

I grit my teeth to keep from retorting. I'm used to Harper's comments. It does no good to respond to her because it only eggs her on—I've watched her with Grayson enough times to know that. The two get along like oil and water.

Another knock at the door saves me from having to make nice, though.

Turning my back to her, a dangerous decision, I walk over to the door, open it, and usher Ellie in.

She's in her fifties, but life has been cruel to her, leaving worry lines creasing her face. Her shoulders are hunched forward from the weight she's carried for so long. First, her husband left, and then she had to deal with her only son dying. The woman deserves the world, but she was handed hell instead. Her gray hair frames her face in a bob, and her shoulders are hunched forward.

Once she's inside, she wraps her arms around me, squeezing tight enough that I might shatter.

"Oh, darling. It's so good to see you."

The tightness of my chest starts to dissipate as I laugh into her hair. "You see me every Sunday, Ellie."

"Oh hush, if I had it my way, I would see you girls every day, but I know you each have your own lives to live," she says, keeping one arm around my waist as she lets go and looks over at Harper.

"Some more than others," Harper says into the drink she helped herself to.

"Harper," Ellie scolds.

Harper throws her hands up, pretending to be innocent. It's her go-to look.

Ellie shakes her head and turns to look at me. "I brought food. It's in the car. Why don't you come help me bring it in?"

I glance at Harper, who's made her way to the living room, picking up items and then placing them back where she got them. I think about the letter I shoved in the book, and for a second, I worry she might find it. It's not that I'm trying to hide it, but Harper is pessimistic about most things. I don't want her to ruin Nate's words to me. The car is just outside, though, and I doubt she will find it in the time it takes for us to go out there and come back.

Giving Ellie a small smile, I take her arm and lead the way.

Outside, I shiver against the night air, rubbing my hands together to keep warm. I should've slipped on a jacket before coming out here. Fall has faded into winter, and the chilliness from the weeks before has taken on a biting edge.

As Ellie opens her trunk and places food in my arms, I can't help but glance over at the main house in search of any sign of life from Grayson. The lights are off, and there's no movement in the windows. It makes me wonder where he is—if he's okay.

Ellie places one more bag in my hand as I firm up my resolve to check on Grayson after Harper and Ellie leave.

"You know she doesn't mean it, right?" Ellie asks, slamming the trunk shut.

I chew on the inside of my cheek, debating the best way out of this conversation. I know Harper is Ellie's daughter and Nate's sister, but the woman is difficult. I don't like putting Ellie in the middle, just like I didn't like putting Nate in the middle when he was alive. Harper has her own issues, but she continuously walks a fine line between making them mine.

Her attitude was one thing Nate and I always fought about. It wasn't that he defended her, but she was better at hiding her disdain for me in front of him. Now that he's gone, she lets her barbs flow freely, and Ellie gets stuck between us. I try to hold my tongue so that she doesn't have to choose because I already lost Nate. I don't want to lose her too.

"I know, Ellie," I say, pacifying her.

There's a knowing look in her eye, though, that makes me wonder if she understands what I'm not saying and the exasperation I have towards Harper.

"Nate would want you to be happy, Georgia. Are you happy?"

I don't answer her immediately, thinking back on the past year. It's not that I'm not happy. It's just that my soul hurts without Nate. Before he died, he asked me to live, and he asked me the same thing in that letter, but I have forgotten how to. I think it's time I try, though.

"Not yet, but I will be," I say, carrying the food in one arm and swinging the other around her shoulders.

She smiles, wrapping one arm around my waist and squeezing.

"I know you will be, sweet girl. I can feel it in my bones."

That at least makes one of us.

Chapter 7

Grayson

Bourbon burns its way down as I sling back the drink. When Georgia left work, I grabbed the bottle and poured myself a glass.

It was only supposed to be one glass.

Now half the bottle is gone, and by that reasoning, I might as well finish the rest.

My life is one disaster away from being total chaos. My best friend died, I'm in love with his wife, and I have a brother who I knew nothing about.

Who am I kidding? It's not one disaster away—it is total chaos.

Pouring another glass, I down it as fast as the last one, except it goes down smoother this time.

I meant to leave the office hours ago, but where would I go? Back to an empty house to wallow in? I can do that just as well here, and I'll already be here for work tomorrow.

Now I'm lying here drunk on the couch beside my desk.

I'm pathetic.

Catching sight of a picture frame on the bookshelf across the room, I rise from the couch, unsteady on my feet. I place my hand on the wall and use it to maneuver until I'm standing in front of the bookshelf. Reaching out, I pick up the picture that perfectly defines my life.

We are at a college football game. I bought season tickets for Nate and me. We went to every game, but Georgia wanted to come to this one, and neither Nate nor I could tell her no. It was two years after we graduated college. My business had started to take off, and I was finally in a good place for the first time in my life. Nate and Georgia were going strong, and I knew that marriage was on their horizon. I just didn't expect Nate to propose that day—or that I would be there when he did.

During the middle of the second half, Georgia was leading the people around us in a cheer. I watched as Nate became so enamored with her that he lowered himself to one knee and asked her to marry him right there. I think Nate was just as surprised by the proposal because he didn't even have the ring with him, but after watching Georgia at that game, half the men in the stadium wanted to propose. Nate was the only lucky one to have the ability to do so.

Someone below us had the foresight to take a picture. In it, Nate is down on one knee, Georgia is smiling at him like he's the sun her world revolves around, and I'm off to the side, smiling at the two. If anyone bothered to look close enough, though, they would see the conflict in my eyes. I loved them both, but my heart broke a little too.

The bookshelf moves in front of me as I try to place the picture back on the shelf. With unsteady hands, I reach out, trying to decide which of the two shelves is the real one. I guess wrong and watch as the picture falls to the ground, glass crashing when it hits.

If that's not foretelling, I don't know what is.

Turning so my back's against the bookcase, I lower myself until I'm sitting on the floor, careful of the broken glass.

I'm spiraling, and I hate that.

When Georgia left the office tonight, it stung that she didn't need me, or maybe it was because I didn't want to admit how much I needed her.

CHAPTER 7

I'm not supposed to need anyone.

I'm Grayson Lewis—a self-made man.

Except I don't feel like that man. I feel like the kid whose anger got him into more fights than he could count and who would have ended up in juvie if it wasn't for his two best friends. Georgia and Nate saved me from a path of self-destruction, and I owe them both for that.

If I had told Georgia I needed her tonight, she would have forgotten her own needs, and too many people ask her to do that already. I won't be another one.

So, I'll sit here and drink until I'm numb instead.

Sunlight pierces into my eyes at the same time an ache runs down my shoulder blade. Groaning, I try to sit up to figure out why I was dumb enough to fall asleep on the floor last night instead of going to bed, but my stomach lurches with the movement. With precise movements, I lower myself back down and try to think around the headache jackhammering into my eyes.

Flashes of tossing bourbon back last night run through my mind, and if it weren't hurting so bad, I'd bang my head against something hard for my own stupidity.

Nights like last night used to happen often. Drinking made things numb, but then I met my dad, and I found out my mom didn't tell me about him because he was an alcoholic. I decided that day I wouldn't be like him, but last night was a moment of weakness—a slip into someone I don't want to be.

There's a knock on my office door, and I wonder for a moment if I could make it in prison because I might kill whoever is banging on the door.

"Go away," I growl, but the banging continues.

Peeking one eye open, I glare at the door before stumbling to my feet again.

My stomach lurches into my throat as I put one foot in front of the other until I'm standing at the door staring at the knob.

It takes all my concentration to make my hand connect with the knob, alcohol still hindering my movements.

When the door opens, Brooks, my little brother, stands on the other side.

There's no denying that he's my brother. If it wasn't for the two years between us, we could have been twins—right down to the way the dimple on our face pokes in when we talk.

I slip my face into a careful mask—careful not to let my surprise show.

"You look awful," Brooks quips as he shoves his way into my office.

"Yes, make yourself at home," I say, sarcasm dripping from my voice.

Shutting the door, I try not to wince at the noise. Brooks lowers onto the couch and spreads his arms across the back.

He studies me as I walk over and sit in the chair behind my desk. I feel like death, and I'm sure my appearance is not far behind. There's a film in my mouth that I'm dying to wash out, but I won't reveal any more weakness to Brooks than I already have.

He hasn't earned that position.

The last time he was in my office, he sat across from me at my desk and was here for an interview. I thought he knew we were brothers, but to my surprise, he didn't. And while he might not have been there to take advantage of the hard work I've put into this company, I still don't trust him. He's called me several times since then, but I haven't answered. I have a family, and while that family has gotten smaller over the years, first my mom and then Nate, I would rather have people around that I can trust, even if that's only one now.

"Where is your watchdog?" Brooks asks.

When we found out about my dad and then Brooks, Georgia was offended that either of them would ask me for anything before actually knowing me. I didn't need her to defend me, but there was a spark in her eye when she put Brooks in his place at his interview. It's the first time I've ever seen her stand up to someone—and it was on my behalf.

"Clearly not here if you got in. Ever heard of scheduling a meeting?"

Brooks's eyes, which are the same color as mine, narrow into slits.

"Ever heard of picking up the phone?" he retorts.

Steepling my fingers under my chin, I throw him a smirk.

"Look at that, we're already fighting like brothers," I say. Then, dropping the smile, I narrow my eyes into a glare and get to the point. "What are you doing here?"

I learned to be intimidating at a young age. It was necessary to survive this town, but to his credit, he doesn't seem fazed. Brooks sits, his mouth spreading into a grin as I continue to glare.

Irritation prickles along the back of my neck. Between that and the hangover, I'm tempted to pummel that smile right off his face. My fists clench against my legs as I wait for him to answer.

"Just checking in on my big brother."

Grinding my teeth, I say, "I don't want you to check in on me. We haven't been part of each other's life this far. I don't see any need for it now."

His grin spreads wider, but his eyes remain icy cold.

"You know, Grayson, regret is something you have to live with forever. Maybe you can live with not getting to know your family, but I can't."

I don't respond, tightening my jaw.

Brooks blows out a heavy sigh and stands. He places his hands in his pockets, leveling me with a stare. "Fine. I can't force you to get to know me, but at least I can say I tried."

He turns to leave, walking over to the door and opening it, but before he walks out, he spins around to face me again.

"We're having a party for my daughter Avery's birthday. It's two months from now, but I figure if I ask now, I'll have plenty of other opportunities to bug you about it until you have no choice but to show up. She's your niece—if that matters to you. I'll text you the date and address. I know you probably won't come, but I want you to know you are wanted there. Do with that what you will."

His knuckles rap against the door frame, and then he's gone.

Chapter 8

Georgia

The numbers above the elevator light up as I wait for it to arrive. Harper and Ellie left late last night, and Grayson's lights were still not on when I walked them to their cars.

I convinced myself he might have fallen asleep early, but my gut tells me that isn't true. Yesterday, when I left work, I was lost in my own grief, but after all the times he's been there for me in the past year, I should have realized that it would have been hard for him, too.

The elevator dings, and I step on, pressing the button for the top floor. Grayson's done well for himself. He built a business from scratch on his own. Before I started working here, I knew that his company was successful, but since I've taken the job, I recognize how much work he's put in to get it to this level of success.

Another ding and the elevator doors open. I step out only to run into a brick wall. Well—it's not an actual brick wall because brick walls don't grunt when you hit them, but it might as well have been. Looking up, I catch a glimpse of dark hair and blue eyes—Brooks. A fresh course of worry for Grayson runs through my stomach, but I school my face so it doesn't give anything away.

"Brooks," I greet.

"Firecracker," he throws back.

"Here to take advantage of your brother again?"

Being around this man brings out the worst in me. Any other person and I'm quick to let things slide, but his effect on Grayson is enough to set me on edge.

The line of Brooks's jaw flexes, but it's the only indication that my barb landed. Otherwise, he's stone. If I didn't already know that he was related to Gray, that would be a dead giveaway. They are both hard to read, hiding behind the icy blueness of their eyes, long lashes, and strong jawlines.

Brooks studies me before one side of his lips lifts into a smirk.

"I see now," he says.

My brow wrinkles, "You see what?"

This time, his smirk comes with a laugh—gruff and dark.

"You'll see, Firecracker. You'll see."

With that, the elevator opens behind me, and he steps through, leaving me questioning his sanity.

I shake my head, my thoughts returning to Grayson, and hurry down the hall to his office. His door is closed when I get to my desk, but with Brooks just leaving, I'm sure he's here.

"Grayson," I call, knocking on the door.

A groan answers me from the other side.

Pushing the door open, I stop when I catch sight of him.

He's lying on the couch beside his desk, with his face down into the cushions. When he hears me step towards him, he turns his head up so I can see his face. I hold my breath so that I don't gasp. It's been a long time since I've seen him like this. His eyes are red from a sleepless night, and the scruff on his jaw is longer than usual. His clothes are rumpled and creased from a night of sleeping in them, and when I get close enough, I can smell alcohol on him.

"Oh, Gray, what happened? Why didn't you call me?"

A mirthless laugh slips past his lips, and he winces at the sound.

"I was coping."

"With which part—Nate or your brother?"

He's been spiraling since the day his dad, Kip Montgomery, showed up in his life, and I don't know if it's because he wants to have a relationship with his dad or because he's so scared to have a family that he might lose. Either way, this version of him scares me. There was a time when Grayson was so lost in his anger that I never thought he would find his way out, but when Nate's dad left, it gave him a reason to be there for someone else. Now he's spiraling again, and I have to find a way to be there for him.

He's all I have left.

"Both," he says, turning his head back into the cushions.

Sweeping his legs off the couch, I sit down beside him.

"I'd be happy to beat Brooks up for you if you'd like," I say, shrugging my shoulder.

A real chuckle shakes his back.

"Easy, Peach." His words are muffled by the cushions his face is shoved into, but I still hear the smile in his voice. I don't want to be the reason he loses that smile, but we need to talk.

"Gray, sit up and talk to me. Why didn't you call me yesterday?"

There's a grunt, and then he's sitting up. His thigh brushes against the outside of mine, and I let my eyes wander over his frame, taking in just how bad the situation is. He looks haggard—like he's lived a thousand lives in the past year.

He's not looking at me when he responds, spreading his legs wide and resting his elbows on his knees so that he's staring at his hands. "You told me what you needed yesterday, Georgia, and I respected that. There aren't many people in this town who respect that you are big enough to make your own decisions, but I do. Nate might have been my best friend, but he was your husband. Yesterday wasn't about my grief. It was about yours. I handled it my way, and you handled it yours. Now, if you had told me you needed me, I would have been there, but don't feel bad because you didn't."

"Gray—" I say, laying my hand against his leg. "You aren't an island, and I'm not so far gone that I can't recognize that other people are hurt by Nate's death, too. I'm not that selfish."

"No one's ever accused you of being selfish, Peach. It's the opposite. You could use a few more selfish decisions," he says, turning his head to look up at me, a smirk causing his dimple to poke in. Something warm settles in my stomach when he looks at me that way—like he can see past the broken shell of who I've become to the girl I used to be before cancer tore my life apart.

I don't ask him what he means. Grayson's been telling me to make more selfish decisions for months, but that's hard. I don't like disappointing people. The most selfish thing I've done my whole life is stay at Grayson's house, and that's only because I can't physically force myself to go back to a house where I watched my husband die.

I think back to the letter still hidden between the pages of my book.

Moving on—loving anyone but Nate—feels selfish.

For a minute, I debate whether I should tell Grayson about the letter to get his opinion, but when I look over, he's already standing and looking a little green. I want to tell him to go home and rest, but he's stubborn, and I would be wasting my breath.

The letter can wait.

"Let's do something tonight in memory of Nate—together," I say.

He stretches his arms above his head, turning to face me. "What did you have in mind?"

A grin spreads across my face because I know exactly what Nate would do if he were here. "Leave it to me."

"Georgia, it's freezing outside. You're going to catch a cold," Grayson calls behind me.

"Oh, come on, you big baby. When did you turn into such a wimp?"

"When I woke up with a hangover."

"And whose fault is that?" I quip.

I turn my head to look at him over my shoulder and come face to face with his glare. Grown men may cower under that look, but I throw my head back and laugh.

Taking a deep breath, I let the cold air burn in my lungs until I have to exhale. Living without Nate has been challenging, but each day, I've tried to find a small glimmer where I can appreciate that I'm alive. This is that moment for me today.

We are heading up to where the old water tower sits just off the road on a beaten path. The days are getting shorter, and we only have about fifteen minutes of daylight left, but I know this trail like the back of my hand. Nate and Grayson used to drag me up here on days when they said my nose had been in a book too long. I haven't been up here since before Nate was diagnosed, though.

With Grayson only a few feet behind me, the water tower comes into view, and I can't help but smile at all the memories that flood my head as I look at it—like the time Nate and Grayson nearly got arrested for climbing it.

Ellie and Clara, Grayson's mom, were spitting mad. For Nate, it was the first time he had ever been in trouble, but for Grayson, it was just one of the many. If Nate hadn't been with Grayson that night, the cop would have arrested him for the mere fact that Grayson was rowdy when he was younger. It bothers me that no one here gives him a break, even now, but they don't know the man that I do. Grayson would give the shirt off his back to anyone who asked. He would just do it with a growl in his voice and a smirk on his face. He doesn't mean it that way. He's just—gruff.

That night wasn't the first time Nate and Grayson came out to the water tower, and it certainly wasn't their last. They just were more careful about who was watching. Sometimes, I would come out here too, and we would sit up top and watch the stars, planning our lives together. There weren't many times in Nate's life that he was a rebel, but climbing the water tower was always one of them.

Grayson must be remembering the same memory that I am because when I stop just at the foot of the ladder that leads to the top of the water tower, he asks, "Are you trying to get me arrested?"

"Come on, Gray. What would Nate do?" I ask, placing one hand and then foot on the ladder.

He grumbles something about being a bad influence, and then he's following me, his hand on my calf as we climb to make sure I don't fall.

When I am at the top, I pull myself up on the platform with a few grunts and groans. I really should work out more, but whenever I allot time for exercising, somehow, it always turns into reading instead. Reading is a form of exercise—for my brain, so I usually can talk myself into thinking it counts. Then I get into situations like tonight, where I actually have to be physically active, and I realize that it doesn't count at all.

Turning around to face the ladder, I offer Grayson my hand. He rolls his eyes and hands me the backpack I made him carry from the car instead.

"You're half my size, Peach. I'd pull you down instead of you helping me up. Then we'd both be in trouble," he says as he pulls himself up sans the grunts and groans.

"Show off," I mutter.

He shoots me a triumphant grin, and I can't help but stare. Grayson doesn't smile often, at least not his real smile. Usually, I'm stuck with smirks and glares that are not half as effective as he thinks they are. But when he does offer a real one, it's something to witness. His whole face lights up, and that shadow that constantly hangs over him fades away. It hints at the real Grayson—the man he would have been if life hadn't kicked him so many times.

That smile does funny things to my chest, causing guilt to eat at my stomach, so instead of taking it in and reveling in it, I busy myself with grabbing the blankets out of the backpack, along with the snacks that I brought for us. I spread one blanket over the cold metal of the platform and sit down, holding the other one. Looking up, I wave my hand and motion for Grayson to sit beside me.

The ghost of that smile is still on his face, and I realize this is one of those moments when my heart doesn't ache as much.

Lowering himself, he sits beside me and rubs his hands together.

"Here, you big baby," I say, handing him the other blanket I brought.

He looks down at the blanket and then back at me. His brows pull together, and then he scoots closer, wrapping it around our shoulders as he pulls me against his side.

"If you think I'm going to let you freeze while I keep the blanket, then you underestimate how much of a gentleman I am," he growls.

A snort slips out of my nose, and I rush to cover my mouth with my hand. Grayson is no gentleman. He's too gruff—his edges too hard—but that doesn't mean he isn't a good man.

Laying my head against Grayson's shoulder, I sigh as I stare at the stars. The sky is beautiful tonight, with stars scattered in every direction. My granny used to tell me that the stars are holes in the sky where heaven peaks through, giving us just a small glimpse of the light that waits for us. I wish that were true. I'd give anything to see Nate one more time, even if it was just through one of those stars.

"Gray," I say, my voice becoming more serious. "I got a letter from Nate."

His body stiffens beneath me, sitting up straighter, and I worry if I should have waited to tell him or maybe I shouldn't have told him at all. I don't know the protocol for receiving a letter from a spouse who's been dead for a year.

"What—uh—when did you get it?"

"Last night," I say. I don't lift my head off his shoulder when I respond, my cheeks flaming despite the cold because I know the question that's coming next. I'm not embarrassed by the letter—just that I've been so predictable. Nate knew how I would react, even a year after his death, and I have to wonder if it's because he knew I wasn't as strong as I pretended to be.

"Where did you find it? I mean, it's been a year. Why didn't he give it to you before he was gone?"

I shrug because I don't know the answers to those questions. "It was in the mailbox when I got home last night. It has a stamp, so I assume it was mailed—not just placed in there."

"Aren't you curious where it came from? What if it wasn't Nate?"

"There's no denying the handwriting. It was Nate. I'm curious about where it came from, don't get me wrong, but at the same time, it wasn't as important as knowing what the letter said."

He nods his head against the top of mine.

"What did it say?" Grayson asks. There's a wavering in his voice that I'm not used to, and I can't place why—hesitation, maybe?

"He—um, didn't want me to lose my faith because of his death. He wrote the letter the day we found out he had cancer. At that time, he still hoped to make it, but he wrote the letter just in case. I think he knew I would be angry if I lost him?"

"Are you angry?"

My laugh is bitter as I pick at the edge of the blanket.

"Of course I'm angry—at myself for being so weak, at Nate for leaving, and at God for not saving my husband—and I hate it because none of that anger makes sense. Nate couldn't help that he left. He was sick, and God—well, I know that he doesn't answer all our prayers in the way we want him to. I feel like a toddler throwing a tantrum because I didn't get my way, but I'm so mad at him."

Grayson's arm squeezes me tight, and I wish it were enough to heal me—to shatter all the hurt that pokes at me like glass.

"I wish I could tell you that anger goes away, Georgia, but I've been angry for a long time. I've heard all my life that God is good by people who have shown no goodness to me, so I'm probably not the person to help you there."

His body heat seeps into mine as his arm stays wrapped around me, muscles bunching as he holds onto me, and I soak in that strength, hoping one day I can find my own.

"There was—uh—there was one more thing. From the letter, I mean," I say, biting the inside of my cheek and debating how to explain the rest. I decide it's best to drop it like a weight, letting the effect hit all at once. "He said I should move on—you know, find someone new to love."

Grayson's body stiffens, not moving a single inch. Even his chest has stopped moving as he holds his breath. With my head still against his shoulder, I tilt my head back, watching as his Adam's apple bobs—once, twice, three times. His arms loosen, and I sit up to look at him. He still hasn't said anything, and worry sits in my stomach, the size of that weight I just threw down.

When another second passes, the silence begins to become too heavy.

"I'm not cheating on Nate," I say, the words harsh even to my ears, but if Grayson can't accept that I could maybe love someone else someday, how am I supposed to?

His face softens, but I look away. I don't want to see the pity there—not from him.

"Georgia, I didn't think that. You just surprised me, is all. I didn't know you were considering trying to find someone else."

"I wasn't—I'm not," I deny. "It's just the letter made me realize that I'm lonely. I miss the connection I had with Nate, but there's no replacing Nate. That's what I would be doing, replacing him, wiping out his memory as if he wasn't one of the most important people in my life."

Grayson clears his throat, considering what I said as he looks up at the stars.

"There's no replacing Nate, Peach. The right person won't let you forget him. They won't be intimidated by his memory. The right person will love him because he loves you," he says to the sky, but when he gets to this next part, he lowers his head so he's looking directly at me. I want to look away, but his gaze is like a magnetic field, pulling me to him. His hand reaches out, and his palm lays against my jaw. My breath hitches, the heat of his hand seeping into my skin. My eyes are drawn to the orchid on his arm. I want to ask him why he got it—if he knows that Nate brought me an orchid every year for our anniversary because it's my favorite—but I don't, too afraid of what the answer will be. "If you ever decide you want to find someone, I'll be here for you. No questions asked. No judgment, but he better be good enough for you."

The muscle in his jaw works as he says that last part. Nate was one of the most important people in my life, but he wasn't the only one. Grayson's been a part of my life as long as Nate. He's always been important, but lately, it feels like his role in my life is changing, morphing into something I don't recognize.

Chapter 9

Georgia,

This is it.

The doctor came in a couple of hours ago and said there's nothing left for them to do. I'm going to die, but before I do, there's something I need to do.

Since the day we found out I had cancer, you've taken care of me. A husband's job is supposed to be to take care of his wife—provide for her—but you've taken on that role because I physically can't. Now it's time I do something to take care of you.

Today, I watched you as the doctor told us that I only have two more months, and my heart broke for you. You were devastated, but I knew you were planning to fight—even when they told us there were no options left. Then I had to tell you that I'm tired. I felt like the biggest jerk in that moment. I know you want me here with you, and I wish more than anything that I could stay with you forever. I would spend lifetimes with you if I could, but our timing is not our own.

When I found out I had cancer, I wrote you a letter, and if you are receiving this one, that means that you've gotten the other one too. I meant every word. Your faith and love are the two most important things you can have in life, and with me gone, I know you will struggle with both.

After writing that first letter, I started thinking of ways to help you move on with life, not just stay stuck in my death.

Because let's be honest, Georgia, you're a hermit. You fold into yourself when you're hurting because you don't want to inconvenience anyone else with your pain, but let me tell you something. That's complete and utter BULL.

Roll your eyes. Go ahead. I know you want to.

Because in order for you to listen to the rest of this letter, I need you to know how well I know you.

Right now, you're probably denying that you rolled your eyes at me calling you out, but I know you—so control your eyes, and let's get back to the point at hand.

(Don't yell at me for that one, okay? See, I told you I know you).

Here's what's going to happen, and no, this is not one of my half-planned ideas. See above—I've been thinking about it for weeks.

I'm going to send you a series of letters I've started writing today, but again, remember—planned for weeks. In each letter, I will give you a task to complete. Don't worry, they won't be hard—probably. Back to the point—this is for your own good, and you have to follow through because this is my dying wish.

Yes, I'm playing that card.

But seriously, Georgia. It's time for you to live, and I'll be right by your side while you do—in spirit, of course, but still by your side. And you'll have Gray, too.

So, with that being said, here's your first task—pick an event, there are plenty of them in this town, and have FUN. I mean it, Georgia. Have fun. Choose something that you will enjoy. Go to a concert, or a football game, or even one of the local festivals. Just do something—anything. Get out of the house. Stop hiding. Because I know you're hiding. I can already see you doing it. When people from town come to visit the hospital, you go into your shell—become a hermit. You haven't been anywhere but by my side in months. You used to love to go out. You'd get all dressed up, even if we were just going to the grocery store. I want that lightness for you again. So find it, okay?

Love,

Nate

Chapter 10

Georgia

Standing on Grayson's porch, I knock hard against the wooden door. My hands are frozen, causing pain to shoot up my knuckles each time my hand meets the wood. The letter is in my other hand, carefully folded into place.

It's been three weeks since I received the last one. I chalked it up as a one-time thing—a way for Nate to have closure. I wasn't expecting another one, but when I checked the mail, there it was, sitting on top, just like the rest.

My knuckles come down again, landing on the wood just as the door is yanked open. I fall forward at the same time Grayson steps into the doorway, and I crash into him, causing him to step back to steady us. It takes me a second to get reoriented. Grayson has his arms around me, holding me, and my hand is trapped between our bodies. I look down, a flush creeping across my cheeks as I realize my hand is pressed against bare skin while the other dangles beside me, the letter still clenched between my fingers.

"Grayson, put a shirt on. It's freezing outside," I say, pushing myself back to put space between us. I swipe my hand against my pants, trying to wipe away the burn of his skin against mine.

Cocking one eyebrow, he watches me as he grabs his shirt from the table in the foyer and pulls it over his head. My mouth hangs open as his head disappears inside his shirt, muscles rippling beneath the tattoos that cover his skin. When the shirt is in place, long sleeves covering all skin—and tattoos, he reaches over and pushes my chin up.

"Close your mouth, Peach," he says with a wink, and dang it, if that wink doesn't make me want to punch him.

Settling, I shove his arm and say, "I'm just amazed that someone who's such a baby when it comes to the cold isn't constantly covered in layers."

He laughs and shrugs. "I was changing, and you kept knocking at the door like a mad woman. I thought something was wrong. You could have just walked in, you know."

"No, Gray, I couldn't. You've done plenty for me. You're letting me live in your guest house. I won't encroach on your life more than I already have."

He starts to argue, but I raise my hand, stopping him.

"I didn't come here to argue with you. Now that you're properly dressed, look," I say, lifting my hand to show him the letter.

He stills, staring at the envelope. "Where did that come from?"

My face is bland as I tilt my head and purse my lips because, really, where does he think it came from? It's not like I run over here with every piece of mail I get.

"Control your face, Peach. I can read it from across the room."

Rolling my eyes, I walk deeper into the house, making my way to the kitchen. Grayson follows behind me, and once we are in the kitchen, I pull out a bar stool, patting the top.

"Sit," I say, shoving the letter at him. "Read."

Grayson obeys, taking the envelope and pulling the letter out while I pace the floor in front of him. His eyes scan the lines of Nate's handwriting as I silently lose my mind.

When he gets to the last line, he repeats what I did, pulling out a stool and saying, "Sit."

I shake my head, refusing. There are too many emotions coursing through my body. With a growl, he stands up, scoops me up in his arms, and plants me on the stool beside him.

"Now breathe," he says, his mouth against the shell of my ear. His voice is deep and commanding, leaving no room for arguments and sending shivers down my spine.

At his command, I take a deep breath in. Satisfied, he steps back, and my next breath comes a little smoother.

Taking his seat beside me, he says, "Tell me why you're so freaked out by this."

"Besides the fact that I'm receiving letters from my dead husband?" I ask, my tone dripping with sarcasm.

"Yeah, besides that," Grayson says, ignoring my attitude.

"It's all of it. Nate had this whole plan, and I knew nothing about it. More letters are coming. And that's another thing—I know I said before that I didn't care how I got them, but that was when I thought there was just one. That information seems important now. But most of all—what if I can't do the things he asks me? Like, yeah, this first one is easy. I can go out in public. I might have a breakdown when I do, but I can do it. What if I can't do the others, though? I'll let Nate down."

Spinning so I'm facing the bar, I let my forehead fall against the cold marble. Out of the corner of my eye, I see Grayson lean back in his stool and place his elbows on the counter.

Cool and unbothered, that's the epitome of Grayson Lewis.

It's infuriating.

"First," he says, reaching over and pulling my ponytail until I turn my head to look at him, "let's start with the obvious. You aren't going to disappoint Nate. He was obsessed with you until he took his last breath—and even now that he's gone, it seems—so get that out of your head. Second, whatever he asks, you don't have to do it alone. We'll do it together."

"Really?" I ask, hope lacing my voice.

He reaches up, shoving his hands through his hair. "Peach, if you have to ask, I've done something wrong over this last year."

I watch as his hand runs through his dark locks, and for a moment—just a millisecond—I wonder what it would feel like to reach up and let my hand follow the path of his, twirling pieces of hair through my fingers until he relaxes for once in his life.

Then I spy that stupid orchid and the moment shatters, a heaviness weighing on my chest.

Grayson watches me, those blue eyes missing nothing, but stays silent, as once again, that tattoo teases me with its untold story.

"Are you ever going to tell me about it?" I asked.

He shrugs, his eyes turning stormy. "Maybe one day, but not today. Today, we're going to focus on you and this letter. I know this is from Nate, and you think you have to do it because it's him, but Georgia, it's your life to live. If you don't want to follow through with these letters, you don't have to."

My hands shake as I sit up and reach for the letter out of his hand, looking at it like it will have all the answers. There hasn't been a moment since I received it that I felt like I had a choice, but Grayson's right. It is my life. I'm the one left here, living it without Nate, and it hits me—that's why I want to do it.

"Nate can't live his life, but I can do it for him," I say, firm in my decision.

Pride and a little sadness shine in Grayson's eyes.

"Then we'll do it together."

"Hello," I call, sticking my head inside the front door of my parents' home.

I visit every week after having lunch with Ellie. It's my way of putting on a face so they don't worry. The first few months after Nate died, it was a constant stream of people worrying. I felt like I was being smothered, so now, even on the days when I'm struggling, I put on that face that says I'm okay.

Sure, I'm not the same Georgia I was before Nate's death—I struggle socially. There are two versions of myself—who I was before Nate's death and who I pretend to be after. Before, I was outgoing. I loved town events and people. Now, I pretend that I will be that girl again someday.

"Back here," Mom calls.

Kicking my shoes off, I walk down the hallway, passing pictures that make my heart ache for the innocence of the girl in them.

The hall opens up to the kitchen. Mom stands at the counter, kneading dough. Her features are sharp—almost severe, a product of her own raising. Her gray hair is styled perfectly, not a strand out of place, and despite her small frame, she's usually the most intimidating woman in any room.

She turns her head when she hears my footsteps, and a smile lights up her face when she sees me.

"Grab an apron," she says, jutting her chin towards the apron hanging on the hook by the pantry door.

I follow her command, setting my keys on the counter and slipping the floral apron over my head.

Without a word, she places a ball of dough on the counter beside her, and I join her, kneading the dough into the flour until it's ready to roll out.

We work in silence, side by side, just like when I was a teenager.

I appreciate the silence. My mom likes to push me sometimes, but she also knows that there are times when I need to come to her. This is one of those times.

"Where's Dad?" I ask, avoiding the talk I really want to have with her.

"He's in the garage. He'll be in soon."

I nod—letting the silence build into an awkward tension until I'm ready to burst.

"Mom," I say, the seriousness in my tone causing her to stop and place her rolling pin to the side.

Wiping her hands on her apron, she rests her hip against the oak cabinets and studies me, waiting until I'm ready to continue. "Do you think Nate would be disappointed in me? You know—in the way I've handled his death?"

In two seconds flat, I'm wrapped in her arms, and she mutters into my hair, "No, baby, I don't."

My throat aches. I didn't tell her about the first letter, and I don't want to tell her about this one. Somehow, it feels fitting to keep it between Grayson and me, but at the same time, I can't help feeling like this is Nate's way of telling me he knew I wouldn't keep my promise to him—like I failed him.

"Look at me, sweet girl," she says, pulling back from the hug and putting a hand on each side of my face. "Healing isn't linear. I know I push you because I'm worried about you. I overstep that line of being there for you and being overprotective because I've not been in your shoes, and I'm trying to be there for you in the best way I know how. Here's what I do know, though. Nate loved you, and he would understand. Don't you ever question that."

"I'm lost without him, Mom."

"I know, Georgia. I know you are, but the bravest thing you can do is find a way to keep breathing. You've been doing that for a year, and to me, that makes you the strongest person I know."

A sarcastic laugh slips out. "Others would disagree. There are so many things I should have done differently—"

"So do them differently," Mom interrupts, impatience hidden under the tough love.

"What?" I ask, my forehead wrinkling in confusion.

"You said there are things you should have done differently. If *you* feel that way, and not because others are making you, then change them. You can't change that he's gone—no matter how much you wish you could—but you can change your choices from here on out. So if you don't like the choices you've been making, then change them."

I scoff, rolling my eyes and returning to the dough on the counter. With the rolling pin in hand, I roll my hands back and forth, pressing down until the space between the dough and the countertop is nonexistent, and still, it's not enough.

"Give me that," Mom says, yanking the rolling pin out of my hands. "You're ruining my dough. Now, you asked for my opinion, and I gave it to you. Don't be getting mad at me because you don't like what I have to say."

"You act like it's so easy—like my whole world didn't change when Nate died," I snap.

I don't know why I'm snapping. She's trying to help—I asked for her help—but her help always comes with sharp edges that make me defensive.

"No, Georgia—I don't. I know it's not easy. I loved Nate because he loved my little girl. I miss the man, too, but I know that my grief is not the same as yours. Change is never easy, honey, but the world doesn't stop spinning because we are sad. All I'm saying is that if the choices that you are making now aren't helping, then maybe it's time to make different choices."

I know she's right, but it stings, making me want to lash out. My relationship with my mom is complicated. I love her. She's always been there for me, but she's blunt. Empathy is not her strong suit. She's not like the other moms who held your hand if you scraped your knee when you were little or bought chocolate when a boy broke your heart. Instead, she told you to get up and walk it off because life isn't fair. Sometimes, I wish for a mom who knows how to coddle me—just for a minute—because life is hard enough without someone there reminding you.

I open my mouth to respond, but the door to the garage swings open, and my dad walks through with a big smile. He must know when Mom and I are at odds because he's always had perfect timing. He is a peacekeeper between us.

Not minding the flour all over me, he wraps me in a hug tight enough to cut my air off, and I feel the tension in my body melt away. My dad gives the best hugs.

"Hey, Georgia Jane. When did you get here?"

"Not that long ago," I wheeze. "Now, would you let go of me? I can't breathe."

He chuckles, stepping back and taking a good look at me. While he's checking me over, I do the same to him.

He's tall, filling the space of the room with his presence and a protruding belly that he's worked on for years. He claims it as his bragging right. Despite his size, he's the most laid-back man I have ever met. It's why he and Nate got along so well. They were one and the same.

"You look to be in one piece at least," he says after a full minute of staring at me. "Are you staying for supper?"

A grin spreads across my face. This is the same conversation we have every week, but it's nice—comfortable. Things in my life haven't been comfortable for a while, but I can always count on my dad to be that person for me.

"I just ate lunch, Dad. It's not time for supper."

His grin is cheeky, like he's in on a secret that I'm not. He leans close to me, and just like all the other weeks, he whispers, "It's never too early to start thinking about your next meal—not with your mom's cooking."

Standing beside him, my mom rolls her eyes and smacks him on the arm with the back of her hand. I take in the scene—emotions splitting me in two. As prickly as my mom can be, my dad loves her. He always has. When I married Nate, I dreamed of having a marriage like theirs. The thing is, I would have. Nate looked at me like my dad looks at my mom. On the day of the funeral, I didn't just bury the love of my life. I buried some of my dreams, too.

Chapter 11

Grayson

Metal clangs against metal as I drop the weights I've been lifting for the last half hour.

I needed a distraction—anything to take my mind off the crushing weight of the elephant on my chest.

A letter—not even one, but two.

I should have seen it coming. I should have known. It's not often I'm caught off guard, but this plan of Nate's hit me like a ton of bricks.

I hate that.

"Dang it, Nate. What were you thinking?" I yell into the air.

Frustration ripples over me, eating at my insides. I'm no stranger to anger—we're old friends—but this is different. The man I'm angry at is gone, and that's like screaming into a void—useless. So, instead, I let the anger choke out my sanity.

I've had a year to tell Georgia about my letter—the one I received days after Nate died—but I didn't.

It would change everything.

I wanted to hide it and pretend it didn't happen, but now that Georgia is receiving letters from Nate, I have to tell her because what if Nate tells her first in one of his letters?

Nate's put me in an impossible situation.

If I tell her, I'll lose the only person I have left, but if I don't, then I face the same problem.

There's no winning for me here—Nate made sure of that—and for the first time since I've known him, I resent him and his meddling.

Pushing off the weight bench, I walk over to the punching bag I have set up in the corner. My fist meets the bag over and over until my knuckles are raw and bloody, creating a scar across the tattoos there.

Nate.

Punch.

Screwed.

Punch.

Up.

Punch.

My.

Punch.

Life.

First, he had to go and die—leaving me without a best friend, and now this.

He couldn't leave well enough alone, which is on par for him. He was always fixing situations—fixing me—and I always told him to stop sticking his nose where it didn't belong. He never minded my gruffness, laughing in my face most times. It made me want to throw a punch to the smugness that always spread across his face every time his plans worked. This isn't one of those times, though. This plan isn't going to work.

Another punch, and the blood starts to pour down my wrist. I should stop—get control of my temper—but rage burns through my veins, sending every other emotion up in flames.

This whole situation is messed up, and the worst part is—I know Georgia needed those letters. She's been floundering, and I haven't been able to help her.

But, dang it, if that doesn't sting.

A roar rips out of my chest as my fists meet the bag, a flurry of motion until I'm standing here with my chest heaving up and down, unable to lift my hands one more time.

Blood is spattered over my arms, dotting the ink etched into my skin and painting it red. I spy it—the orchid setting just above my wrist. Red is smeared over the purple ink. It's the only tattoo I have that's in color. The symbolism of my blood smeared over the tattoo, meant to be a promise to Nate, doesn't escape me. The only way I'll ever get the girl of my dreams is at the expense of my friend.

An hour later, after washing away the evidence of losing my control, there's a knock at my door. I know it's not Georgia because when she left, she said she was visiting Ellie and her parents today. From experience, she won't be back until late tonight, so whoever is standing on the other side of my door is either brave or stupid.

My house is my refuge—a place away from this town's drama and the stress of my job. There aren't many people I let come here—one, I let one person here.

Swinging the door open, I cross my arms over my chest, making sure that the bruises on my knuckles are showing. When I see the man on the other side, my jaw flexes, and I itch to reach out and split my knuckles open one more time—preferably on his front tooth.

Kip Montgomery stands on my stoop, looking, for all intents and purposes, like the loving father he never was. I can't blame the man. It's not like he knew I existed, but his very existence irks me, prickling at my nerves until all that's left is a fire of resentment burning in my gut. With him standing here on my front porch, it feels like a betrayal to my mom.

"What do you want?" I ask, lowering my voice and flexing my bicep.

"I was in the neighborhood," he says, his blue eyes twinkling under a set of gray bushy eyebrows.

Those eyes are an exact replica of mine and Brooks's. Most kids can't wait to be like their dad. I want to be nothing like mine. He was such a sot my mom left him when she found out she was pregnant with me. She was protecting me, but the life we lived without him was just as hard.

"And I'm sure you can find your way out of it too." My face is stone, giving nothing away—not to this man.

He's about to open his mouth, but a little voice behind him says, "Papaw Kip, I thought you said there was a bathroom here."

I look down to find a little girl with blue eyes that match mine and a halo of blonde hair. I haven't been around many kids in my life, but I would guess she is about three or four. She stares back at me, cocking one eyebrow with mischief sparkling in her eyes. I almost laugh when she scrunches her nose and examines me like she isn't quite sure she likes what she sees. She reminds me of Georgia—the Georgia before Nate died, fiery and full of life.

"Can we at least use your restroom?" Kip asks, pulling me out of my scrutiny of the girl.

Frowning, I move aside to motion them in. "Bathroom—then you leave."

I don't know what game Kip is playing here, but I'll win. I'm not accustomed to losing, and I don't play fair. Life taught me that lesson.

I don't want him in my space.

Once inside, I point to the half bath on the other side of the hall, and the little girl skips down the hall, closing the door behind her. I turn back to Kip, ready to face off now that we don't have an audience. He's looking around the foyer like he can learn something about me in this eight-foot opening.

I hate to tell him, but almost everything he sees here is Georgia's doing. I may have done all the work to fix this place up, but Georgia made it a home for me. The first time I invited her and Nate over when the house was complete, they brought pizza, and we sat on the floor eating in the living room. It's one of the few times I remember feeling content in my life—like I wasn't going to break under the pressure. As we sat on the ground shoving pizza in our mouths, Georgia jumped up and stared down at Nate and me. Excitement glowed on her face as she bounced on her toes.

"Let's go shopping," she'd said, on the edge of combustion.

Nate and I glanced at each other and then back at Georgia, wondering if she had finally lost her mind.

"For what?" I'd asked.

She'd looked at me like I was the one that was crazy.

"Well, we can't sit on the floor every time we come over, now can we? It should feel like home," she insisted.

And that's how every personal touch in my house ended up coming from Georgia. We all three went shopping that night. I handed over my credit card and let her fill the space. I didn't tell her it already felt like more of a home than I had ever had because it wasn't tainted with memories I never wanted to relive. I let her have her fun, and now, every day when I come home, I get a piece of Georgia that I would never have gotten otherwise.

I clear my throat, and Kip turns back to me. He sends me a sheepish grin, but I ignore it.

"What are you really doing here, Kip?"

He's smart enough to wince at my tone before he says, "I wanted to check on you."

A bitter laugh slips past my lips, breaking some of the emotionless mask I always keep in place. "I'm thirty-one years old. I don't need my daddy checking in on me."

His shoulders tense as he considers me. "Maybe you don't need it, but everyone wants it—someone around just to stop in and see how you are."

I let the silence hang around us, glaring at him because he's got it wrong—that's not a need or want for me.

After a beat, Kip nods, accepting what I'm not saying. Defeat sinks his shoulders as he glances down the hall to see if the bathroom door is opening yet.

"That's your niece, you know? Her name's Avery," he says, not looking back at me.

"Sort of figured from the eyes," I say, bored.

He expects that to mean something to me—like I'll drop everything and gush over this little stranger I know nothing about—but he doesn't realize I'm good at shutting people out.

Clenching my jaw, I refuse to take this conversation any further. I don't know what it is about Kip and Brooks dropping in unannounced, but it gets under my skin. I didn't seek them out, looking for a relationship with my long-lost family. Life taught me several times that the people you care about eventually disappoint you. I'm not looking to add anyone else into my life.

The door to the bathroom slings open, and Avery skips out the same way she skipped in, oblivious to the tension swirling through the air. She stops when she's standing directly in front of me and then reaches into her pocket, pulling out a piece of paper.

"Here," she says, shoving the paper towards me. "This is for you."

I take it from her, pinching the edges between my fingers and glancing up at Kip. He's watching us now, and when I cock an eyebrow in question, he merely shrugs.

Unfolding it, I stare as glitter and scribbles come into focus.

Not taking a second to breathe between her sentences, she says, "It's an invitation. I made it myself. I heard Daddy tell Mommy he invited you to my birthday party but that you probably wouldn't come. I figured it was because he didn't give you a real invitation. My grandma says that every party should have an invitation. I decided to make one when Papaw Kip said we were stopping by your house today. I'll be four."

She throws all that at me like a rabid animal, and I'm left stunned, grasping for something to say to this nearly four year old.

"I'll—uh—have to check my calendar," I say, unsure what to do with this paper that's leaking glitter all over my original hardwood floors.

Avery nods as if my answer is acceptable, then turns back to Kip.

"I'm ready now, Papaw Kip," she says, her chin lifted high like a queen, and like an obedient subject, Kip takes her hand and walks to the door.

When they are about to walk through, Kip turns back to me, leaving me with one final parting blow. "Grayson, your last name may not be Montgomery, but that doesn't negate the fact that you are one. We are here for you, Son—whenever you want us to be."

Avery tugs on his hand, and then they are out of the door, walking to the truck. I watch a moment as Kip lifts Avery, placing her in the car seat and dropping a kiss on her forehead before I slam my front door shut.

The paper that Avery gave me is still in my hand. I don't know what makes me do it—maybe it's the thought of all the effort she must have put into it—but I walk to my kitchen and hang it on my refrigerator, right beside a picture of Nate, Georgia, and me.

Chapter 12

Grayson

The man in front of me sits squirming in his chair as I stare down at him over the bridge of my nose.

I can't stand incompetence. It irritates me because, at the core of it, it's just laziness—pure and simple.

Sitting back in my chair, I steeple my fingers under my chin and study him, debating how to handle this situation. While I hate incompetence, I also realize that people rely on the jobs I give them. I'm not a man to be trifled with. The work we do is important to millions of homeowners. One mistake on our part means that a family buying a new one may experience a home emergency they aren't financially ready for. It could mean ruin for them. I expect my employees to know what they are doing so that doesn't happen, but at the same time, I had a mom who provided for her family on her own. We struggled, and because of that, I try to employ what little patience I have when dealing with my employees' mistakes.

"Do you want to explain how you missed this?" I ask, setting the papers down on the desk in front of me.

The man looks like he might cry, and dang it, if that doesn't anger me further.

"I'm—I'm sorry, sir."

"Sorry?" I ask, controlling my tone. "Sorry doesn't fix the twenty thousand dollar mistake you missed."

"I—um—I," The man stutters.

"Enough." My voice is low. My patience is quickly running out, and if I don't get this man out of my office soon, I will fire him—no questions asked. "Here's what's going to happen. You're going to take a few refresher inspecting courses. The company will pay for them. Then, for the next six months, you are on probation. That means that each time you inspect, you will have a superior there with you. If a mistake this big happens again, you will be fired immediately."

"You're—" he stops, considering me, then swallowing hard before continuing, "You're not firing me?"

"Not this time, but the ice you're walking on is very thin. You would do well to remember that. Now go," I say, pointing towards the door.

He stands, stuttering out several thank you's as he makes his way out of my office. Georgia walks in as he walks out, closing the door behind her.

"And they say you don't have a heart." She grins. Walking over to me, she places a cup of coffee in my hands and sits on the corner of my desk. Her legs are on display beneath her black pencil skirt, making my throat bob as I clear it and look away.

"They would be right."

Her hand reaches out, tousling my hair, and the feel of her fingernails scratching against my scalp almost sends me over the edge of sanity.

"I don't think so, Gray. You just like to hide it, so it's hard to find."

The sadness in her voice has me turning back to her. There's a smile on her face, but her eyes glitter with pain. Reaching out, I grab the papers that I placed on the desk earlier and clench them between my fists to stop myself from pulling her into my lap and holding her until all that pain is gone.

"I must be really good at hide and seek then because I've hidden it so well, even I can't find it."

"You will," she says, holding my gaze. "One day, you're going to find a girl to love, and it will be impossible to hide that heart of yours."

I give a gruff acknowledgment because I can't tell her I've already found that girl—she's sitting across from me, forever out of reach.

"So," she says, clapping her hands and jumping off the desk. I think my lucky stars because if she had sat there one more second, I might have been tempted to reach out and run my hand over the smoothness of her skin. "I need a favor."

Arching my brow, I wave my hand, urging her to continue. She takes a deep breath, her lips parting and drawing my attention to them. There hasn't been a single day that I haven't wondered what it would be like to taste them—to feel them pressed against my own—but each time that thought crosses my mind, it's like a punch to my gut, reminding me that she's my best friend's girl.

"Do you remember how you said I wouldn't have to do these letters alone?" she asks.

"Yes." Her question is like a bucket of water being poured over my head. She's still grieving, and all I can think about is pressing my lips to hers.

"Well, I think I know what I want to do for the first one." She's nervous. I can hear it in how her voice wavers as she speaks, her hands rolling the end of her hair between her fingers.

"What's that?" I ask cautiously.

"There is a winter festival that the church is putting on, and I thought maybe we could go because there's going to be funnel cake, and rides, and games. There will be a big crowd because people from across several counties are coming, and I thought maybe it would be easy to get lost in that crowd—that way a ton of people aren't attacking me with a hundred questions." The words bubble out of her mouth at a speed that makes it hard to follow. When she's finished, she bites her lip and digs her toe into the ground.

My brain finally catches up to the words, and a sense of dread settles into my chest. I know I told her that she didn't have to do this alone, and I meant it. I just didn't expect the first place she'd want to go would be a festival filled with people who can't stand the sight of me and vice versa, but I made her a promise. I won't back out just because of my aversion to people.

"When is it?" I ask.

She meets my gaze, still chewing on her bottom lip, and I have to physically restrain myself from getting up and tugging it out from between her teeth.

"This Saturday."

I nod and turn away from her, back to my desk. "I'll put it on my calendar."

For the second time in a matter of days, I'm caught off guard as she rushes over to me and slings her arms around my neck. Heat rushes through my veins from the feel of her cheek pressed against mine. She turns her head, presses a kiss on my cheek, and whispers, "Thank you" against my skin.

And—if I thought I knew guilt before, it's nothing like what I feel now because I don't know if there's a possibility that I can go my whole life without finding out what it's like to have Georgia's lips on mine.

The cold nips at my skin as I walk out of my house and across the driveway to Georgia's. Sometime over the course of the last year, I stopped thinking about it as the guest house and started thinking of it as Georgia's. She could live here a hundred years or move out tomorrow, and I would still consider it hers from now until forever.

It's the day of the festival. Not a single fiber of me is excited about this, but I know Georgia is. After she asked me, she spent the rest of the week talking about the funnel cakes and rides and everything else that will be there. She was like a kid on Christmas—pure, unadulterated excitement.

I might resent the letter Nate sent me, but I'm not fool enough to ignore that the two that Georgia received have healed a part of her soul.

Rapping my knuckles against the door, I step back, waiting for Georgia. When the door swings open, my breath is knocked out of my lungs.

The woman is beautiful.

Her dark hair tumbles around her shoulders and frames her face with her toboggan pulled down low over her ears. She smiles at me with pink cheeks, and my heart stutters in my chest. When I get to her eyes, though, they are rimmed with red. She has been crying.

My brow furrows as I try to comprehend what's happening.

"What's going on? Why have you been crying? I thought you were excited."

"It's nothing," she says, closing the door behind her and locking it.

She tries to push past me to go to the truck, but I slide in front of her, blocking her path.

"Hey, don't do that. Don't push me out."

Blowing out a breath, she stares at a spot right over my shoulder, refusing to make eye contact.

"I was excited, but now that today's here, I'm just not sure I'm ready."

Keeping my hands carefully by my side, I step closer to her and say, "We don't have to do this if you're not ready."

Her mouth twists as she contemplates what I've said, and then she spins on her heel, marching back to the door.

Catching her hand, I spin her back to me until she crashes into my chest. Her hand lands directly above my heart, and I pray she can't feel how fast it's beating.

"We don't have to go *if* you aren't ready, but Georgia, you are. That excitement you've felt all week—that's your gut telling you that you are. Be brave, Peach."

Our breaths tangle as she looks up at me, three inches separating her lips from mine. All I would have to do is lower my head, and my lips would be on hers. I could finally know what she tastes like, but a voice in the back of my head screams that she isn't in a place for that.

Stepping back, I give her the space that we both need. Her chest heaves up and down, breathing hard from our closeness—or maybe it's from the decision that she has to make. This isn't just a decision to go to a winter festival or not. This is a decision to either move on or stay stuck in her grief, and I can't make it for her.

Finally, after what seems like hours, she nods and says, "I'll go."

Chapter 13

Georgia

Noises and lights swirl around me as Grayson and I walk through the entrance to the festival. The church has been putting the event on every year since I can remember. It's filled with vendors, food, activities for the kids, music—and most importantly, people. When I decided to follow through with the request in Nate's letter, I knew I needed a place where I wouldn't be smothered. Maybe it's strange that I chose the most crowded event of the year, but in my mind, it meant I could get lost in the sea of the crowd with Grayson. It's not just our town that comes to this thing—it's people from all over, making it one of the biggest tourist events of the year. It's a bump in our economy right before the holidays.

A twinge of dread runs through my body as I think of facing another holiday without Nate.

I take a deep breath to center myself, filling my nose with the sweet scents of fried food. Grayson's eyes dart towards me, his mouth dipping in concern, and I shake my head. I don't want to do that tonight—be the look of concern. Tonight, I want to do like Nate asked me and live. I can be sad tomorrow, but I want to be present today.

"Georgia," a voice calls from somewhere in the crowd behind me. "Oh, Georgia."

Turning around, I scan the crowd, looking for where the voice came from. I don't have to look long because the woman it came from is anything but discreet—that goes for the pack following along with her, too.

Four elderly women cling to each other, arm in arm, pushing through the crowd—pushing may be too tame of a word, more like they are tackling anyone who gets in their way on their mission to get to me. Our mayor may hold the keys to the city, but these women run it.

"Mrs. Adams, how are you?" I ask, pasting on a polite smile as they shove closer.

She's a spry old woman with naturally gray hair and a penchant for being a menace—the leader of her girl gang. Her voice sounds like she smokes a pack a day, which she does, but she likes to tell everyone at church that she quit twenty years ago. She doesn't mean any harm. The woman could boss the president around if she wanted to. But her bossiness is her way of caring for the people around her. Some people are an acquired taste, and she's one of them.

"Oh, you know how it is. But enough about me," she says, batting away my question like a fly buzzing around. I want to tell her I don't know how it is, but it won't deter her from what I know is coming. Instead, I keep quiet and wait for her to continue. "We are all so glad to see you here. Right ladies?"

The women around her nod like bobbleheads. I worry their heads might fall off when the nods continue past what should be socially acceptable. They are Mrs. Adams's loyal followers. If she says jump, they say how high. If she jumps off a bridge, they are going with her—literally. They all went bungee jumping at Mrs. Adams's insistence two years ago. Sometimes, I wonder if the woman is certifiable. Yet, despite her eccentricities, she's good for the community—arranging fundraisers, heading festivals, dropping in several times a month to check on the woman who lost her husband to cancer. She hasn't missed a month since Nate died, and she never comes empty-handed, always bringing apple pie—Nate's favorite.

"Well—thanks," I say, drawing the words out and waiting for the other shoe to drop because, with her, there's always another shoe.

"Since you're here—" Mrs. Adam starts—and there it is, the other shoe. "We need someone to man a booth for us. Lucille here doesn't draw in the customers as much as a young, pretty face would."

She gestures to the woman standing to her right, who looks suspiciously sheepish. Grayson grumbles under his breath beside me, but I don't catch what he says. Neither Mrs. Adams nor any of the other women have bothered acknowledging Grayson since we've been standing here, and as much as I like Mrs. Adams, anger at her blatant slight towards the man who has been there for me the last year bubbles in my chest. I hate it when the townspeople treat Grayson like he's still that lost kid who caused trouble. He hasn't been that person in a long time, but they never let him forget it.

I open my mouth to respond, but she barrels over me like a freight train. "Besides, we have some young bucks we would like to introduce you to. It's about time you start to move on."

At that, she's taking my arm and pulling me along with her. I should tell her to stop, pull my arm away, walk back to Grayson, and continue our night, but my mind is frozen from the audacity.

Throughout this whole grief process, there's always someone telling me how I should grieve. What's appropriate at what time, and I hate it.

I hate it so much.

Their intentions are pure. I know they are, but that doesn't stop me from wanting to rage and throw things every time it happens. The problem is that I hate disappointing people—especially those I love. It makes my skin crawl just with the thought of it, so I've let them shove their opinions down my throat. But this—this crosses a line.

"That will be enough."

Grayson's voice is low and dangerous, just barely heard over the noise of the crowd, but it causes Mrs. Adams and her posse to stop in their tracks. A shiver runs down my spine when I catch a glimpse of Grayson's face. It's stone cold. His blue eyes flicker with fire—dark and dangerous—a soldier standing ready to save the day.

He stalks towards us—his careful control over his anger is apparent with each step he takes. The thing about control, though, is, one slip—one tiny nudge—and then it's gone, and you're left with mass destruction.

"Georgia will not be going with you. She didn't come here to work, and she sure didn't ask you to set her up. When she is ready to move on, she will, but until then, you will back off. Am I clear?" Grayson says, all while staring Mrs. Adams down. He doesn't blink, letting the flame burn brighter in his eyes until his irises are consumed with his anger.

To her credit, most grown men would cower under Grayson's demanding presence, but she doesn't bat an eye. Staring him down the same way he is her.

I watch as the muscle in his jaw jumps once, grinding his molars together, and then his body relaxes, letting the anger melt from his body and leaving frustration behind.

After a moment, she gives him a nod of acceptance. Letting go of my hand, she turns and shoves through the crowd, her gang of women following closely at her heels.

Turning to Grayson, I see his fists clenching at his sides, the only remnants of his anger. Taking careful steps, I approach him until I'm right in front of him. He doesn't move, head still held high, but his eyes dip down to mine.

He looks like a wounded animal. I lift my arms slowly as if he might dart if I move too fast. He flinches but otherwise remains immovable until my arms wrap around his waist. He's pure muscle in a 6' 3" form.

"Thank you for always saving me," I whisper into his chest.

As my breath fans across his chest, that stone facade crumbles, and he leans into me, dropping his chin so it's pressed against the top of my head. His arms wrapped around my shoulders, squeezing me tight to him.

"Anytime, Peach."

I should pull away. We are in a crowd of people who thrive on gossip, but I can't make myself—not yet.

It's been a year since I felt cherished, and I want that connection again, if only for a moment. So, I let myself be selfish.

"I've been worried about you," I say against his chest.

"You don't have to worry about me, Georgia."

"But I do, Grayson. I was there for all the times your anger got you in trouble. Don't get me wrong, I know you had a reason to be angry, but you've made so much of yourself. I don't want to see you go back."

He jerks back as if I've slapped him, and as he stares down at me, there's hurt written across his features.

"Are you—" he starts and clears his throat to try again. "Are you scared of me?"

My hand finds the line of his jaw, and he relaxes into it just a little bit.

"No, Gray. Your anger has never hurt anyone but yourself. You self-sabotage, and after Nate and finding out about your family—well, I've just been waiting for that to happen so I can help you pick up the pieces like you have for me."

The muscle on his jaw relaxes, and his face softens.

"That won't happen, Peach. I've grown up a lot since my teenage years. Sure, I still have moments I get angry, especially when old women try to pimp you out, but I can control it now. I have things to take care of now—more than myself."

I nod because that makes sense. He has a whole business where employees rely on him. He cares about that business and his employees, even if he's not one to wear his feelings on his sleeve and show it.

"Right, your business. How do you do it? Let go of that anger? I watched just now as you were consumed with it, and then it was like a blink of an eye, and you relaxed. You were still frustrated but not angry. So what worked for you?"

"Are you asking because you want to know about me, or are you asking for yourself?" he asks, staring down at me.

Shrugging, I say, "A little of both. It's no secret that I've been angry since Nate died. But I also want to know about you, too."

He studies me a moment before saying, "I don't know—I guess I just try to be mindful now. When I feel that heat burning deep in my gut, I take one deep breath and think about where I am and if it's worth being this angry. Usually, the anger simmers to frustration. It doesn't always work, mostly when I'm around Kip and Brooks, but for the most part, it cools me down enough to let me think."

"I'm glad you've found that part of you, Gray, but if you ever need me to pick up the pieces, I will," I say, squeezing my arms around him and holding him until the crowd pushes against us and we are forced to break apart.

I don't look at Grayson. I can't. Instead, I look around the festival, searching for a distraction for both of us. Catching sight of a booth labeled hot chocolate, I motion towards it and say, "Let's go grab some of that. I'm freezing."

Grayson nods, refusing to make eye contact with me either.

Besides the run-in with Mrs. Adams and her posse, this isn't as hard as I thought. For the most part, people have left me alone, waving as they walk by and then moving on. Whether that's from fear of Grayson's glare or because they are busy with their own lives, who can tell, but it's been nice.

The hot chocolate stand is to the left of the grandstand, where several mid-size performers are taking the stage tonight. The mic on stage crackles to life, announcing the schedule for the rest of the night as we wait in line.

Grayson stands beside me, his hands shoved in his coat pockets, warding off the cold. Objectively speaking, he really is handsome, his dark hair a shocking contrast to those blue eyes. His eyelashes are long and dark, causing every girl to hate him for the mere fact they would kill for natural lashes like that. He's caught the eye of several women here tonight, but he's remained oblivious to it. My heart aches a little when I think about losing the only friend I have left to another woman someday.

"Why do you never date anymore? Before Nate died, it seemed like you went out with a new girl every weekend."

I instantly wish I could shove that question right back into my mouth. Heat rises in my cheeks, and I'm thankful for the bitterness of the night so I can blame my blush on the cold. It's none of my business why he doesn't date, and if I'm honest, I also don't want to know.

Grayson's eyes narrow just a fraction, but that one movement makes it feel like he can see right through me.

"I got tired of going out with the wrong girl."

"What do you mean?" I ask, scrunching my nose. "I never got the impression that you wanted to settle down."

"It's not like I haven't thought about it. It was impossible not to think about being around you and Nate, but I watched my mom make all the wrong decisions—and look at Kip. I'm pre-genetically disposed to screw things up."

"Gray," I say, pulling him so he's facing me. "You know that's not true."

He shrugs, and irritation crawls over my skin. Reaching up, I flick him on the tip of his nose.

"Hey," he cries, rubbing the spot. "What was that for?"

I lower my brows and glare at him from below my eyelashes. "For thinking that's actually true."

"Fine—then let's just say I haven't had the chance with the right girl, " he says, a smirk taking over his full lips, causing his dimples to poke in under the scruff along his face.

My heart rate kicks into overdrive, and I hope he can't see what that one little smile does to me. His choice of words seems intentional, but I can't figure out what he means by them.

Instead of asking, I say, "You'll get your chance."

His smirk grows into a full-blown smile, and at this point, my heart might fall right out of my chest.

"Yeah, Peach," he says, studying me. The clearness of his eyes darkens into stormy puddles when he continues. "I think you're right—I just might."

I don't know what to say to that, so I let the conversation go.

The microphone on the stage begins to crackle as someone taps their finger against it. Looking over, I recognize Pastor Greer, a middle-aged man with a large stomach, salt-and-pepper hair, and a kind smile.

"Good afternoon, folks," he says into the microphone.

The crowd answers him with several good afternoons resounding around them. Grayson and I grab our hot chocolate. I try to offer my money to the vendor, but Gray shoves it away and slips him a twenty. Not waiting for the change, he places his hand on the small of my back and guides me towards the stage so we have a better view.

I try to pay attention to where I'm going, but all I can focus on is Grayson's hand pressing softly into my back, guiding me. He saves me from bumping into people a couple of times, and then we are standing still, listening to Pastor Greer continue.

"I would like to thank everyone who came out tonight to make this festival a success. We have a lot of people here who worked very hard to put this event on for you tonight."

The crowd cheers, but I'm having trouble concentrating. Grayson's hand is still resting against my back, and when I glance at him, it looks like he has no intention of moving it.

"Before we continue with the festivities, I want to say a couple more things. When we started this festival many years ago, we wanted a way to gather and fellowship with one another. What we didn't realize at the time was that it would turn into a way for us to spread God's love for us. So—with that in mind, I want to share one last thing that's been weighing on my mind. There are some of you here today who are struggling—maybe it's a struggle to accept the Lord, or maybe it's your anger that you're holding against him, but I want you to know that you are loved by a high and mighty God. He did not promise that he wouldn't give you more than *you* can handle, but he did promise that he wouldn't give you more than *HE* can handle. That—my friends—that makes all the difference. So, if you are struggling today, I want you to know that there is a light at the end of that tunnel waiting for you to find him."

With Grayson's hand forgotten for the moment, tears pool in my eyes. There are hundreds of people here, but that message felt like one God intended for me to hear. There have been many times over the last year when I thought I was going to be pulled under the current of my grief. People would placate me by saying that God wouldn't give me more than I can handle. I thought I was broken—that I was weak—but Pastor Greer's words settle in my chest, loosening the knot that's been there.

I'm still angry. I can't understand why Nate had to die, but maybe I'm a little less mad at God and more just angry at the situation itself.

Leaning into Grayson's hand, I take comfort in his strength.

It's late when we pull into the driveway. I'm slumped down in the front seat, with the top half of the chair leaned back for me to rest.

Rolling my eyes towards Grayson, I yawn. "Tonight was fun."

We'd stayed and listened to several of the singers before calling it a night. I might have even seen a Grayson smile once or twice.

"It wasn't terrible," Grayson agrees.

Sitting up, I reach for the handle, ready to get inside, kick off my shoes, and lie in bed. Today was fun, but it was also mentally draining.

"Wait." Grayson's hand shoots out, grabbing my wrist and pulling me back. "Stay there."

He jumps out of the truck and rounds the front, stopping at my door. Through the window, I watch him run his hand over the scruff on his jaw and up the back of his neck, grumbling to himself the whole time. Then he's opening the door and offering me his hand. I take it, placing my fingers in his palm and letting the heat of his skin ward off the chill in the air. When my feet are on solid ground, he places his hand on the small of my back, just like at the festival. It's a small gesture with no real significance, so why am I obsessing over it?

I've spent the last year missing Nate's touch, so maybe my obsession stems from that loneliness.

I miss the companionship of having a partner.

At the front door, I search my purse, looking for the key—prolonging the moment.

When I walk inside, I'll forget the way Grayson's smile was like tape over the cracks in my heart tonight or how the warmth of his hand sends goosebumps over my arms. I'll forget all those things because tape does nothing to hold together shattered glass.

Nate asked me to move on, but that won't happen. I'm too broken for anyone to put back together—especially my husband's best friend. Tonight was fun, but it doesn't change the fact that as a person, Nate's death changed me, and there's no going back to the girl I was before. I'll go along with his letters, put myself back out there, and find myself again, but the girl I find will always be a broken version of the one I was before.

Grayson clears his throat, and I look up at him. It's a full moon, and the moonlight behind his head creates a halo around him. I can almost imagine that he's my guardian angel, sent to protect me from myself this last year.

"You were brave tonight, Peach. I'm proud of you."

The wind blows a stray hair across my face, and Grayson reaches up, sweeping it behind my shoulder. A cold chill runs from the crown of my head all the way to my toes.

Chapter 14

Grayson

The cold burns my lungs as I pick up my pace—a punishment for my stupidity.

I let myself pretend for one night that Georgia could be my girl. I held her close, placed my hand on her back, and stood tall for everyone to see she was there with me. In the end, the only one who was fooled by my game was me, and now I can't stop thinking about what it would be like if I could do that for real—if I could take her in my arms and swipe my lips across hers without anyone blinking an eye.

Stupid. I was stupid.

My legs ache as I push them through the final curve of my run.

I've run the same route since I was fifteen, and I haven't missed a day in the last two years. Nate and I started running this route during our freshman year of high school. He wanted to join the football team, dragging me along with him. I didn't realize I would also fall in love with the game. We ran this route a lot over the years. When he got sick and couldn't run anymore, I ran every day for him, and I haven't stopped, no matter what the weather calls for.

A brick house lies just ahead, and I angle my body towards it—Nate and Georgia's house.

Georgia hasn't been here since the day of the funeral when I drove her over here, but I've come over periodically over the year to keep it up. It will be ready for her when she's ready to return. It's the least I can do, and with the weather dipping into freezing temperatures, I want to make sure the heat is on so none of the pipes burst.

This morning, the weather channel was calling for snow that was supposed to start late into the night, but it looks like they were off by a few hours because flakes are falling around me, landing on my eyelashes. I blink them away, jogging a few more steps until I stand on the front porch. Reaching for the front door, I slip the key from under the rug and shove it in the lock. My hands are frozen, so it takes me a couple of times before I successfully unlock the door and shove it open.

The house is older, with a brick exterior and white shutters framing the windows. The inside is cozy, with a fireplace in the living room and an updated floor space, so it's open to all the other rooms. When Nate died, Georgia asked me to take the life insurance and pay off the house. It's the only good thing that's come from his death.

Finding the thermostat, I turn the heat on and head over to the fireplace to get it going. The cold permeates the air, and I flip the hood of my sweatshirt up to ward it off. As the furnace and fireplace run, I take a minute to look around.

Nate haunts the walls of this house. I've left everything the way I found it, only cleaning up where it needs it. Nate's jacket lays across the back of the couch, where Georgia always kept it for the days after chemo. Pictures from their wedding hang on the wall behind the couch. Nate's happiness that day was contagious. There are even a few shots of me hanging on the wall, and what's more, I'm smiling.

Georgia asked me why it had to be Nate once, and the truth is, it's an answer I want myself. I don't understand why one of the best men I've ever known was taken while I got to stay. I wish it had been me instead of Nate—for Georgia's sake. She deserved to have her happily ever after. Not that she can't still have it. I know she doesn't see it yet, but one day, she'll heal. Someone else will love her, but there will always be a blip in her life where her happily ever after was tainted.

The idea of her loving another man causes jealousy to burn in the pit of my stomach, but I knew Georgia deserved better in high school, and that's still true today—no matter how much holding her last night, defending her, felt right. Just like I did with Nate, I'll cheer on the next man that comes into her life—as long as he's good to her.

There's a recliner next to the window that Georgia used to curl up in and read. I sit in it, glancing at the snow floating down and blanketing the grass beneath it. There's a table next to the chair, and I reach over, grabbing the bible lying on top. Turning it in my hand, I run my fingers over Nate's name engraved into the leather. Flashes of Nate on one of his many trips to the hospital, sitting in the bed reading this book, run through my mind. Even until the end, Nate kept his faith.

Flipping it open to where the bookmark lies, I begin to read the first verse I come to aloud.

"To every thing there is a season, and a time for every purpose under the heaven: a time to be born, and a time to die, a time to plant, and a time to pluck up that which is planted. A time to kill and a time to heal."

The last words stick in my throat. Unable to read further, I close the book and place it back where I got it.

A time for everything.

The thought almost makes me laugh. In my life, there's only ever been a time for heartache—first as a kid, then when my mom died, and now that Nate's gone. I'd like to know when the healing time is coming because it seems long overdue.

The sun is starting to set when I get back to my house. I haven't heard from Georgia all day, which is strange. She usually always checks in at least once—not that she has to. She's entitled to a day without me in it, but when Nate first died, she sunk into this hole I was afraid she would never find her way out of. I made her go to the doctor, and they diagnosed her with depression. She started taking medicine and checking in with me every day.

Looking towards the guest house, I notice that none of the lights are on. Her car is still in the driveway, though, so where is she?

Unease settles in my gut.

"There's no need to get ahead of yourself, Grayson. She could be out with a friend," I grumble to myself, even though I know that's not true. Aside from last night, she doesn't go out.

Veering off the sidewalk that leads to my front porch, I walk over to Georgia's door, careful of my footing as the snow starts sticking, making the concrete slick.

Once I'm in front of her door, I raise my hand and knock, waiting for some kind of life from the inside, but there's nothing—not a sound. I pull my phone from my pocket and swipe so it brings the screen to life. I was hoping I'd missed a call or text on my way home, but again, there's nothing.

Tapping my finger against the screen, I debate my next plan of action.

On one hand, I could be overreacting, but my gut tells me I'm not. I've learned to listen to that feeling a lot over the years—it's the one thing that's never failed me.

Swiping my thumb across the screen, I dial Georgia's number and press the phone to my ear, waiting for it to ring. This time, I do hear noise inside the apartment. Her phone rings from inside, and that knot in my gut squeezes a little tighter.

There's a flower pot just outside of the door. I keep an extra key under there just in case of emergencies.

Bending, I grab it, then hesitate. Right now, there's a line between Georgia and me labeled Nate's girl, but that line has started to blur for me. If I barge in to check on Georgia, will I be going as Nate's best friend or something more?

The answer has me hesitating a few seconds longer until a running memory of Georgia lying in bed with the lights off for weeks runs through my mind.

I unlock the door and step inside.

The first thing I notice is that the house is clean, which means it's at least not as bad as the last time. The second thing I notice is the sob coming from the bedroom.

Not waiting any longer, I flip the hallway light on and walk to the back room. My heart isn't ready for what I see.

The hallway light shines into the room, casting a sallow glow across Georgia. She's lying in bed, her hair a mess, and last night's makeup still on her face. Black streaks coat her cheeks from the remnants of her tears.

She leans up for a second to glance at me and then lies back down as if the effort to hold her head up is too much. That one motion splits my chest in two.

What happened between last night and today? She hasn't had a day like this in months.

My tennis shoes thud against the hardwood as I walk towards her—each step in time with the beat in my chest. She doesn't bother looking at me as I approach. Carefully, I sit on the edge of the bed and swipe my hand over her matted curls.

"Peach," I say, my voice broken. I hate seeing her like this. It breaks a piece of me every time I do.

She doesn't look—just lies there with her eyes turned toward the ceiling.

"Come on, Peach. It's me. Let me help." At this point, I'm practically begging. I want her to hand over her pain and let me share the burden, but still, she doesn't move.

Not bothering to kick off my shoes, I sling my legs onto the queen-sized bed, lie beside her, and pull her into my arms.

Her chest moves up and down against my arm—the only sign that she's alive.

"Georgia," I plead. I will not plead with anyone else for anything, but this—for her—I will.

It's her name on my lips that finally breaks her from her trance. Big, gulping sobs pour from her mouth. Her whole body shakes, and I pull her closer, wrapping my body around her. My legs tangle with hers. My arms hold her. In another lifetime, this would be everything for me, but in this lifetime, she's a broken woman, and I'm the defective glue trying to hold her together.

"What, Peach? What happened between the time I left you last night and now?"

She shrugs, the sobs still leaving her body, but that answer isn't good enough for me—not after I've seen how far she can fall.

"Tell me," I demand. It's not harsh, but it catches her attention. I won't let her go back there.

"I knew yesterday would be hard," she hiccups, "but then I got there, and I had fun. It was fun. I was happy when I got home last night. Then I walked inside, sat on the couch *alone*, and it hit me out of nowhere."

"What did?" I ask, my voice smoother than before.

"That I was happy."

My brows pull together. "I don't understand why that led you here, Peach."

"Because I was happy, Grayson," she says, pounding her fists against my back. I let her. I'll be her punching bag if that's what she needs. "I was happy, and Nate's not here. I was happy without Nate."

Her fight fizzles out as understanding dawns on me.

"Georgia, baby, look at me."

She lifts her chin, turning her face away from me. The woman is as stubborn as a mule. Untangling one of my arms, I pinch her chin between my thumb and forefinger, turning her head until she's facing me. Still, she lets her eyes wander to everything in the room but me.

"Georgia," I growl.

A small shiver runs over her body. If she weren't so close to me, I wouldn't have noticed, but she is, and I did. I store that information away for later when there's a more appropriate time to analyze what that small reaction means.

She stares behind my head, then slowly pulls her eyes towards mine. I swear sloths move faster than how quickly the woman meets my gaze.

When I have her full attention, I take advantage of it.

"Nate wants you to be happy. It's the whole point of the letters. But I also know that guilt—and grief—can't be explained or willed away. So today, you're going to take the time to grieve the happiness that you didn't get with Nate, and tomorrow, *we* are going to get up and put one step in front of the other because that's all life is, Georgia—putting one foot in front of the other."

Her breath stutters as she tries to hold back her sobs, but I don't want her to hold it back. I'm selfish—I want all her pain and happiness too.

"Let go, Georgia. I've got you."

She drops her head to my shoulder, and tears soak into my sweatshirt. It's then that I realize that I'm never going to not love this girl. I've tried so hard not to love her—to only see her as a friend because I know she deserves better—but I want days like this where I get to be her strength and nights like last night where I got to be a part of her happiness.

We lie there for over an hour, our limbs intertwined and her hands clutching my shirt, and when I'm sure that she has no more tears left to cry, I stand up.

"Where are you going?" she croaks, her voice ragged from her sobs.

"I'll be right back," I say, turning and walking out of the room to the bathroom across the hall.

Flipping on the light switch, I search through the vanity until I find what I'm looking for. Then I walk over to the bathtub and turn on the water, checking it to make sure it's set to the right temperature. When the tub starts to fill up, I dump in the bath salts I found under the sink.

Leaving the water to run, I return to the bedroom and sweep Georgia out of the bed into my arms.

"Hey," she protests, but I ignore her.

Tonight, I'm taking care of her.

I carry her to the bathroom and then place her on her feet.

"Stay right there," I instruct.

Her eyes narrow at me bossing her around, but she doesn't protest.

In a flash, I run to the kitchen, grab a candle and a lighter, and then I'm back in two seconds flat. I set the candle on the vanity, light it, and dim the lights.

"Now," I say. "I'm going to close this door and give you some privacy. After that, you will get in that tub and soak for as long as you need. When you're done soaking, you're going to wash your hair because you always feel better when you wash your hair. In the meantime, I'm going to make supper because I'm sure you haven't eaten all day. Am I right?"

Her mouth hangs open at my demands, but she nods her head anyway.

"Good." Smirking, I drop a kiss on the top of her head and then close the door behind me.

For a long time, I've not felt worthy of Georgia. I still don't, but it's past time I start trying to be because, as she was wrapped in my arms today, I realized I couldn't let her go.

Chapter 15

Georgia

The water is cold when I finally press my foot against the drain and step out of the bath. Wrapping a towel around me, I walk over to the door and grab the clothes Grayson set outside—an oversized t-shirt and leggings, comfort clothes.

Wiping the steam from the mirror, I study myself. My hair drips down my shoulder from where I washed it. Grayson was right. It did make me feel better. I wouldn't have gotten out of bed today if it wasn't for him. Things have gotten better than they were when Nate first died, but there are still days when getting up to start a shower feels too much.

Today was one of those days. I went to bed with a sense of dread sitting on my chest, and then this morning, when I woke up, it all was just too much. I could have called Grayson and told him how I felt, but I didn't want to bother him. When he showed up, I didn't have time to hide, not that I could—not from him.

Once my clothes are on, I wrap a towel around my head, grab my leave-in conditioner and brush, and walk out to the kitchen where Grayson is standing.

His back is to me, and he doesn't hear me approach. It gives me a chance to study him without him noticing. He must have gone home to change while I was in the tub because he's no longer wearing his running gear. Instead, he has on gray sweats and a black hoodie. I don't want to analyze why my heart skips a beat in my chest seeing him like this—in clothes that would make any girl drool and standing at the stove cooking.

It's domestic—a word I've never used to describe him before.

Swallowing hard, I step the rest of the way into the kitchen.

"Hey," I say.

Grayson turns his head, and I swear his smile is devastating.

"Do you feel any better?"

Pulling out a bar stool, I put the bottle of conditioner and brush on the counter in front of me.

"Maybe a little."

"We'll get there."

And that's the part that confuses me. He never acts like my pain is just mine to handle. We were friends before Nate died, but he was always more Nate's than mine. I don't get why he's done so much for me, but I also don't have enough energy to question him today.

Turning from the stove, he slides a plate of spaghetti and garlic toast in front of me.

"Eat," he demands.

His voice is forceful, but his eyes soften when he says it.

"I'm not hungry," I protest.

"Georgia, you're going to eat if I have to feed you myself. I'm not letting you fall into the hole of your depression again. I didn't notice last time until it was too late, but I see you this time—so eat."

He holds my gaze in a test of wills until, finally, I blink.

"Fine, but I have to get the knots out of my hair first," I say, pointing to the brush on the counter.

Without a word, Grayson walks around the counter until he's standing beside me. Then he picks up the conditioner and spritzes it into my hair. The brush is in front of me, and he picks it up, gently stroking it through my hair.

My eyes drift close, and a content sigh slips past my lips. Having someone brush your hair is a different type of intimacy. Grayson's fingers follow the path of the brush, massaging my scalp as he works the tangles out.

"Gray—" I whisper.

"Shh, Peach. Just let me take care of you."

And because I am powerless to resist this man, I do.

Everything around me is white. The floor blends in with the walls and the ceiling, making it hard to determine where one starts and the other ends.

A figure steps out of the brightness surrounding me, and my heart pitter patters to an unnatural rhythm.

Nate.

I know I'm dreaming because I only ever see him in my dreams anymore, but those dreams have started to become few and far between. I'm forgetting him, and that hurts.

"Hi, baby," he says, drawing closer but staying just out of reach.

I want to reach out and touch him, feel his skin against my hand, but every time I've tried, my hand passes through him—a mirage, like all the dreams we planned together.

"I miss you," I whisper.

"I miss you, too—-more than you can ever know, but you have Grayson now. He's taking good care of you. Let him, Georgia."

My eyes fly open, and Nate disappears into the recesses of my mind. Every night I go to sleep, I crave these dreams—one more night I get to spend with Nate, even though I know it's only in my mind.

Tonight's dream falls under the umbrella of guilt. I don't know when it happened, but Grayson has started to feel less like a friend and more like—I don't know. I don't know what category he falls under anymore, making my stomach churn whenever I think about it.

Gray took care of me last night. After he finished brushing my hair, we ate in silence, and then he guided me over to the couch, stuck a book in my hand, and turned a movie on for me.

It was comfortable. My chest ached a little less when he was there.

Then, when I fell asleep reading, he scooped me up in his arms again and carried me to my bed. That was the second time he had carried me. The first time, I was too lost in my fog to notice, but the second time, all I could focus on was how his biceps bunched against my side.

He had laid me in bed, pulled the covers up to my chin, and pressed a kiss to my forehead.

My chest had tightened from both the warmth that spread through me from being taken care of and the guilt I felt because of that.

Groaning, I turn on my side and look at the clock.

It's one a.m.

I won't be able to go back to sleep for a while. I'm always wired after I dream about Nate, and tonight, the memories of Grayson and Nate are clashing together, each warring for dominance.

Throwing the covers back, I slip on my slippers and pad to the kitchen for a glass of water. When I reach the end of the hall, though, I nearly jump out of my skin.

Grayson's lying on the couch, fast asleep. He's lying on his back with his head turned to the side. One arm is draped across his stomach while the other falls to the floor.

What's he doing here? Why didn't he go home?

Quietly, I tiptoe over to the couch.

He looks peaceful while sleeping, none of the usual lines of grumpiness marring his face.

Leaning down, I run my hands through his hair like he did to me hours before, careful not to wake him up.

For a moment, I wonder what it would be like to lay down beside him while he sleeps. The feel of him holding me in his arms while I cried earlier haunts my memories—making me ache for a future that I gave up when Nate died.

If I let myself, I could love Grayson, and that terrifies me.

So, instead, I pull my hand from his hair, gently kiss the scruff on his jaw, and grab the blanket lying across the back of the couch, pulling it over him.

I don't look back as I silently walk back to my room.

I could love him, but I'll never let myself.

Chapter 16

Georgia,

Hi, pretty girl. It's me again. By this point, I hope you're okay with receiving these letters. I know the first one was probably a shock. I'm doing it for your own good, though, so keep that in mind when I ask you to do this next thing, okay?

I'm going to tell you a story—it's important, so listen up.

We were young when we first started dating, so I really didn't know what dating was supposed to look like. But, being the book nerd you are, you were in love with love and romance.

There was this one day in college—we were sitting on the grass outside your dorm. It was late spring. While I studied, you were reading one of your romance books. You couldn't quit talking about the date the male character set up for the female lead. You glowed talking about that book, and I vowed that day that I would learn everything I could about romance so that I could be the one to make you look like that.

You didn't know it, but the next time I was in your room, I took a picture of your bookshelf and read every romance book you had. I took notes. Then, when I was ready, I set up the perfect date.

Do you remember it?

I found this little coffee shop that doubled as a bookstore. I didn't have a lot of money then, but I had enough to buy you the book you had been talking about for weeks. We went to the coffee shop. I bought the book and read it to you while we sat in that cafe. I've never been much of a reader, but seeing how you smiled that day was worth it.

You read all these fairy tales about love and romance, but the thing is—it's better when it's real.

I told you before, and I'll tell you again, you are a girl who's supposed to be loved, and because of that, I'm going to ask you to do something hard. Don't hate me for this.

Go on a date, Georgia.

It's time.

I let you dip your toes in the water with that first task, but now it's time for you to dive head-first into moving on. It doesn't have to be serious—or lead anywhere—but you need to put yourself out there. One day, it will be serious, and I want you to be ready for that.

Love,

Nate

Chapter 17

Georgia

The breeze blows through my hair as I stomp to Nate's grave.

I'm so mad I could spit fire.

How dare he do this. When he mentioned it in the first letter, I thought it was a joke—the ramblings of a dying man—but now, well—if he hadn't already died, I'd strangle him with my bare hands.

My hair swings behind me as I walk, and when I'm standing in front of the tombstone, I let go.

"What were you thinking, Nate?" I yell at the sky. "I did what you asked. I got out of the house, but this? This is too much. I'm not doing it. I refuse."

I stomp my foot on the ground, and it sinks deep into the snow.

When I woke up this morning, Grayson was gone, and for reasons I refuse to examine, it was the start of my bad mood. Then I found the letter, and my mood went from gray to pitch black. Add in the snow that keeps coming in spurts, and the whole day is spiraling out of control.

My husband has some nerve in asking me to go on a date with someone else—like he isn't the only person I've ever dated.

Besides Grayson in middle school, I never had the desire to date anyone else. Nate and Grayson were the only two people I hung out with. It's not that I don't love the people in my town. I did and still do.

It's just that those experiences of going out always left me in a funk the next day. Social interactions just drain my battery, and that got worse when Nate died—last night being a prime example.

Nate was the social butterfly who could spend all day talking to people. I was content to love them from the side, but for some reason, when people clung to Nate, they clung to me, too.

He says it's because I'm supposed to be loved, but what he doesn't get is that I was supposed to be loved by *him*—no one else.

Despite the cold, anger burrows under my skin, heating it.

"I hate these stupid letters, Nate," I say, stubbornly crossing my arms across my chest.

Even as I'm saying it, I know that's not entirely true. I don't hate them. I've loved having a small piece of my husband again, but I hate that the letters are pulling me out of my comfort zone—pushing me past my grief. I wanted to stay stuck there because Nate's there, and if I move past it, that last thread that's tying me to him will be gone.

We had talked about kids, but the timing was never right for us, and then we found out he was sick. Selfishly, I wish it had happened for us because then I would always have part of him with me, but at the same time, I would never want my kids to know what it feels like to live without their dad.

"Do you remember that one time we went to the beach? It was the first time either of us had ever been, and it was just the two of us. We packed our stuff early in the morning and drove five hours so we could spend the day there. The whole day was just about the two of us. We played in the sand and the waves, letting the sun warm our skin. Then, that night, we sat on the sand, your arms wrapped around me, and watched the sunset. I remember thinking I could live every day like that—just the two of us in our little bubble. But now, you aren't here, and you're asking me to live outside that bubble. This one is not fair, Nate. I can't follow through with it. I'm sorry."

My knees buckle, and I fall to the ground in front of his tombstone. The chill of the snow sneaks past my snow pants, taking all the heat of my anger and the rest of my energy with it.

Pulling off my gloves, I trace the letters of his name.

"Please don't make me do this," I whisper, but as I sit here with my fingers gliding over his name, I know I will. I'll do it for him because he asked me to, but not just for him, for me too.

That bubble we lived in that day on the beach popped, and now it's time for me to find out what's outside it.

Sitting there a few more minutes, I let the cold seep into my bones, and when my body is numb, I know it's time for me to go.

Leaning over, I press my forehead to his tomb. "I'll try, Nate."

Rising to my feet, I slip my gloves back on my hands and then turn to leave.

Acid burns my throat as I walk back to my car because although I took my anger out on Nate, I am actually angry at myself. A small part of me is excited to go on a date—no matter how much I want to deny that. The problem is, there's only one person I want to go with, and he's my husband's best friend.

As I get in my car, I chew on my cheek, contemplating the mess I've gotten myself into.

I realized last night that my feelings for Grayson have changed—grown. I didn't want to admit how much, but when I read that letter today, butterflies filled my stomach. For one second, I let myself imagine going on a date with Grayson—how his hand would feel in mine or how his lips would be soft when he pressed them to mine at the end of the night. Then I snapped out of it and realized what I was doing. Guilt melted into anger, and I grabbed the letter and came here—letting out my frustration that I only have myself to blame for.

Putting the car in drive, I pull out of the parking space as the snow begins to fall.

CHAPTER 17

Nerves skitter across my skin as I take turn after turn, leading me away from the cemetery. I should have been smarter about coming here today. The roads were slick, but I needed a place for my frustration.

Taking another curve, the car starts to slide, careening.

I slam on my breaks, trying to prevent the inevitable, but it only makes it worse. The car skids across the road, and in that moment, I do something I haven't felt like doing in a while—I pray.

"Please, God, please."

The prayer isn't eloquent or long, just a repeat of the same words over and over until the car stops in a ditch on the opposite side of the road.

My heart hammers in my chest as I try to catch my breath.

Swallowing hard, I look up and whisper, "Thank you."

Tears stream down my face as the knot of anger in my chest loosens. I've held onto my anger at God. I couldn't understand what he was doing, but as I was sliding across the road, praying, I felt peace.

Easing my grip on the steering wheel, my hands shake as I bring them away and reach for my phone, only to find it no longer on the seat beside me. Leaning over, I see it lying haphazardly on the floorboard. I reach over, plucking it from the ground.

Through the windshield, I can see the front of the car is pushed into the bank.

With a groan, I contemplate calling a tow truck, but it could be hours before they arrive in this weather. I could call my dad, but he's getting older, and with the roads as slick as they are, he'd probably break a hip trying to help. That only leaves one option.

I wince as I pull up Grayson's number and wait for it to ring.

"Georgia," he says as a way of answering, his voice smooth and warm.

Goosebumps prickle my skin, and I'm thankful that it's cold, so I can at least try to blame it on that.

"I need your help. I went to the cemetery."

"I'm on my way," he says without hesitation.

My teeth chatter as the cold permeates the air of the car. It's been thirty minutes since I talked to Grayson.

He's coming, but I might freeze before he arrives.

The rumble of a truck catches my attention, and I turn to see Grayson pulling up behind me.

I watch him through the back windshield as he steps out of his truck. His brows are pinched, and his lips are smashed into a grim line. Annoyance radiates off of him as he walks around the car, assessing. Black clouds follow over his head, his anger palpable. He stomps through the snow, making eye contact with me as he approaches the front. His glare sears into me, landing somewhere in the area of my heart.

I glare back. He can just take that annoyance and shove it because I'm not having the best day, either. I wouldn't have called him if I'd known it would be such an inconvenience to him.

Shoving the car door open, I step out of the car as he approaches the driver's side door.

"Are you hurt?" he asks once we are standing face to face. The tip of our boots touch, and his eyes roam from my head down to my feet and back up.

Now is not the time for the tingles that run down my spine when he does that, but my body doesn't care. There's an appreciative glimmer in his eyes under all that annoyance, and gosh, if that doesn't make my heart feel like it might beat out of my chest.

"I'm fine." It comes out barely above a whisper. I clear my throat and try again. "I'm fine." This time, it's louder, but the husk in my voice is undeniable.

"Are you sure?" His voice is rough, holding back the anger that radiates off him, but I'm tired of him holding back. He doesn't see the man I do, and I want to push and prod until he explodes, letting go of all the weight he holds on his shoulders.

Irritation prickles across my skin. Letting out a huff, I cross my arms over my chest. "I said I'm fine."

He ignores the annoyance in my voice, letting his eyes travel to the car behind me, and that irritates me further.

"Don't ignore me," I say, shoving his shoulder to get his attention, but he must be made of stone because he doesn't budge. The only sign he noticed at all is the slight twitch in his eye.

Remaining silent, he returns his gaze to me, and that look freezes me in place. There's rage in his eyes, bubbling just below the surface and on the edge of breaking free.

I'm driving the man crazy—becoming more of a handful than he is ready for, but I tried to warn him it would happen the day of the funeral.

He said he could handle it—handle me—but I see now that I've become too much, and soon enough, I'll lose him too.

Narrowing my eyes, I glare at him as I step forward and poke a finger into his chest.

"If you've got something to say, say it," I say, my voice low and controlled.

I'm actually surprised by how much control I have over my temper because inside, I'm a volcano—one that has been dormant for a long time and is now ready to erupt. I've held it all in, been the grieving widow, but now all those emotions are about to get messy.

"What were you thinking?" he asks. The timbre of his voice is dark and vibrates with the tension surrounding us. The air around us is alive, sparking with both our anger.

"Not that I have to explain myself, but I was mad—at myself, and Nate, and you. I was mad, and I needed to yell and scream and get it out, so I came here—hoping that I could make sense of things."

He steps closer, narrowing the space between us. I fight the urge to step back, refusing to give him the upper hand.

"Make sense of what, Georgia?"

The use of my real name sets me off, causing me to explode. At this point, I hardly notice the cold, my anger running through me like lava.

"I received another letter today," I say, reaching into my pocket and slapping the envelope against his chest. He doesn't bother looking at it. Instead, he brings his hand up and presses it over mine, right over his heart.

"What did it say?" he asks. His face is stone, revealing nothing, but his heartbeat gives him away, beating erratically in time with mine.

I smirk, giving him his own signature look before saying, "Wouldn't you like to know?"

It's petty, but this isn't one of his business meetings where he can glare and get whatever he wants. If he wants to know, he's going to wipe that irritation right off his face before he gets a word out of me.

"Yeah," he says, gravel deep in his voice as he lifts his hand from mine and leans forward. He braces himself with his hands resting on the top of the car, bracketing me between his arms and forcing me to step back. My back hits the car. There's nowhere for me to go—not that I want to go anywhere. Being around Grayson makes me feel normal. My breath comes in spurts as he leans his face towards mine, stopping when they are inches apart. "I do want to know, and Georgia, you're going to tell me because I'm barely holding myself together right now. So tell me what it said before I lose control and do something we'll both regret."

He's so close that his breath kisses my face with each word. Biting my lip, I close my eyes and try to gain control of the situation, but even though I can't see him, I know I'm never getting that power back, not with him this close. When I open my eyes, he's watching me, studying every inch of my face.

I open my mouth to respond, and his eyes follow the movement, never leaving as I speak. "If you want to know, you can read it yourself."

My hand is still pressed to his chest, and I feel it rumble when he lets out a growl of frustration.

"No, Peach—not this time. Tell me what it says."

Every one of my senses is on overdrive. It's overwhelming, making my thoughts a jumbled mess. Not even an hour ago, there was a ball of anger rooted deep in my chest, but now all I can think about is how maybe going on a date wouldn't be so bad—especially if it's with this man in front of me.

"It—uh—Nate, that is, said I should go on a date. That's my next task—a date."

"Look at me, Georgia," he commands. Refusing, I lift my chin and stubbornly stare past him. One of his hands leaves the car and grips my chin. His touch is soft as he tilts my face so that I'm looking at him. "Why did that make you angry?"

"Because it's something I want to do, and I'm mad at myself for that. I promised Nate forever." My answer is soft, a whisper against the wind, but Grayson hears it. His face softens, and I watch the muscles in his neck move as he swallows my confession.

"You gave him his forever, Georgia. Your forever just lasted longer, and that doesn't mean you have to be lonely."

His thumb slides across my skin, tracing my jaw, and I worry I might melt in a puddle right there.

"That—um—isn't the whole story, though," I say, trying to concentrate but finding it hard to focus on anything other than his skin against mine.

"What else? Lay it on me."

"I—I don't want to go with a stranger."

He leans closer, whispering against my lips, "Ask me, Peach."

"You've already done too much for me," I protest.

"Ask me."

I swallow, gathering all my courage, then ask, "Will you go on a date with me, Gray?"

A sly smile crosses his lips. There's a spark that makes me giddy with excitement, "I thought you would never ask."

Then he's leaning in and pressing his lips to mine.

Chapter 18

Grayson

I'm going to be struck by lightning. Not only am I kissing my best friend's girl, but I also haven't told her about my letter yet.

If I'm going out, though, this is the way I want to go.

Georgia's hand slides up my chest, around the back of my neck, pulling me closer—pulling me home.

I've dreamed about this girl, but I didn't want to taint her with my darkness. I can't go back now that I've tasted her lips on mine. There will never be another lifetime where I can resist holding her in my arms.

She deserves the world, but all I have to offer her is mine.

The kiss slows, and I pull back just enough to rest my forehead on hers. The frozen air clouds as our breaths mingle together.

"Peach." Her name is a whisper against my lips, begging her to tell me she was there in that moment with me—that I wasn't alone—but she shakes her head, not ready to talk yet.

My throat aches as I swallow, praying she doesn't regret that kiss because even though I should feel guilty, I can't force myself to.

I nod and step back, placing distance between us. There's a war on her face that I can understand—I've been fighting the same one. Only hers is between honoring her husband and fighting the feelings she's trying to hide from me.

She could choose anyone for this date, but the difference between me and every other guy she could choose is that I will honor her husband's memory because he's part of mine. I loved him, but I love her too. I always have, and because of that, I understand that she needs me to go slow.

I won't rush this because you can't rush forever—and I plan to give her my forever. There's no more holding back for me—only waiting for her to catch up now.

"Come on," I say. "I'll call someone to pick up the car and bring it to the house."

Placing my hand on her back, I guide her to my truck, careful of the slick spots. She's remained quiet since the kiss ended. I want to know how she's feeling and what she's thinking, but I can give her time.

I open her door and take her hand as I help her in. Once she's situated, I grab the seat belt and lean across her to buckle her in. Her breath stutters as my body brushes against her, and it's enough for me right now. She was just as affected by that kiss as I was.

Leaning back, I brush her hair out of her face, taking her in. Her cheeks are flushed, and her hair is damp from standing outside in the snow, causing it to curl on the ends. I have to physically restrain myself from grabbing a piece and twirling it between my fingers. Swallowing hard, I lean back, throw her a wink, and shut the door—putting space between us so I can get my head on straight.

The drive back to my house is quiet, filled with an awkward tension that I hate.

This is not the first nor will it be the last time I've wished I could read a woman's mind.

My thumb drums against the steering wheel. I should turn on some music, but then Georgia might think I don't want to talk about what happened, and I do—I really, really do. I'm not a man typically known for sharing my feelings, but for Georgia, I can—I will. I may not be good enough for her, but I'll spend every day trying to be.

Out of the corner of my eye, I see Georgia wringing her hands. Without thinking about it, I pull one of mine off the steering wheel, reach over, and place it over hers. She glances down at our hands and then at me.

The confusion in her eyes is gut-wrenching. She's conflicted, and I hate that I've made her feel that way.

She starts to open her mouth to say something at the same time I pull into the driveway. She closes it when she sees the truck sitting there, a family standing outside of it—my family to be exact.

A growl resonates from my chest—frustration blooming. I'd be annoyed that Brooks is standing in my driveway with his daughter and what I assume is his wife, unannounced, on a normal day, but especially today, of all days when all I want to do is drag Georgia inside my house, figure this thing out, and plan a date—one that has the power to change our whole future.

Georgia's fingers slip between mine, squeezing. Seeing Brooks here at my home was like a shock to my system. I'd forgotten I'd placed my hand on hers, but now, with her fingers laced with mine, it's all I can concentrate on—releasing that anger crept into my body at the sight of Brooks.

When Georgia told me that she was worried about me at the festival, I realized that she was right—parts of who I used to be have been slipping out since Nate died, but I want to be the better man for Georgia—I'm going to be that man. So, with her fingers in mine, I focus on reigning in the frustration of having Brooks on my step—but it doesn't mean he doesn't still annoy me. Apparently, that's part of having a brother, or so I'm told.

She squeezes again, and I turn my head to look at her.

"You've got me," she says. There's a dip in her voice—a tiny inflection—that has me hiding my smirk. She may not know it yet, but she put more weight behind that statement than she realized.

I nod, swallowing my response as I put the truck in park. Through the windshield, I see Brooks lift Avery in the air and twirl her around before dropping her down in the snow. Avery giggles as Brooks's wife stands by and watches on. There's a content smile on her lips, and for a second, jealousy burns deep in my gut.

Growing up, I dreamed of that kind of family for my mom and me—one with stability and love. It wasn't that my mom didn't love me, but life hardened her. Her idea of showing love was working long days so she didn't have to be home with me and yelling at me when I got in trouble. I gave up on the idea of family, at least for me, but looking at Brooks and his family, there's a longing deep in my chest that I thought was dead.

I rub my hand over the scruff on my chin to clear my head. My neck pops as I tilt it from side to side, relieving some pressure before shoving my door open and walking to the passenger side. I take my time helping Georgia out of the truck, keeping my back to Brooks and his family until I fully have my emotions in check. There's no chance I'll let my estranged little brother see one ounce of emotion from me. It would give him the upper hand.

Swinging the door open, I place my hand in front of her. She puts hers in mine, and the smoothness of her palm against mine is enough to calm my racing heart. I school my face, so it's a cool mask of indifference, but Georgia sees straight through me. With her feet on the ground and one hand in mine, she lifts the other to caress my jaw. Leaning into the warmth, I close my eyes and just breathe.

"I know your worth, even if you don't. I've got your back," she says.

My eyes flash open, and I study her face. I'm not used to relying on people. I try not to because I get tired of being disappointed, but I can see the sincerity shining in Georgia's eyes.

"After this, can we talk?" I ask.

I need to tell Georgia about my letter. If I ever want this to be more, she has to know—even if it means she never talks to me again. First, I have to get through whatever my brother is here for.

One problem at a time.

She nods, and I turn and walk towards Brooks, keeping Georgia's hand in mine. Brooks eyes us as we approach, zeroing in on our linked hands. He's wearing a strange smirk, and just like when he was in my office several weeks ago, I want to knock that smirk right off his face. Georgia squeezes my hand and gives a subtle shake of her head as if she can read my mind, and I grind my molars together to keep my temper in check.

"Brooks," I say as a greeting when we stand a few feet apart.

His smirk turns into a full-blown smile, and I swear it only makes me want to punch him harder. The glint in his eyes is knowing, like he takes pride in raising my blood pressure. I have to say that having a younger brother is not all it's cracked up to be. Irritating is a better word for it.

"We hope we're not intruding," his wife says beside him. "But we had some errands to run today and thought we would stop by. Had we known the weather was going to be like this, we probably would have stopped another day."

I turn my attention to her, carefully keeping my face in a stony mask. I let the silence set for a minute as I study her, making sure that there isn't any question that they are intruding. She's pretty, with blonde hair framing her face, causing her green eyes to pop. She's out of my younger brother's league, that's for sure—but I choose to keep that comment to myself. If I stir the pot, they won't leave.

Georgia must know that I'll let the awkwardness stretch out for as long as it takes because she steps forward, extending her hand to Brooks's wife.

"Hi, I'm Georgia."

Brooks lets out a harsh laugh as his wife takes Georgia's hand.

"Oh, she knows who you are, Firecracker. I've told her all about you."

With a swift smack to Brooks's arm, his wife rolls her eyes and says, "Ignore him. I'm Emryn."

"I'm Avery," a voice pipes up behind Brooks and Emryn.

All eyes turn towards my niece, who is lying on the ground making snow angels.

Georgia lets out a soft laugh from beside me, and from the way she's watching Avery, I can tell she's already besotted with her.

I have to admit, it's hard not to find the pipsqueak charming. She must get that from her mom because it definitely didn't come from her dad.

Letting go of my hand, Georgia walks over to Avery and bends down beside her. A secretive smile lights up her face as she looks down at her, and in a flash, images of Georgia as a mom, holding our kids in her arms, run through my mind. I might as well have taken a bullet to the chest because the thought of it takes my breath away.

Offering her hand to Avery, Georgia says, "Why don't we go inside and get some hot chocolate? I know where your grumpy uncle keeps the good stuff."

Avery jumps up, cheering, and Georgia throws me a conspiratorial look. I don't know what her plan is, but it looks like my brother and his family are staying.

Resigned to my fate, I stomp up the steps, unlocking the door and stepping back for everyone else to enter. Avery leads Georgia by the hand, pulling her up the steps of my porch. Emryn follows them, that smile of contentment still on her face. As she passes me, she places her hand on my shoulder, leans in, and whispers, "You're more alike than you think." Then she continues, following behind her daughter and

Georgia.

Bringing up the end, Brooks stops in front of me, working his jaw as he watches his wife disappear into the house.

"She's not wrong, you know. We are a lot alike, but the difference is I'm the handsome brother."

He slaps my shoulder and walks through the door, grinning.

Sticking my boot out, I catch his foot as he crosses the threshold into the house. He's not expecting it, so he doesn't gain his balance in time. Instead, he flails for a minute before crashing to the ground, barely catching himself with his hands. Too bad—I was hoping he'd catch himself with that handsome face of his.

I stand over him, smirking as he looks up at me in surprise. The shock quickly fades, and he narrows his eyes, looking for a weak point he can attack. I slide my hands in my pockets and lead my shoulder against the door frame, kicking one foot over the other and whistling as I wait for him to decide what to do.

Still on the floor, he pushes up his sleeves over his forearms. My eyes follow the motion, but I remain impassive until I see it. Dark ink runs over his forearm from his wrist to his elbow. Jeremiah 29:11 is written in block letters. He didn't have a tattoo the last two times I've seen him, so it must be fairly new.

Tipping my head towards the ink, I say, "Trying to be like me, little brother?"

Sarcasm oozes through my voice, but I still don't move an inch.

Brooks glances down at the tattoo and then back at me before rolling his eyes and pushing to his feet.

"You know, Grayson, not everything is about you," he says, walking away.

"That's what you think," I call after him.

I make a mental note to ask Georgia about the meaning of Brooks's tattoo later and follow behind him to find the women.

In the kitchen, Georgia is ruffling through cabinets, pulling out coffee cups and all the fixings for hot chocolate. She looks at home—like she belongs here—and it does funny things to my chest.

Avery is sitting at the bar, and I pull out a chair beside her. Emryn is on the other side of the kitchen helping Georgia. Brooks walks over to his wife and pulls her into a hug. She giggles, and I try not to gag.

My skin prickles with unease as if someone is watching. Turning my head, I come face to face with Avery's blue eyes. She's so close that I jerk back. My stool careens, and I have to place my foot out to keep from falling. Avery isn't fazed, her icy blue eyes staring into my soul as wisps of blonde hair fall out of her ponytail.

"Do you always look this grumpy?" she asks.

"Yes," I reply, my voice gruffer than I meant it to be, but she merely nods, a serious look on her face—now that she takes from her dad's side.

I don't know what to do here. I've never been around kids, only adults, and even then, I don't like the majority of the adults I talk to—besides Georgia. She's the exception.

"When I'm mad and scrunch my face up like yours, Mommy tells me mine will get stuck like that. Is yours stuck like that?"

My brows dip lower, and I watch as horror fills her eyes. I'm pretty sure that's a tear in the corner.

Panic seizes my chest. When did I start keeping the house so warm? Sweat trickles down my back as I roll up the sleeves of my hoodie, pushing them over my forearms.

This is only the second interaction I've ever had with my niece, and it's going to end in tears—hers and mine.

Thinking quick, I force a smile on my face, but that only causes her lip to wobble.

"It—it is stuck that way," she cries.

Helplessly, I glance over at Georgia, sending her a pleading look. She shakes her head and gives a subtle tilt of her head toward my niece.

I'm going to have a heat stroke. The sweat is beading on my forehead now.

There's a smug humor in Brooks's eye, but I don't have time to think about that right now. I have to fix this before there are actual tears. I've been in boardrooms with grown men who are less intimidating than this.

Thinking quickly, I spy the highlighters I left on the kitchen table. I'd been working on board reports when Georgia called earlier, but there was so much panic in her voice that I'd dropped everything and left.

Turning back to Avery, I hold out my hand like a stop sign and say, "Stay." Then dash over to the kitchen table.

The other three adults in the room watch me with a mixture of horror and fascination on their faces as I grab the highlighters and then run back to where Avery is sitting, her lip still wobbling.

"She's not a dog," Brooks grumbles under his breath. I send him a scolding look before turning my attention back to Avery.

"Do you like coloring?" I ask, holding the highlighters out to her.

She gives me a quizzical look before nodding warily.

"Here," I say, pushing my sleeves up further on my arms and pointing to my tattoos. "You can color these while you wait for your hot chocolate."

Avery's eyebrows dip as she studies my arms, but her lip is no longer wobbling. I'm counting it as a win. The look reminds me so much of myself that I have to bite my tongue to keep from laughing.

"Why did you color on yourself? When I do that, mommy yells at me."

The question catches me off guard.

"Do you want to color or not?" I ask, avoiding the question.

She considers it for a split second before her face lights up in a blinding smile. I stretch out my arm as she uncaps a highlighter. When she starts to color, I look over at Brooks, Emryn, and Georgia. They are all wearing varying expressions on their faces. Brooks looks like he might burst out laughing at any moment. Emryn looks like she might strangle me, but Georgia—she's looking at me like I'm the sun that her world revolves around.

Chapter 19

Georgia

"He's not what I expected, you know?" Emryn muses from beside me.

I'm leaning back against the counter, watching Grayson and Avery as I wait for the hot chocolate to simmer. Growing up, mom always made homemade hot chocolate, turning her nose up if the quick powdered version was even mentioned. Unfortunately—or fortunately, depending on how you look at it—it made me a hot chocolate snob.

"What do you mean?" I ask, turning my head towards Emryn but keeping one eye on Grayson and Avery. With each tattoo she colors, Grayson regales her with the story of why he got it. I can't decide if he's being a good influence or bad. Brooks has joined them, sitting on the other side of Avery, and from the look on his face, I would say that he's leaning towards bad.

Serves him right.

Meeting Avery and Emryn has put Brooks into perspective for me. I believe him now when he says he was just trying to take care of his family the day he showed up for the interview. Pure love shines in his eyes whenever he looks at his daughter and wife, but I still don't regret defending Grayson that day.

"Well, I've known Kip for most of my life, and I've loved Brooks since I was six. Don't get me wrong, both men are—hardened, for lack of a better word, but there's a soft side buried underneath. When Brooks told me about what happened at his interview with Grayson, I wasn't sure if that soft side existed in him, but I was wrong," she says, dipping her head in Grayson's direction, where he sits laughing with Avery.

My heart does a funny flip in my chest, and that guilt I've been feeling all day digs deeper into my stomach.

"Yeah, I agree. He's pretty great when he lets you see what's underneath that grumpy mask he likes to wear," I say, heat flooding my cheeks. Turning to stir the hot chocolate, I try to avoid eye contact with Emryn, but I can feel her eyes on me. When I turn, she's wearing a knowing look that makes me nervous.

"What?" I ask, swiping my face in case I smeared some of the cocoa powder across my cheek while mixing it.

"I don't know your story, Georgia, but I'm going to give you some advice that I learned the hard way. Don't miss what's right in front of you because I promise you'll regret it." There's no hint of judgment on her face as she says it, and I wonder what it would feel like to have a friend like her.

Nate and Grayson were my best friends growing up. Sure, I had girls who I talked to in school, but time and time again, they used me to try and get close to Grayson and Nate. By the time Nate and I started dating, I was tired of it. I gave up trying to find the friendship I saw other girls have. Nate and Gray were good enough for me. I didn't need anyone else, but now, talking to Emryn, I wonder what it would be like to have a girlfriend I could talk to.

It sure would have come in handy today when Grayson kissed me like his life depended on it after I had just visited my husband's grave. Add on the fact that I asked him on a date—well, kind of—and I'm a ticking time bomb, ready to explode with everything I'm trying to hold in.

I suppress a groan. There's not a friend in this universe who would know what to do with that drama.

"I don't know what you mean. Gray and I are just friends," I say, turning the burner off and pouring the hot chocolate into cups. When the cups are full, I place the pot back on the stove and reach for the whipped cream. Emryn's quicker, though. She puts her hand on mine, giving it a gentle squeeze. I look up at her, and there's a sad smile on her face.

"That's what I mean. By the way, you two keep stealing secret glances at one another when you think the other isn't looking. I figured something complicated was happening between you two. Believe me, I know complicated when I see it. I've been there, done that, but that man looks at you like you are the oxygen he needs to breathe." She stops and shrugs before continuing, "And maybe I'm wrong, but I think you feel the same way about him."

"You don't even know me," I argue. "We're practically strangers."

She smiles. There's a story in that smile, but I don't ask for it.

"You're right," she says, patting my hand. "I don't know you, but I do know love. I've been in love with the same man since I was six years old, and I know how I look at him when I think he's not watching. Just think about what I said."

She gives my hand one more pat before gathering up three of the cups in her hand and walking over to her daughter and husband.

When she gets to him, Brooks takes the cups out of her hands, places them on the counter, and then wraps her in his arms, pressing a kiss to her lips that leaves no question of how he feels about her.

My throat aches at the sweetness of it all, but also because it's not Nate I'm thinking about when I wish for what Brooks and Emryn have.

Feeling like an intruder in their moment, I turn away from the scene and grab mine and Grayson's cup. He smiles when he sees me approaching, and gosh, if that doesn't make the conflict coursing through my veins even worse.

Sitting his hot chocolate in front of him, I pull out the bar stool on the other side of him and sit.

"Thank you," he says, taking the cup up in his hand that isn't being colored on.

I mumble some kind of acknowledgment, but I'm too lost in my head to notice my surroundings.

That kiss is messing with my head, making it hard to determine what's real and what isn't. Yes, Grayson kissed me, but he was mad—so was I, for that matter. We got caught up in our emotions, letting them win. That's the only explanation for what happened, except it doesn't explain how Grayson's lips were like fire against mine, waking up a part of me that's been sleeping since Nate's been gone. I felt loved and cherished, but that has to be because it's been so long since I've been kissed, right? Not because it was Grayson.

Avery's voice breaks me out of my musings, pulling my attention to her.

"What's this one?" she asks, pointing at the orchid at the base of Grayson's wrist.

My heart slams into overdrive. He's told her the truth of every other tattoo that he's gotten. Will he tell her the truth about this one? Will I finally get to know the story too?

"It's a promise to my best friend," Grayson says after a minute of silence. His voice is low, like a rumble of thunder off in the distance.

I'm positive Brooks and Emryn can hear my heart beating in my chest from the other side of the bar.

Avery leans in and whispers conspiratorially, "Mommy says that Daddy is her best friend. Is Georgia your best friend?"

I don't think it's normal for a person's heart to beat this hard. I might be having a stroke.

Grayson gives a sad shake of his head. "No—well, not exactly. She's one of them, but this was my other best friend. He died last year."

Avery scrunches her nose. "What does died mean?

Beside me, Grayson's shoulder stiffens, but I'm too busy trying to survive my stroke to come to his rescue on this one.

Brooks runs a hand over Avery's ponytail. "It means he went to heaven, honey."

There's a look of pity on Brooks and Emryn's faces as they study Grayson, and it makes me want to claw their eyes out. I hate pity. What good does it do? It doesn't bring Nate back.

One side of my face is going numb—nope, not a stroke, just a panic attack.

Avery gives a grave nod as if that's settled the matter, and then she scrunches her nose again.

"What's a promise?" she asks.

"It means that I gave him my word that I would do something, and the tattoo reminds me to keep that word."

"What did you tell him you would do?"

Avery's questions are innocent, the curiosity of a child, but they feel like the tip of a blade pointed straight at my heart. One wrong answer, and I'm gone.

Grayson turns to face me, keeping his eyes on mine when he answers Avery, "I promised I'd take care of his flower."

My breath stutters, but I refuse to let the panic attack pull me under. Focusing, I start to use another technique the therapist taught me.

Five things I can see: His eyes—that's the first thing I take note of. They're Nordic blue today—clear crystals that let me see all of him. There's a compass on the back of Grayson's forearm that Avery has colored green. It's one of my favorites. He got it when his business started to turn a profit. It was his reminder that no matter how lost you feel, there's always a new direction. My eyes are drawn to the sleeves of his hoodie. They're pushed up past his elbow and reveal cords of muscle on his forearms. He works his hands in and out of fists, causing the muscles to flex, and I nearly swallow my tongue. Two more things—I need two more things. Pulling my eyes away from his arms, I continue to let them roam. A hole in his jeans' knee is starting to fray, and I wonder how he got it. He's meticulous about clothes. He wouldn't have bought them with the hole in it. One more thing—just one. My eyes travel back up and land on his lips. The bottom one is full, pouting out just a little more than the top, drawing my attention to it. Biting my lip, I remember what it felt like to have his pressed against mine.

This is not helping my heart rate.

I need four things I can touch. The mug in my hand is warm, taking away some of the chill in the air. That's one. Reaching out with my other hand, I run my hand against the scruff of his jaw, letting it prickle against my skin. Grayson watches me, but I ignore him, searching for two more things. The drawstring of his hoodie is tucked into his shirt, so I move my hand down his jaw to the v in his hood, pinching the string between my fingers and yanking it out. The fabric slides against my fingers until I reach the knot at the end. Grayson's hand covers mine, and I can feel the callouses scraping against my skin.

Why is this not working?

Three—I'm at three. I need three things I can hear. Closing my eyes, I listen as I try to ignore Grayson's hand still on mine. Avery's gone back to coloring, clearly satisfied with Grayson's answer. I hear the click of the lid of a highlighter as she makes a new color choice. Brooks and Emryn's voices weave together as they talk, blissfully unaware of the atomic bomb that's about to explode in my chest. Grayson's not, though, because I hear his molars grinding as he waits for me to gain control. He's not very good with patience. We should work on that.

I'm at two. Opening my eyes, I bring my mug to my lips and take a sip, letting the aroma of the chocolate fill my nose. When I pull the mug away, I take a deep breath, and the spice of Grayson's cologne is a sharp contrast to the sweetness of the chocolate.

One thing I can taste. I need this to work. My eyes snap back to Grayson's lips because even though I've been sipping on the hot chocolate, the taste of Grayson's kiss still lingers on my lips. It's the only thing I can taste.

Zero—there's nothing left to count, but I'm still struggling to breathe. I'm the flower Grayson's talking about. Did he make Nate an actual promise, or is this one of those times that he took it upon himself—a way to still be in touch with his best friend? What does that mean for our date—and that kiss?

A thousand questions swirl through my mind, blocking everything out until both Grayson's hands come up and bracket my face.

"Breathe, Peach. Breathe."

At his command, it's like the fist around my lungs loosens, and I can get air all the way to the bottom of my lungs. When I do, my surroundings come into focus. Grayson, Brooks, Emryn, and Avery are all staring at me with looks of concern on their faces. Heat flames my face.

I really am socially incompetent.

Leaning back, I pull my face from Grayson's hands and clear my throat. "I—uh—sorry."

If the ground could open up and swallow me whole, that'd be great.

Grayson's back is to Emryn, and when I look at her, she dips her head towards him. There's a sly smile on her face as she wiggles her eyebrows up and down.

I give a subtle shake of my head.

After the way this morning started, I expected chaos for the rest of the day, especially when we pulled up to find Brooks and Emryn here, but surprisingly, my heart doesn't hurt as much as it did when I found Grayson gone and a letter from my husband in my mailbox. I've lived lifetimes since this morning. There are a lot of things Grayson and I still need to talk about, but one thing is for sure: lately, he's the reason I can breathe.

"They're gone," Grayson says, standing in the doorway of the kitchen after he walked his brother and his family out.

I'm wiping down the countertop, and I don't look up when he speaks. I can't because I know what's coming—a conversation that's well overdue, but it will change everything. In a matter of one day, years of friendship will be laid on the line.

"Georgia," Grayson urges.

I scrub harder. There's a stubborn stain that won't get the best of me.

"Peach." This time, his voice is sharp and demanding.

Throwing the towel down on the counter, I lift my head, defiance burning in my eyes, but I'm not ready for the sight that greets me.

Grayson's standing in the doorway, his arms stretched above his head, resting on the top of the door frame. My mouth goes dry when I catch a glimpse of the toned muscle peeking out from where his shirt doesn't quite meet the line of his jeans.

When I don't answer him, because—hello, I can't—a rumble of frustration reverberates from deep in his chest. He yanks his arms from the doorframe and stalks towards me. His movements are slow—predatory. He's the lion, and I'm the innocent prey waiting to be devoured. Except, I'm not afraid of being devoured by him. What does that say about me?

"Wait," I squeak, raising my hand so he doesn't come any closer because if he does, I can't be held responsible for my actions.

He pauses, stopping a few feet away, but judging by the look on his face, he's not stopping for long.

"Why an orchid?" I ask.

There's a dangerous glint in his eye as he says, "Because it's your favorite flower. Nate's not the only man that knew that."

I swear my heart stops beating.

"How did you know?"

"Peach, I've watched you from the sidelines since we met, but I can't stand on the sidelines anymore."

He takes another step forward, and I take one back, hitting the counter.

"Did Nate make you promise to take care of me?"

A flicker of emotion crosses his face, but in a flash, it's gone, replaced by an intensity so bright, I'm afraid I might burn from it.

"Not in so many words." His answer is vague, leaving me with more questions than answers, but before I can ask what he means, he says, "Last question—better make it a good one."

"Is that why you kissed me?" My heart is pounding so hard I'm afraid it might burst out of my ears. If he says yes, a piece of me will crumble. "Is that why you've done everything for me this last year?"

"No," he answers. His voice is rough, sending goosebumps down my spine.

"Then why?" I demand, standing taller.

He looks me straight in the eyes and answers, "Because I've been in love with you most of my life."

I don't think before I lunge and crush my mouth to his.

We're like fire and ice, melting into each other.

He wraps his arms around me and lifts me up on the countertop, pulling his lips away from mine and peppering them along my jaw.

"We should probably talk about this," I say, my breath harsh, even to my ears.

"About what?" He murmurs against my jaw.

I can't think. My mind is a jumble, only concentrating on the scruff of his beard against my skin.

"Hmm," I hum.

His laugh is deep and infectious, spreading through my veins and causing my heart to skip.

"Am I distracting you, Peach?" Grayson asks, his breath fanning against my skin.

My only response is a harsh swallow, followed by another laugh from Grayson.

"I guess I know what to do in the future for those panic attacks of yours."

That's like a bucket of cold water over my head. He starts to bring his lips to mine again, but I push myself back further on the counter.

"Wait—wait, Gray. We have to talk."

He studies my face, taking in the seriousness of my expression, and rubs his hand across his mouth as he steps back. His face is a careful mask, devoid of any emotion. It makes my chest ache.

"Don't do that, Grayson."

He doesn't let anyone in—no one has ever asked him to—but I'm asking now. For that to happen, though, we have to have everything out in the open, with no secrets between us.

"Do what?" He asks casually, shoving his hands in his pockets like he isn't pulling away.

"Act like I'm telling you no."

He shrugs, "Aren't you?"

Jumping off the counter, I stand in front of him and run my hand along his jaw.

"No, Gray. I'm not."

"Why?"

The question is simple and heartbreaking. It shows me so much of this man that I never saw before.

"Because you're one of my best friends, and sometime over this year, my feelings for you have started to change. But—I need you to be patient with me. I'm this mix of guilt and excitement, and I don't know what to do with that. I can't define this feeling yet, Gray, but I can tell you it's more than friendship."

His breath fans across my face as he lets out a huff—a mix of frustration and acceptance.

"I can understand that."

"Good because I'm not going anywhere, but I need time. I can't say I'm not grieving Nate. It wouldn't be fair to either of us. When I got that letter this morning, I was conflicted because I made vows to my husband, but I also recognized that my feelings for you have grown. Just—be patient with me, okay?"

I watch as his lips tip up in the smirk that I've come to love, a dimple poking in on his cheek. His hand reaches up, smoothing my hair behind my ear, and my goodness, I must have been starved for human touch because I feel that one touch through my whole body.

"I can do that," he says, leaning forward and pressing a kiss to my forehead.

A happy sigh escapes from my lips. It's strange how today is a drastic contrast to yesterday, but honestly, that's grief. Some days, it's like being pulled down by the tide, while other days, I can keep my head above water. But today, it finally feels like I'm happily paddling to shore.

"Can we talk about your family for a minute?" I ask.

Grayson scrunches his face up in a grimace. We've avoided discussing this situation since Kip showed up that first day. He filled me in on the basics enough that I was protective of him, but meeting Brooks, Emryn, and Avery today changed how I see things. Grayson may not realize it, but there was a peacefulness about him that I've never seen before as he let his niece color on his skin. I think she filled a piece of his soul that's been missing for a long time.

"I suppose we have to since they keep popping up and encroaching on my space."

Smiling, I run my finger down the bridge of his nose. "I think you secretly love that they do. They're growing on you."

He narrows his eyes in a glare, but he can't hide from me—I see him.

"Yeah—like mold," he grumbles.

A full belly laugh bubbles out as I smile up at him. His face remains passive, but a slight twitch in his mouth and a crinkle at the corner of his eyes give him away.

"Personally, I think you are more like your brother than you want to admit. I wasn't Brooks's biggest fan at first, but this is the second time he's sought you out. He wants to be a part of your life. I'm not saying you have to let him in all the way, but maybe start small." Tilting my head towards his refrigerator, I smile. "There has to be a reason you still have that birthday invitation up there."

"Yeah, I needed a little decoration."

The man is stubborn.

"You keep telling yourself that," I say, patting his chest.

He glares down at me before his face turns pensive.

"Can I ask you something while we are on the topic?"

"Of course," I say, pulling out a bar stool and sitting down. I can see the wheels turning in his mind as he shoves his hand through his hair. He's never been much for talking, so I'll wait until he's ready.

"It's stupid, but Brooks got a tattoo on his arm. I saw it today before we came into the kitchen with you guys. It's a bible verse. I guess I could have asked him what it meant, but I refuse to give that little annoyance an inch more than he's already taken. He might think I like him or something, so I was wondering if you could tell me."

It's not what I was expecting, and I'm probably not the best person to talk to him about this. But—I can hear Nate's voice in my head asking me not to lose my faith before he died. I did, though. Today, when my car was sliding across the road, it was the first time I've talked to God in a long time. Maybe talking to Grayson about this is the next step in slowly finding my way back to my faith and God.

"First off, you won't be able to hide from Brooks forever. He's kind of like you—stubborn. Second off, what verse was it?"

"Jeremiah 29:11."

"Do you have a bible here?" I ask.

He looks at me sheepishly, a blush creeping along his face before he nods and sprints out of the room. I can't think of one time I've ever seen Grayson blush. Now, I'm curious.

Grayson's back within minutes with a bible in his hand, and I instantly understand his embarrassment. I bought the bible for Grayson during our freshman year of high school. My mom and Nate's mom gave us new bibles at the start of our freshman year. They wanted us to start our high school experience on the word of God. They had mentioned what they were doing to Grayson's mom, but they were poor—really poor. So when Nate and I got our Bibles, and Grayson didn't, I took all my allowance and bought him one, too. I'll never forget the look on his face when he opened it up. He looked at me with pure adoration, and that was the first time I knew what it felt like to be loved by Grayson Lewis—even if I didn't recognize it for what it was at the time.

He hands the bible to me without any comment, and I let it go because I can tell that it makes him uncomfortable.

I run my hand over the smooth leather and then flip to the verse and start to read, "Jeremiah 29:11—For I know the plans I have for you, says the Lord, plans to prosper and not to harm you, plans to give you hope and a future."

My voice trails off, the weight of that verse sitting like a ton of bricks on my chest. I look up at Grayson, and he's standing with his hands in his pocket, swallowing hard.

"What's the story behind that verse?" Grayson asks.

"It's been a long time since I've read it, but I remember the basics. God's people were exiled—as a result of their own sins—but God wanted them to know that he was still sovereign and faithful. He said he would return in seventy years and perform his good word. In the meantime, he wanted them to live their life—marrying and making homes and most of all praying for the peace of the city they are in."

Grayson sits beside me and pulls the bible into his hands, skimming over the verses.

"I guess I still don't understand."

I sigh because the truth is I don't either. I don't understand a lot of the things that have happened over the last year.

"I think that the point of the story is to show the people that in the midst of the chaos we create, he is still good and patient—even at the times we least deserve it. There may be times when our life is hard, but there is hope in the future."

He lays the bible on the table and turns to me, slipping his fingers through mine.

"Do you believe that?" he asks, and I wish he hadn't.

"I want to because I've created a lot of chaos for myself in the last year—"

"But—" Grayson prods.

"But I can't figure out how to get rid of this anger that's still swirling in my stomach. Some days, I think I'm not angry anymore, and then it hits me out of nowhere. How can I be angry and pray for peace, too?"

He nods his head but remains silent. I don't know if I've helped him or confused him more, but I hope for his sake I've pushed him toward finding the peace I've been searching for the past year.

Chapter 20

Georgia

A text pings through my phone in the other room.

It's been a week since that kiss—or, I guess, kisses—with Grayson. He's professionally distant at work, but every night, he comes to my apartment. We eat dinner together and talk, but he hasn't mentioned the date again—and he doesn't touch me. I'm starting to wonder if he has his own form of guilt because I know I do. As we sit talking over dinner each night, I can't help thinking about how Nate probably didn't mean for my date to be with his best friend.

Would he be disappointed? Betrayed? I hate that death doesn't offer closure. I can't call and ask him like I would if we had broken up.

Walking into my bedroom, I find my phone lying on the bed and swipe my finger across the screen. There's a notification from Grayson. I type in my passcode and then pull up the text.

Grayson: *There's a package for you outside.*

Georgia: *For me?*

Grayson: *No, for the other person who lives in my detached garage.*

The snark on this man. Rolling my eyes, I text him back.

Georgia: *Grumpy.*

Grayson: *Just go look at the package.*

When he tries bossing me around, it makes me want to plant my butt exactly where I am and not move—which happens a lot because, technically, he is my boss. A please wouldn't kill the man. I've tried to teach him manners, but that's like communicating with a caveman. He operates in grunts, growls, and demands.

Georgia: *Only after you ask me nicely.*

Grayson: *Peach...*

Georgia: *Still waiting.*

Grayson: *Georgia, will you please go outside and look at the package at your door?*

Georgia: *Well—since you asked so nicely.*

Throwing my phone back on the bed, I walk out of my bedroom and open the front door. Just like he said, there's a package with a note on top. I wasn't sure what to expect from the package, but it definitely wasn't a dress box from the high-end boutique in town. Grabbing the note and the box, I take it inside back to my bedroom.

Georgia: *What is this?*

Grayson: *Did you even bother reading the note? Let me answer that—no. Otherwise, you would know. Now read the note and do what it says. Goodbye.*

I'm going to strangle the man. Pulling the note off the top of the box, I take my time unfolding it. I don't know why I'm suddenly nervous—but butterflies dance in my stomach.

Peach,

It's time we go on that date.

Put on the dress.

I'll pick you up at 7.

Love,

Grayson

Laying down the note, my hands tremble as I reach for the ribbon wrapped around the dress box. This is it—I'm going on a date with someone who isn't my husband. I'm going on a date with my husband's best friend. This is crazy. What am I thinking? A thousand doubts run through my mind, but they all become silent when I pull the lid off the box.

Placing my phone on the bed beside the note, I reach in and pull out the prettiest dress I've ever seen. The material is black velvet, and when I hold it up against me, it drapes to the floor with a slit that runs up the side of one leg. The sleeves pillow until they end in a cuff for each wrist. The sweetheart neckline is modest but enough to make anyone feel beautiful if she wears it.

Pretty isn't a strong enough word for this dress.

It's gorgeous—stunning—and way too much.

I gently fold the dress back into the box before picking up the phone and dialing Grayson's number. The phone rings twice before he sends it to voicemail. Then, in quick succession, a text comes in.

Grayson: *Put it on, Peach. I'll see you tonight.*

I don't know when the man learned to read my mind, but it's annoying.

Huffing, I look at the clock on my bedside table—five o'clock.

The dress probably won't even fit. It's not like Grayson's ever bought me clothes, so I doubt he knows my size. If it doesn't fit, maybe we can just stay in—watch a movie this time—because then I can pretend, just for one more night, that I'm not letting go of Nate.

Slipping my clothes off, I grab the dress and pull it over my head. The inside is lined with silk, and the fabric is soft against my skin. It fits perfectly.

There's a mirror on the other side of the room beside my dresser. My steps are slow and measured as I walk over to it. When I'm standing in front of it, I nearly cry.

The woman in front of me looks healthy. The darkness that's lined my eyes since Nate's been gone has faded. I've put on some of the weight I'd lost, and there's a pink glow in my cheeks. The sparkle in my eye makes me look alive. I look like the girl I was before—a woman

I never thought I would see again. But I'm not that woman anymore. My throat aches as I look closer. There are wrinkles in the corner of my eyes from all the days I spent worrying about Nate, and the harsh set of my mouth tells the story of all the grief I've endured. There's no going back. Death shapes and molds you, and I'm starting to realize that it's up to me who it will mold me into. For a long time, I've hidden from everyone—including myself—but as I stand in the mirror, I see a woman ready to stop hiding and feel wanted again.

Turning to see the back of the dress, I spot Nate's last letter on my dresser, and my wedding rings lay beside it. I took my rings off six months ago. They were a constant reminder of the life I wouldn't have. Picking them up, I slip them on my finger. They fit, just like they always did, but now their weight feels wrong, like I no longer fit into that life.

I expect that to make me feel guilty, but for once, it doesn't. When I dreamed about Nate that night, I think it was my subconscious telling me what I'd been trying to deny. Nate would be okay with me falling for Grayson because he loved him. I've been placing the guilt on my shoulders—not giving myself a real chance to move on, but that ends tonight.

Squaring my shoulders, I march into the bathroom to get ready.

Tonight, I'm going to allow myself to heal.

There's a knock at my door at exactly seven o'clock. Nerves turn in my stomach as I walk to answer it.

Taking a deep breath, I reach out and turn the knob, but that breath is knocked right back out of me when I see Grayson standing on my doorstep in a tux.

I've seen him dressed up a thousand times at the office, but this is different. The man is all sharp lines and hard muscle, but a softness in his eyes makes me want to lay my heart in his hands.

"Hi," I greet him. It comes out breathless, a whisper against the cold night wind.

The muscles in his throat tighten as he swallows, looking me up and down. His eyes stop at the slit of the dress that ends just above my knee, and his breath stutters as he tries to settle himself before dragging his eyes back to mine.

"You're beautiful." The sincerity in his voice sends shivers down my spine. "Shall we?" he asks, holding out his hand for me to take.

I place my hand in his and step through the door into a new life—one where I'm stronger and less jaded. He reaches behind me and closes the door. Slipping his hand from mine, he places it on my back and guides me to the truck. The driveway is slick, though, and heels aren't made for snow. With one step forward, my foot slides out from under me. I jerk back, bracing myself for the fall, but Grayson's there. His hand that was on my back wraps around my waist and pulls me against him.

"There you go, saving me again."

"Always," he says as he picks me up and carries me to his truck. I wrap my arms around his neck and hold on to him. "Open the door for me, sweetheart."

Reaching out, I pull the handle to the truck. When the doors open, he places me gently on the seat and reaches over, buckling me in. It's a repeat of the day he first kissed me, and like then, he takes over all my senses.

When he pulls back, the smell of his cologne surrounds me, filling my lungs. Grayson closes my door, and I shake the nerves from my hands as he walks around the front of his truck.

When he's in his seat and settled, I turn so my body is angled towards his.

"Where are we going?" I ask.

He sends me a scathing look and says, "Do you really think I will tell you and ruin the surprise?"

"What if I ask really nicely?" I stick my bottom lip out and open my eyes wide, looking innocent. I lean in closer and beg, "Pretty please."

"I'm a professional negotiator, Peach. Your little puppy dog eyes won't ruffle me."

"Oh, yeah?" I ask, unbuckling and sliding closer across the bench seat.

"Peach," Grayson warns. "Buckle up."

"I am. You'll pop a blood vessel one day with the amount of worry you take on." Buckling the middle seat belt across my lap, I lay my hand against his bicep. His muscles flex under my fingers. "Now, where were we? Oh yes, I remember. You were about to tell me where we are going."

"The answer is still no, Peach."

"Ah, Gray—you're no fun, but I kind of figured the answer would still be no. I just wanted to sit closer to you."

I look up at him and give him a cheeky smile. When he glances down at me and chuckles, another piece of my heart heals.

Chapter 21

Grayson

The place I'm taking Georgia is an hour away. One of my clients told me about it three weeks ago. I knew Georgia would love it as soon as I heard about it, but we weren't even an option at that point. I bought the tickets anyway, hoping to find a way to convince her to come with me as just a friend.

Then she told me about Nate's next task for her—the date—and I knew the contents were as much for me as they were for her—there are too many ties to my own letter. My options were either to step up the way Nate asked me to or let her go out with another man.

To me, it wasn't even a choice.

I won't be able to handle watching her love someone else a second time. The first time, it was my best friend, but this time, it might be some stranger who won't treat her like she's the best thing that's ever happened to him. She may deserve better than the man I am, but I'll spend every day trying to prove to her that I can be who she needs.

Her head is lying on my shoulder as I drive, and I swear I could spend forever like this. We take one more turn, and I slow the truck. Georgia lifts her head and glances around her, confusion marring her pretty face.

There's a sign in front of us with the words Clayton County Memorial Library written in block letters. The building itself is bigger than any library I've been to.

"What are we doing at a library?" she asks.

I smile down at her as I pull up to the valet stand and put the truck in park. Confusion draws her brows together as she looks at the valet and then back at me.

"I don't understand."

"You're not supposed to," I say, placing a simple kiss on the crown of her head before getting out and walking to her side of the truck. Opening her door, I put my hand out and help her down.

She doesn't release my hand when her feet are on the ground. Men and women swarm all around us, exiting their cars in formal wear, and as I look around, I can't help but think I'm the luckiest man here.

Georgia is beautiful. The dress I had delivered compliments her pale skin, and her hair is pulled back into a slick, high ponytail, revealing the smoothness of her skin, but it's not just her outward appearance. It's everything about her. Her soul is beautiful, even with the scars life has left on it.

"Do you trust me?" I ask, tilting my head towards the steps everyone else is ascending.

She squeezes my hand and whispers, "Always."

Stepping in front of her, I pull her along as we take the steps two at a time. Then, we are standing at the top. The doors are opened for us by men dressed in tuxes just like me, and when we step through into the library, Georgia's breath stutters as she takes in the sight.

"What is this?" she asks, her eyes wide as she takes in the library.

The library is an older building with stairs that descend into the main room. The ceilings are tall, and the walls are lined with shelves filled with books. All the tables have been cleared from the center of the room, leaving a wide open space where men spin their women around on a dance floor. To the right, a fireplace is lit, and couches are scattered around it, with women sitting down and reading a book from one of the shelves.

"It's a book ball. A customer of mine mentioned it a few weeks back. There are some local authors here who will be doing book readings by the fireplace," I say, reaching inside my pants pocket and pulling out a folded paper. "Here's the itinerary for all the authors who will be here."

Georgia's mouth sets ajar as she stares at the paper I'm holding out for her to take. I clear my throat as she continues to stare.

Maybe I messed up, and this is too much for a first date. I'm about to take the paper back and tell her we can go, but then she places her hand on my arm. Her soft touch sends a shot of electricity straight to my heart.

"It's perfect. Thank you."

Her lips tip up on one side, and it hits me that it's genuine. I've missed seeing smiles on her face that aren't forced because she thinks she has to.

She takes the paper from me and studies it, and I watch her closely, waiting until she gets to the last name on the list. I see the exact moment that she reads the name. Her eyes widen, and her head snaps up to look at me.

"Ava Carson is here? Are you kidding me?"

Georgia's hands shake as she tries to stop herself from jumping up and down in excitement. Ava Carson has been her favorite author since we were in high school. Every time she releases a new book, Georgia has it in her hand within the week. It's another reason I brought her here. I knew she wouldn't miss a chance to meet her favorite author.

"Nope—not a joke."

At this point, she can't contain her excitement. She's bouncing up and down on her toes before finally flinging her arms around my neck. Placing both my hands on her back, I hold her close, relishing having her in my arms.

"This is the best date I've ever been on."

As soon as she says it, her whole body tenses against mine. The regret is instant.

"Georgia, I will never make it a competition between Nate and me. You have your memories with him, and they are good. We will have our own memories. It doesn't dilute your ones with him—they're just different. That's all. You can love this date and the ones you went on with him, too."

She nods against my shoulder, taking in what I said, and I turn my head to whisper in her ear.

"Will you dance with me?"

She pulls back and smiles at me, and I know I'll spend the rest of my life trying to put that smile on her face.

"You can dance?" she asks, and I scoff.

"Of course, I can dance. Who do you think taught Nate?"

Her giggle is a balm for my soul.

"Well, if you're the one who taught him, then I feel sorry for my poor toes tonight. He was abysmal."

Wiggling my brows, I send her a smoldering look and tip my lips up in a smile.

"He was just a bad student, but I have skills. Just you wait."

She purses her lips, trying to hide her smile, but fails miserably.

"I guess you'll just have to prove it then." She takes my hand, walking us to the dance floor.

Once we are in the middle of the crowd, I pull her to me, placing one of her hands around my neck and keeping the other in mine. I slip my arm around her waist, lightly placing my hand against her back, and when the music changes beats, I lead us around the dance floor, gliding between the other dancers. Georgia's eyes go wide as she lets me lead. We move together like we were meant for each other, and I can't ever remember another time when I've been as happy as I am at this moment. The thing about guys like me, though, is that it all comes crashing down sooner or later, but until that moment, I'll enjoy the feel of Georgia in my arms.

"I'm going to grab us a drink," I say to Georgia, bending my head so she can hear me above the noise. "I'll meet you over at the fireplace."

We've been on the dance floor for over an hour. Tendrils of hair have escaped from her ponytail and curl around her face. Her cheeks are red from exertion, and she's prettier now than when we started the night.

Georgia nods, and I leave her to find a place to sit while I weave through the crowd to grab us drinks. The bar is crowded when I reach it, and I have to squeeze in between two other men for the server to see me. I lift my hand to flag him down, and he gives me a nod of acknowledgment, letting me know he will be over when he's done with his current order.

Turning, I rest my elbows on the bar and take in the people around me. Being an hour away, there's no one here that we know, but that doesn't stop the feeling of inadequacy from creeping up and smothering me. Despite having more money than I could ever spend now, I still feel out of place in a room full of people who have it. They can smell the lower-class blood that still runs through my veins.

As I take in the room, someone slides in beside me at the bar. I turn my head, and there's a woman there, pressing closer to me than necessary. I try to step to the side, but people on the other side prevent me from putting any space between us.

"Hi," she says, placing a hand on my arm resting on the bar.

"Good afternoon," I say, standing so her hand falls away.

Her face falls for a second before she gives me a sly, flirtatious smile that I've seen on a hundred other women, but just like this one, they never impress me because all I can imagine is Georgia's green eyes and dark hair staring back at me.

I've been on a hundred dates, but nothing compares to Georgia's smile.

My eyes travel across the room, searching for Georgia and effectively dismissing the woman beside me. I find her sitting on the couch closest to the fireplace, a book already in hand. She's immersed in her book, but she must feel the weight of my stare because, after a couple of seconds, she glances up and looks straight at me. Unfortunately, the woman beside me chooses that moment to rest her hand on my arm again.

Georgia's brows dip, causing a pucker between them before she pulls her attention back to the book in her hand.

Grinding my molars, I look back to the woman who is not getting the hint.

"Remove your hand from my arm."

My voice is deadly. The woman looks taken aback but drops her hand immediately. A few people around the bar stop and stare, but I don't care. Annoyance causes every one of my muscles to tighten as I take in the woman beside me.

"I apologize. You seemed like you could use the company," she giggles.

"You see that woman right over there?" I ask, pointing to Georgia. "That woman is my company. Take it from me: when a man wants your company, he won't shy away from your touch. Now, if you'll excuse me, I'm going to join my girl."

The server approached while I was speaking, so I place my order, hand over my card, and within minutes, I'm on my way back to the girl of my dreams.

When I get closer, though, her brows are still pinched together. I watch her as I approach. She reads the same page at least twice before huffing and closing the book.

"I got you a drink," I say, offering her the glass as I sit down beside her.

Taking a drink, she sits silently, looking around her.

"You want to tell me what's going on in that pretty head of yours?" I ask.

Tilting her chin up and away from me, she says, "Not particularly."

"Too bad, Peach," I tease, tugging on her hand. "Now spill."

She tugs her lip between her teeth, worrying it, then says, "It's just—this last year is the first time I haven't seen you with a rotation of women on your arm, and I get it, Gray. You were a single man, and look at you—my goodness, look at you. Women can't help but throw themselves at you, but I'm not made for casual. I know what you said in your kitchen that day, but you've never had a serious relationship. What if you get bored? I don't want to lose you, too—and I just assumed this is a relationship. I'm going to go die of embarrassment now."

Her words spill out without a breath in between, and when she's finished, she slings herself back against the couch and covers her eyes with the crook of her elbow.

Pressing my lips together, I try not to laugh because if there's one thing that Georgia is not, it's dramatic, so for her to be now says a lot.

"Where is this coming from?"

She lifts her arm just barely enough to show one eye and glares. "I think you know," she says, glancing at the bar and then back at me.

I do know, but I'm selfish. I want to hear her say it.

"I don't," I prod, feigning ignorance.

"Fine, Gray—then I'll tell you. Women do everything they can to get your attention when you are in public, and that makes me—I don't know, ragey. I've never been ragey before—why do I feel that way?"

This time, I can't hold it back. My laugh slips out, and I reach over, pulling Georgia into my lap so I can hug her. She lays her head on me, and it fits perfectly between my shoulder and chin.

"I think the word you are looking for, sweetheart, is jealous. And make no mistake—this is a relationship. I won't get bored of you, Georgia, because I meant what I said. I've loved you most of my life, but Nate was my best friend. He was what you deserved. But since he's gone, I promise to try to be a better man for you."

I mean that promise with every fiber of who I am. I will be a better man for this woman in my arms because she deserves a man who can love her purely, without reservation.

"Gray," she says, lifting her head to look at me. "You are a good man. You don't have to try. The last year is proof of that. I trust the things you are telling me—but those women still make me a little ragey."

"Okay, fighter," I say with a chuckle. "Let's get you over to your favorite author before you get us in trouble with all that rage."

I stand, lifting her with me and placing her on her feet. There's a smile on my face that not even my father could wipe off because this woman in front of me is incredible, and for the first time in my life, I don't feel broken.

Chapter 22

Georgia

Georgia: *You busy?*

It's Sunday—the day after our date. According to every romance novel I've ever read, I should wait two to three business days for Grayson to text me first, but our relationship is far from the norm. It's messy and chaotic, but it's not silent. I refuse to sit around and wonder if he will text or call—which, judging by his admission last night, he will—but the thing is, I can, too. I shouldn't just place the success of this relationship on his shoulders.

Grayson: *Never too busy for you. What's up?*

Georgia: *I ran out of books to read and need groceries. Want to go to town with me?*

The read receipt pops up as soon as I send it, and three dots appear within seconds. I kick my feet up and down as I chew on the side of my nail. He read that so fast that it's evident that he was waiting for my reply. I forgot how it feels to have these nerves of excitement when you first start dating someone. Nate and I had become comfortable with one another, which wasn't bad, but this is nice, too.

Grayson: *Didn't you just get a new book last night from Ava Carson?*

Georgia: *I read it this morning. Are you judging my reading habits?*

Grayson: *Never.*

Georgia: *You still didn't answer the question. Is that a no?*

The three dots dance across my screen again, appearing and then disappearing, and I swear if he doesn't answer soon, I'm going to march over to his house and kick his butt.

In three…two…a message appears, saving him from my wrath.

Grayson: *The answer is always yes to you, Peach.*

I smile and squeal like a teenager before texting back my reply.

Georgia: *Meet me outside in five. I'll drive.*

Grayson: *Absolutely not. I've seen your driving. You still have a car in the shop from your driving abilities. I'll drive.*

Rolling my eyes, I grab my coat and run out the door to beat him outside.

He's opening his door by the time I've closed mine, and when he sees me running at a full sprint to the driver's side of his truck, he jumps off the porch, skipping the steps, and takes off at a dead run. He has the advantage because his truck is parked closer to his side, but I refuse to let him win.

It's a good thing some of the ice has melted because if not, I would be flat on my back when I pick up the pace to beat him.

My hand touches the handle of the driver's side door at the same time he reaches the truck. I'm about to pull it open when he picks me up and throws me over his shoulder.

I squeal, pounding on his back as he carries me to the back of the truck, opens the tailgate, and sits me down.

"You cheated," I say, shoving at his chest.

He doesn't go anywhere. Instead, he ignores it and steps closer, laughing as I cross my arms and huff.

"Did you really think I would let you win, Peach?" He lowers his head and runs the bridge of his nose against my jaw, causing me to shiver. "I'll tell you what. I'll let you drive, but I need a consolation prize."

"Oh, yeah? What's that?" I'm breathless as I ask the question. My hands are wrapped into his hoodie like if I let go, he'll disappear.

"One favor—no questions asked, and I can call it in whenever I want." It's a whisper against the shell of my ear, and I can't take it anymore.

"Yeah, yeah. Sure, one favor. Now kiss me."

There's mischief in his eyes as he leans in and kisses me, but I figure I'll worry about that later. Right now, I can only focus on the pure happiness running through my whole body as I smile against his lips.

"Are we there yet?" Grayson asks from the passenger seat of his truck.

His eyes are closed, and he's holding on to the handle above the door with a grip so firm that I worry he might break it. When I don't respond, he peeks one eye open to look at me, keeping the other one tightly squeezed shut.

"We're here, you big baby. I'm not that bad of a driver."

"The near heart attack I had back there says otherwise."

Rolling my eyes, I open the truck door, grab my purse, and hop out. Grayson meets me at the back of the truck and scoops my hand in his, intertwining our fingers.

I look down at our hands and then back at him as we walk across the parking lot toward the grocery store door.

"Is this okay?" he asks, holding our hands up to indicate what he's talking about.

"Why wouldn't it be?"

He pulls me to a stop just outside of the door, a serious look on his face.

"Because you know as soon as we step through those doors with me holding your hand, the whole town will know about us. If you aren't ready for that yet, I'll understand. We're doing this on your timetable, not mine."

I don't know how this man can't see how good he is, but it's the truth—he is. Sure, he's grumpy, but he's willing to give up his happiness if it means I'm comfortable.

Squeezing his hand, I smile at him and say, "I'm okay with it. Now, come on. I need groceries so I can cook us supper."

"Your cooking is even worse than your driving," he groans as I pull him behind me into the store.

"It is not," I laugh over my shoulder, "and you better not let my momma hear you say that, either. I like you, but I can't save you from her wrath. She taught me everything I know."

We make our way through the store, piling groceries into the buggy as we go through each aisle, and it hits me that I don't dread coming into public like I have every day since Nate died.

Healing is funny that way—it's gradual and unnoticed until one day, it doesn't hurt to breathe anymore.

The problem is that healing doesn't take nosy neighbors into account.

As we round the corner into the frozen aisle, I spot the one person in town I try to avoid—Ms. Taylor. She's an elderly woman, and if there's a secret to be told in town, she's the one to do it. She's not shy about making her opinion on the topic known, either.

I know I told Grayson that I don't mind people knowing about our relationship, but I wasn't expecting her to be the first person we tested it out on.

I'm about to back up and go down another aisle when she turns around and spots us.

"Oh, Georgia," she calls.

My shoulders tense, and Grayson must notice because he pulls me into his side, slinging his arm around my shoulders and placing a kiss against my hair.

I keep my gaze on Ms. Taylor, whose eyes widen as she takes in Grayson beside me.

Pushing the cart closer to her, I wait for what she has to say, knowing that it's never good.

"As I live and breathe, it's Georgia Evans in the flesh—or did you change it back to Williams now that Nathaniel's gone?"

Grayson tenses beside me, and red seeps into the edges of my vision at the gall of this woman. I keep my hands in fists next to my leg so I don't accidentally punch an old woman in the grocery store.

That would be bad, right?

"It's Evans, ma'am," I say through clenched teeth.

"Humph," she hums.

When she doesn't elaborate, I can't help but feel like this has gone easier than I thought it would. I'm proven right when the next thing out of her mouth is, "Well—I couldn't be sure, seeing as how you're here with that Lewis boy. It didn't take you long to move on, did it? In my day, we knew how to mourn a person."

Her tone is condescending as she looks at Grayson's arms around my shoulders with her nose scrunched up in distaste. I feel him take a deep breath beside me, and I know he's pulling himself together—reigning in the old Grayson so that the new one can stand tall beside me.

I'm about to rip into her—not for what she said about me, but for how she talks about Grayson like he's not there—when a voice comes behind us.

"When was that Delilah? Biblical times?"

Mrs. Adams stands beside Grayson, patting him on the cheek before turning back to Ms. Taylor.

"Well, I never—"

"Was taught manners. We're aware, Delilah. Now, if you don't mind, I'd like a word with the youngsters here," Mrs. Adams says, turning her back to Ms. Taylor and effectively cutting her off.

Ms. Taylor stomps her foot with a huff and storms off in the opposite direction.

The smile that creeps over Mrs. Adams's face is mischievous. The woman knew what she was doing. It makes me wary of what's to come now that her sights are set on us.

She lets her gaze fall to where Grayson's arm is still around me, and that smile of hers cranks up a few notches.

"Well, it's about time," she says with a wave, and then she walks away as if the sight of us together isn't the biggest piece of gossip this town has had in months.

When I look over at Grayson, there's a mixture of relief and happiness on his face because whether she realizes it or not, Mrs. Adams made him feel accepted in this town for the first time in his whole life.

Turning back, I watch as Mrs. Adams walks down the aisle, and when she's almost at the end, she looks over and gives me a wink.

Oh, yes—that woman knows what she's doing.

Chapter 23

Georgia

Mondays have to be the longest day ever. Nothing will convince me they are not thirty-six hours long instead of twenty-four.

Grayson and I were run ragged today, not getting time between clients to see each other. The poor guy is still at the office in meetings. He texted me around five to tell me that his meetings were running late and that I should go ahead and head out.

I was grateful for the reprieve, but as I'm driving home to sit at an empty house alone, I have the sudden urge to turn around and wait for him to join me.

That would be crazy, though. We already live beside each other, and I see him every day at work. We've been friends forever, but it's different now that we are in a relationship. I've needed him a lot this past year. I can't recall him ever having one serious girlfriend. I don't want to be one of the girls he gets tired of because I don't give him space. I'd even thought about finding a new job, but honestly, even taking Grayson out of the picture, I love this job. So, I'll just make sure to give him space in other areas—not waiting around the office or texting him 24/7—and maybe it's time to start thinking about going home. I've intruded on his space for a year. Plus, the idea of going back to the home where Nate and I experienced both life and death doesn't seem so hard anymore. In fact, it feels like the next step of healing for me. I'll mention it to Grayson next time I see him.

Despite all that, I still don't want to go home tonight and sit in a house alone, so instead, I find myself turning onto the road my parents live on.

I haven't seen either of them since Grayson and I started dating. I know they've heard the rumors, but I artfully dodge their questions when they call. It's not because I don't want them to know, but Mom has a way of ruining what she doesn't approve of. I don't know if she would approve of this, so I've been avoiding it.

But I can't avoid it forever, and I don't want to. I'm not trying to hide Grayson. He has been my rock for a long time, and that's not something I'm ashamed of.

When I pull into their house, the lights are on in the living room, but I keep my car running for two minutes while collecting myself. Reaching for my phone, I start to text Grayson to tell him where I am, just in case. When I slide my thumb across the screen, though, the red battery pops up. I have got to start remembering to charge it at night.

Throwing it into the cup holder, I place my hands on the steering wheel and let my head follow. Coming here may have been a bad idea.

Nerves prickle my skin. I wasn't afraid of the whole town finding out we were dating when we went to the grocery store, but the first time I have to face my mother, all bets are off.

"Get it together, Georgia," I say, giving myself a pep talk in my rear-view mirror. "You can do this. They are your parents, and they love you."

With one more deep breath, I step out of the car and into the cold—without my winter jacket on, because I despise wearing it while I'm driving. The cold air stings through my sweater. Running up the porch, I sling open the door and burst into the living room as if someone were chasing me.

CHAPTER 23

My parents sit in their recliners, and they startle when I run in.

"Georgia Jane," my mother scolds. "You scared the dickens out of me. What are you doing here? We weren't expecting you."

Her hand is over her heart, and I feel a little bad because her face is pale. I should have called.

My dad, ever the peacemaker, sits up straight on high alert. "What is it, Georgia? Is something wrong?"

Giving him a sheepish grin, I tuck my hair behind my ear and say, "There's nothing wrong. I just missed you guys. Plus, I left my coat in the car, so sorry for bursting in and making you worry."

As expected, my mom huffs in annoyance and rolls her eyes, going right back to the sewing kit in her lap. My dad, though, grins and pats the arm of the couch beside him.

"Well, now that you're here, come take a seat."

I slip my shoes off at the door and pad across the well-worn hardwood until I'm sitting on the couch right beside my dad.

He's watching a game show. My parents have a routine for every night. On Monday night, they eat supper at precisely four o'clock, clean the kitchen together, and then Dad watches a game show while Mom sews. I don't know that I can ever remember a time when they deviated from that schedule, not even when I was living at home.

After I'm settled on the couch beside him, my dad wastes no time getting to the question I know they've both been dying to ask.

"So—how's Grayson?"

I have two options: pretend that I'm oblivious to the real question he is asking, or rip off the bandage and get it all out there. An overwhelming need to have Grayson here beside me hits me right in the gut. Taking a deep breath, I decide to use some of the strength he always seems to lend me.

"I know that you know, Dad."

He chuckles and says, "You got me there, kiddo."

In the other corner of the room, my mom drops her sewing into her lap and studies me. Her face is hard to read, and I try not to squirm under her scrutiny. She has a way of seeing right through me—I haven't mastered my poker face when it comes to her.

Finally, right when I'm about to jump up and confess every bad thing I've ever done, she says, "Why didn't you tell us? Did you think we would be mad?"

I can't stand the disappointment in her eyes. Looking down, I pick at one of my nails so I don't have to face it.

"At first, I didn't tell you because I wasn't sure what I felt—or if he felt the same way. Grayson's been there for me every day during the worst time of my life, and I didn't recognize that my feelings were changing until one day, I couldn't deny it anymore. Then, when I found out that we felt the same, I guess I was protective of it. I didn't want the world ruining it for me, and I was proven right when I ran into Ms. Taylor at the grocery store."

My mom screws her face up in distaste at the mention of Ms. Taylor's name.

"What did that horrible woman say?" she asks

The pure venom in her voice surprises me. When I look up at her, though, there's a softness in her face that I'm not used to.

"She accused me of not grieving Nate long enough. She made me feel like I'm betraying him."

A moment passes where the only noise in the room is the television, and then I witness something I think will only happen once in my lifetime—my dad loses his temper. He slings the footrest of the recliner closed and hops up out of his chair. His face turns red as he paces and mumbles a couple of incoherent sentences, "Why I ought to…that woman's biding her time…"

The scene is so shocking that laughter, unbidden and uncontrolled, slips out. When I look over at my mom, she's staring at my dad like she's looking at an alien, which only makes me lose it further. There's a stitch in my side, and tears pool in my eyes as I lose control.

"Dear, you're going to give yourself a heart attack," Mom says in a voice that doesn't match the expression on her face. "Please, do sit down."

And as proof of how long my parents have been married, my dad sits back in his recliner, still grumbling all the time.

My laughter starts to subside, and it hits me just how long it's been since I've laughed like that.

"Now," my mom continues as I settle down and my dad's grumbling comes to an end. "That woman's had it coming to her since she stole my apple pie two years ago at the church's homecoming dinner and pretended it was hers—like anyone would believe it. Since then, I've been planning my revenge, biding my time, but this really amps things up."

Mom rubs her hands together as she plots, and I wonder if my parents have lost their minds. This is not how I imagined this going.

"Uh—Mom, I don't think—"

"Hush now, I'm thinking," she says, waving me off.

Shaking my head, I recline back against the couch with a grin. My dad reaches over and pats my hand, and I turn my head to look at him. The weathered lines of his age run across his face as signs of what a good life he's lived, and there's a happiness in his eyes that never seems to fade, even when my mom is concocting plans to threaten old women.

"Are you happy, kiddo?" He asks, not taking his gaze from my face.

"Yeah, Dad. I am."

Driving home from my parent's house, I feel lighter than I have in a very long time.

My relationship with my mom might be prickly sometimes, but I can always count on her to be on my side when I need her. It's just taken me a long time to learn that.

It's a fifteen-minute drive from my parents to Grayson's, and I'm counting down the minutes until I can take off my shoes and throw some pajamas on. Taking the last turn, I can see Grayson's driveway up ahead. His truck is parked there, but all the lights in his house are off. Glancing at the clock on my dash, I see it's only eight o'clock. Maybe this day got to him, too, and he went to bed early.

But that theory is put to rest when I pull into the driveway and see him sitting in front of my door, his back resting against it and his head hanging in his hands.

There's an ache in my throat because, for once, the strong Grayson Lewis looks a little broken.

Grabbing my stuff, I step out of the car and shut the door.

Grayson's head pops up when he hears the noise, and the pure fear in his eyes has me sucking in a breath and taking a step back.

He pushes himself off the ground and steps towards me—his steps slow and deliberate. I force myself to stay where I am. I don't know what happened between the time I left the office and now, but something did. For as many times as he has taken care of me, now's my turn to take care of him. I can't make any sudden movements, though, because I know Grayson. He needs to come to you. So I'll stand and wait for as long as he needs.

When he's finally standing in front of me, he reaches his hand out and twirls my hair between his fingers, but that touch must not be enough because I'm suddenly in his arms, being crushed against him in a fiercely protective hug.

I wrap my arms around his neck, holding him so he doesn't break.

"What's the matter, Gray? It's freezing out here. What are you doing sitting outside?" I ask.

His heart beats fast as he tilts his head so it lays in the crook of my neck.

"Gray," I urge. "You're starting to scare me."

"I thought—I thought—"

"What, Grayson? What did you think?"

"On the way home, I flipped on the radio. There was a wreck, and it matched the description of your car. I tried calling a hundred times, but your phone went to voicemail. Then I came here, and you weren't here. I thought I lost you. I can't lose you too."

His voice is grave as he tightens his arms, and it hits me that Grayson's biggest fear is losing someone else.

He spends all his time caring for me, but he's never had someone take care of him.

"I'm not going anywhere, Grayson. I'm right here," I say, dragging my fingers through his hair and massaging his scalp. A shiver runs through him, and he nods against my neck.

"Come on. Let's get you inside." Pulling back, I take his hand and drag him behind me. He follows like a lost puppy. I've never seen Grayson like this. He usually keeps his feelings close to his chest, never letting anyone in on his weakness, but I should have seen this coming after we lost Nate. A breakdown from him is past due.

Unlocking my door, I lead him to the living room and pull him down on the couch beside me. He must not think that's close enough, though, because he pulls me closer until I'm sitting in his lap with my arms wrapped around his neck.

"I just need to be close to you right now," he whispers.

And I get that because lately, being next to him is all I can think about.

"Have you eaten?" I ask, twirling the hair at the base of his neck between my fingers.

"No."

"Do you want me to make you something?"

"No."

"Do you need anything?"

"Just you, Peach. Just you," he says, laying his head against the couch and closing his eyes.

As I study the strong line of his jaw and how the tension releases from it, I rub my hand over his hair. His shoulders start to relax, and his breathing becomes even as he slips off to sleep.

I hate that he carries so much on him—that people can't see the man that I do. He's paid a lot for mistakes he made as an angry kid, and because of that, he thinks that he doesn't deserve good things in life—or worse, that the good things he has will disappear.

Leaning down, I gently kiss his forehead and whisper three words that I've been too afraid to say aloud, "I love you, Gray."

I hope one day soon I'll be brave enough to say them to him when he's awake.

Chapter 24

Georgia,

I hope this letter finds you starting to heal—going out more, enjoying life, and maybe finding love again, but there's still one more thing I need you to do. You already know what it is, don't you? This one's the most important. I wrote the other letters as a warm-up because I know this one will be hard for you, but you've made it this far—I think you're ready.

Heal your relationship with God, Georgia.

The day we found out I was terminal, I asked you not to be mad at God for my cancer, but I could see in your eyes that you already were. I fought so hard not to leave you because of that. The anger in your eyes scared me because I wasn't sure how I would help if I was gone.

You're strong. You don't need me there to heal, but you do need God. You can find yourself everywhere else, but it all means nothing if you don't find yourself with him again.

Go to church—let it heal you completely.

Please don't spend the rest of your life being angry when you can see me again when you get here.

I love you, Georgia, and God does, too. He didn't do this to hurt you, but he can heal you.

Don't get me wrong, I know that this one will be the hardest task I give you, but I promise that healing will be worth it.

Love,
Nate

Chapter 25

Georgia

At this point, I should be used to receiving letters from Nate, but every time I see his handwriting on another envelope, there's a drop in my stomach. I didn't think much about where they were coming from at first, but now I can't help but wonder who else knows about them.

"What are you looking at?" Grayson asks, coming up behind me in the kitchen.

He hugs me from behind, and I let my head drop to his shoulder. I can't help remembering how we stood here in this kitchen a year ago after Nate's funeral. It was a day I never thought I would heal from, but I have. My steps are slow, but I'm getting there, mainly with the help of the man behind me. And the more I think about Nate's letter, the more I realize he's right. I also have to heal my relationship with God, so my next step is going to church.

"Another letter."

"What are we doing this time?" There's no hesitation in his question. He'll help me without even knowing what the letter says.

"I don't think you'll like this one," I say, turning in his arms and offering him the letter to read.

Church for Grayson means a lot of people who wrote him off, but if he can help heal me, maybe I can help heal that church hurt for him.

He winces as he reads over it, then looks at me.

"I'll go with you, but you're right—I don't like it."

"Gray, I know you're angry, but have you ever stopped to consider that you're angry at the people and not at God?"

His body stiffens against me. It's a topic he doesn't want to talk about, but he's not getting out of it so easily.

"Come on. Talk to me," I say, reaching up and tugging on his jaw so he's looking down at me.

"I quit caring about what the people in this town think a long time ago."

The sadness in his eyes is crushing—though he's trying to hide it—but I can still see that little boy who acted out every chance he could to get someone's attention. That boy has just become a man who throws himself into creating a successful business, so those people still see him.

"That's not true, Gray," I say. "And you know it."

Wrenching out of my arms, he turns so his hands rest against the counter.

"Why do you have to push this?" he asks, anger lacing his voice.

It's the first time I've ever seen him mad at me. Business partners? Sure, all the time. People in town? Probably more than that. But me? Never.

"Why are you getting so mad?" I counter.

His shoulders are rigid. He's trying to push me away—to shut off the conversation before he has to talk about how he feels—but I won't let him. I run my hand over his back. He stiffens even more, but he doesn't pull away.

"Talk to me. Let me see all of you," I beg.

"I don't want to care, okay? I am a grown man. I don't need the people in this town to approve of me, but for some unknown reason, I want them to. And as for God, didn't you just tell me that you were still angry at him, too? Why am I not allowed to be?"

"Look at me, Grayson," I say, pulling on his arm until he turns around. He refuses to meet my eye, though, looking off to the side and clenching his jaw. "I'm not saying that you can't be angry. The people here have been unfair to you, but God isn't the sum of those who pretend to know him. I at least know what much. And you're right—I'm still so angry that I think it might suffocate me, but I know if that I don't eventually get over that anger, then I'm never going to heal—and healing for me means being with you, so I'm willing to work on it. I'm going to trust that Nate understood something about faith that I still haven't learned. What about you? Are you willing to heal?"

Pursing his lips, he huffs out a breath.

"I guess we're going to see, aren't we?"

His answer isn't exactly what I hoped for, but it's a start.

The white building looms ahead of me, making me a little queasy. The last time I was here was Nate's funeral, and I think I must have disassociated from the events of that day because I can only remember them in little snippets—the color of the coffin, the paleness of Nate's face. All the things I do remember play over in my nightmares sometimes, so I've avoided this building, going as far as driving out of my way to avoid it. I was afraid that if I passed it, I would remember more things from that day, and the nightmares would get worse.

But I haven't had those nightmares in months—not since the letters. With Grayson by my side, I feel a little braver than I would if I were standing here alone.

Squeezing his hand, I ask, "Are you ready?"

"As I'll ever be." His voice is devoid of emotion, and when I turn my head to look at him, his face is set in stone—the mask is back. I hate that he feels he has to put on his mask walking in here, but I also understand why he's doing it. It's his way of protecting himself, and I can't fault him for that.

"We'll be okay," I say as we walk up the stairs hand in hand. I might have said it to him, but it's also a reminder to myself. I can't expect this one visit to fix all my problems, but it's a start—just like the festival and the date. They were both a place to start. This is just another place—except it's the most important place: no pressure or anything.

Once we are up the steps, Grayson lets go of my hand and opens the door for me. Shaking the nerves out of my hand, I step forward, but as I do, Grayson leans in and whispers, "You're strong, Peach. Don't let anyone make you think otherwise."

Then, his hand is on my back, leading me into the church's foyer. We are met by a gaggle of older women, all waiting to greet us as we try to make it to the back pews.

There's a variation of greetings, but each one ends the same—with a sharp glance at Grayson's hand on my back.

I have to physically bite my tongue to keep from lashing out at these women who are supposed to know better than to judge. Grayson's mask stays firmly in place, ignoring the women as we push through the crowd.

I'm afraid we will never make it to our seats when all of a sudden, Mrs. Adams appears—an angel disguised as a feisty elderly woman—or at least she would be if the next thing out of her mouth wasn't, "You heifers get back to your seats and stop staring. Jesus doesn't like ugly."

I have to hold my breath to keep from laughing.

Most of the women scurry away, afraid of the wrath of their precious leader, but a few straggle behind, pretending to read the bulletin board when really their attention is on us.

Mrs. Adams doesn't stop to consider the ones still watching. Instead, she walks right up to Grayson, wraps her arms around him, and says, "I'm glad you're here, son."

The stone set of Grayson's mask starts to crack, and with that hug, the boy begging for acceptance starts to heal.

Tears sting my eyes, and I have to turn my head to keep Grayson from seeing them. He won't like that I'm getting emotional on his behalf. When I have myself under control, I turn back to them, and Mrs. Adams is stepping away. Grayson stands there, stiff and awkward, but there's a lightness in his eyes that wasn't there before.

"Now come on," Mrs. Adams chides, "before we're late to the service."

She spins on her heel and marches into the sanctuary, expecting us to follow.

I look over at Grayson and mouth, "Bossy."

He throws me a wink, and his lips tip up in a crooked grin that nearly splits my chest in two with happiness.

Chapter 26

Grayson

I thought that walking into this church would feel like walking into my execution, but oddly, it doesn't.

I've been around these people thousands of times, and I've always been the outsider. The thing about being an outsider, though, is that it teaches you lessons. I learned a long time ago that you can't control how people feel about you—you can only prove them wrong—and walking into this church with Georgia by my side is my way of proving them wrong.

No one here ever thought I would be good enough for the girl by my side—including me—and I may never be. But, I will spend my whole life trying to be.

Mrs. Adams leads us to a pew in the middle, and I have to hold back a groan. The back would have been preferable as no one could shoot daggers at my head with their eyes if I'm sitting behind them all, but Georgia happily follows her in—and where Georgia goes, so do I.

Despite the padding, the pew is hard underneath me. My leg bounces up and down as I look around, trying to get an idea of who I'll be dealing with today. My eyes land on Harper and Ellie sitting in the row across from us, and when Harper realizes I'm looking at her, she sends me a glare. I smirk back at her, knowing it will get under her skin. A huff and an eye roll later, she looks away. Ellie is staring at Georgia, a wide grin spread across her wrinkled face. Georgia's parents are sitting a few rows in front of Ellie and Harper, and even from here, I can see tears sparkling in their eyes.

My leg bounces harder, jostling Georgia as Pastor Greer takes his pulpit. She places a hand on my knee, steadying me. I'm supposed to be comforting her today, but instead, she's comforting me.

"Welcome, friends and family. It's nice to see everyone here today."

A chorus of greetings resounds around the room as the congregation settles down in their seats.

"If you will open your bibles to Romans chapter 5, I would like to get started."

There's a rustle of paper as people flip through their bibles, looking for the page. Reaching into the inside pocket of my winter vest, I pull out the bible Georgia gave me so long ago. It was the first gift I had ever received from anyone but my mom, and even then, the gifts from her were few and far between. So when Georgia laid the bible in my hands that day, I couldn't help but fall in love with her a little more.

I let my hands run over the smooth leather as I flip through the pages, looking for Romans, and when I finally find it, I glance up at Georgia. She's staring at me with pure adoration shining in her eyes. And even though she hasn't said it, I can't help but feel like a man that's loved. It's a new feeling that doesn't mesh well with the perpetual grump that I usually am.

"Before I read the scripture to you, I would like everyone to close their eyes and bow their heads as I lead us in prayer."

Georgia bows her head, and I can't help taking one more glance at the lingering smile on her face before I close my eyes.

"Dear Heavenly Father, we come here today to worship you and to lay it all at your feet. I pray that as we get into the service, this message from your word will reach the ones who need to hear it. Amen."

Georgia's hand is still on my knee, so with my bible in one hand, I use the other to scoop her hand up and link my fingers through hers, needing the contact.

"With a show of hands, how many of you have ever felt like the burdens you've been given in life are too much for you to bear?" Hands around me shoot up in the air as Pastor Greer steps down the stairs of the altar and stands in front of the congregation, studying each person as if he can see their pain.

I dip my head when he gets to me. The people I let see my pain are few and far between, and one of them is sitting beside me.

"Romans five verses one through four say, 'Therefore being justified by faith, we have peace with God through our Lord Jesus Christ: by whom also we have access by faith into this grace wherein we stand, and rejoice in hope of the glory of God. And not only so, but we glory in tribulations also: knowing that tribulation worketh patience; and patience, experience; and experience, hope.'" He pauses there, letting the reading sit in, and it does—like a boulder in my stomach. Georgia's hand tightens around mine, and she leans forward, bringing me with her as the pastor continues, "Now, I don't know about you, but those verses send cold chills over my skin when I think about them. Not only does he offer us peace during our tribulations, but we stand within his grace. It doesn't matter what we've done in our life—or how much we think we don't deserve it—we have his grace. And those tribulations we're going through—those storms we think we will never make it out of—teach us patience and can eventually lead us to one of the best places of our lives here on Earth. Maybe you can't see it now because you're in the eye of the storm, with the rain beating down all around you, but oh, when that storm breaks up, does he have a plan for you."

Mrs. Adams gives a loud "Amen" and claps her hands, giving me a pointed look as she does—one that screams, "Are you listening, you fool? This is for you."

The woman is the strangest person I've ever met, but she has a way of seeing what you need and giving it to you with her own special twist. She sends me a wink, and I find myself growing fond of the old woman—despite her crazy.

By the time the sermon ends, Georgia and I look like we've been through an emotional wringer. I've run my hands through my hair more times than I can count, causing it to look like I just rolled out of bed, and she has lines of mascara streaming down her face from the tears she cried.

As she stands, I tug on her hand and pull her to me, taking my thumb and wiping over the smudges under her eyes.

"You okay," I ask, letting my hand trail down her face and over her shoulder until our fingers are interlaced.

"Mm-hmm. Or at least I will be. It hit a lot harder than I prepared myself for, but can we talk about it later? I'm going to talk to Ellie before we go," she sniffs. "I'll meet you outside, okay?"

I nod and watch as she walks away. Ellie throws her arms open as Georgia approaches and hugs her tightly. Georgia's parents stand behind the pair, watching their daughter.

Sometimes, I wish I had been the guy Georgia deserved back in high school—the only one she's ever loved because I'm selfish and want everything she is willing to give me. Watching her with Ellie, though, is another reason I know she needed Nate first. She won't have a loving mother-in-law with me, and as for a father-in-law, well—who knows with Kip. I haven't contacted him since the day he showed up at my house. It seems Brooks didn't fall as far from that tree as he had hoped, but after Brooks's visit with his family, there's been a niggling in the back of my mind, making me debate reaching out—to both Brooks and Kip. Maybe it's time I stop being so hard on the pair.

"It's a scene worthy of a picture, isn't it?" Harper asks, sarcasm oozing from her voice as she slides up alongside me. I look over at her, but she isn't looking at me. She's looking at Georgia wrapped in Ellie's arms. Harper rolls her eyes when she sees Ellie caress her hand over Georgia's hair.

"What is it this time, Harper? Jealous?"

The look she sends me is scathing.

"Of Georgia? Absolutely not."

"Just bitter then," I throw back.

She tilts her head, cocking one brow as her lips flatten into a mirthless smile.

"You're one to talk—but I guess it's worked out well for you—stealing your best friend's girl and all. Tell me, Gray, how long did you wait after Nate was gone to go after Georgia?

She says my name was such condescension that it takes everything in me not to reach out, wrap my hands around her neck, and shake her until she gains a little bit of common sense.

Through my teeth, I grit out, "You have no idea what you're talking about, Harper. Maybe you should worry about your own relationship for once."

The insult is weak, but Harper has a way of digging under my skin and chopping at every nerve I have left. Part of that is because we're too much alike, but the other part is because of the way she treats Georgia. I've chalked it up to jealousy over the years. Harper would have done anything to have her dad stick around so she could have the kind of family that Georgia does. Georgia's mom may be tough, but she loves her. Neither of her parents walked out on her like she wasn't good enough. That's a pain that sticks with you—even after you find out it wasn't true and they just didn't know about you. Then Georgia started dating Nate, and all the attention that Nate used to give to Harper got split between the two. As a teenager whose dad walked out without a word, I can see how that would have been hard for Harper, but as a fully grown adult, it's time she let go of grudges that aren't there.

Her laugh is harsh as she flips her hair over her shoulder to look at me. The smile on her lips is poisoned with bitterness, and whatever arrow she's about to shoot will be deadly.

"Enjoy it while it lasts because you and me—" she says, wagging her finger between the two of us, "we aren't so different, and despite how blind you are, little Miss Perfect over there won't stick around for someone like us."

Harper knew exactly where she was throwing to get that barb to stick. It hits me right where she intended because she's not wrong. I've known it since I met Georgia. It's not that I think she will walk away, but someday she might see through to the guy underneath, the one the rest of the town sees. When she does, I can't expect her to stay because that guy has never been good enough for anyone else to stay. That thought doesn't make me bitter, though. I'll selfishly soak up all the time she'll give me, and when she's done, I'll let her walk away and cheer her on from the sidelines, even though it will kill me.

Harper doesn't bother sticking around for my response. She knows she won't get one.

Georgia finishes talking to Ellie and her parents, and when she comes back to me, her smile is so bright it sends a pang to my chest. I would let her ruin me as long as I could see that smile on her face every day.

Chapter 27

Georgia

After church, Grayson and I came back to his house to fix lunch. We kept it simple with sandwiches and soup, taking them to his living room and snuggling up on the couch to eat.

"Want to watch a movie?" Grayson asks, handing me the remote.

"Absolutely," I say, clicking through the movies.

Grayson finishes his food as I scroll through the options. He stands to take his plate to the kitchen, and I call, "Will you grab me a water while you're in there?"

"Of course."

He returns and stands behind the couch. I tilt my head back on the couch to look up at him. He bends to place a kiss on my forehead and drops the water on my lap. I close my eyes at the feel of his beard scraping against my skin. Out of all the ways he's cared for me, this simple act feels the most domestic. I wait for the guilt and fear to crash into my stomach with the realization, but it doesn't. Instead, contentment settles in my veins, thrumming through my whole body.

Grayson walks around to the front of the couch and sits beside me again. Lifting my head, I flip through the channels again, searching for something to watch.

"How did you feel about church today?" Grayson asks, tracing patterns on my arm with his fingertips.

"I feel like I should be asking you that. You weren't exactly ecstatic to go."

"Honestly," he says, his fingers stilling. "It wasn't as bad as I thought it would be. It was kind of nice to see Mrs. Adams put people in their place. That woman is a terror when she wants to be."

I let out a gentle laugh because it's true, but I love her for making Grayson feel seen.

"What did you think about the message?" I ask.

His hand leaves my arm, and he squirms in his seat.

"I think that I wasn't asking for patience—my whole life has been a lesson in that," he mutters.

Smacking him on the chest, I shake my head.

"Come on, seriously, what did you think?"

"I guess—that I would say before today, I didn't feel worthy of a whole lot, and if I'm honest, I don't think one church service can change that, but I will say that I'm starting to feel like I can be more than my mistakes."

"Oh, Gray," I say, laying my head on his shoulder. "You've always been worthy. There's never been a question of that. Those mistakes are not the sum of who you are. You are so much more."

He rests his chin on my head. From his silence, I can tell he doesn't believe me, so I wrap my arms around him, praying he feels at least an ounce of his worth through my arms.

"Do you remember the night that the gazebo in the town square burnt down?" he asks, his voice contemplative.

"Yes." I'm not sure where he's going with this, but I don't think I will like it.

"It was me." His answer is whispered into my hair, but I still hear him.

A gasp slips past my lips before I can't stop it, and I jerk back, knocking his chin against the top of my head.

"Grayson," I chide, rubbing at the spot on my head where his chin hit.

He acts like he didn't notice my head hitting his chin at full force because he continues to talk. "It was an accident. Now sit back, and let me tell you the rest of the story. Watch where you're throwing your head, too."

His fingers wrap around the top of my arm and tug me towards him. I go willingly, but all my nerves are on edge. I still don't believe that Grayson's worth is equal to the mistakes of a teenager, but I can't say I'm not shocked. This is the first time I've heard about this particular mistake. When the gazebo burnt down, many people in town accused Grayson, but nothing ever came from it. I just assumed they had been wrong and moved on. Besides, I thought he would have told Nate and me if it had been him, but I guess I was wrong on both accounts.

"Okay," I say, settling back into his chest. "I'm ready now. I was just a little surprised before."

He makes a sound of amusement in his throat before he continues. "Think really hard. Do you remember what else happened the night that the gazebo burned down?"

My brows dip together as I do what he asks. Then it hits me—that was the night Nate and I had our first date, but I don't see how they are connected.

"It was my first date with Nate that night," I supply.

He nods. "It was. By the time Nate asked you out, I had already decided that I would never be good enough for you, but my best friend was. I was happy for him—for you—but I also felt like I was mourning you guys a little bit. Our friendship dynamic wasn't going to be the same anymore, and I hated change—"

Shifting, I look up at him. "Why didn't you tell us you felt that way?"

"Because I was just as invested in your relationship working as you guys. If you and Nate didn't work out, I wouldn't have let you fall in love with another guy. I would have been selfish and never let you go."

I can't decide how that makes me feel because, on the one hand, I had Nate, and I would never trade my time with him, but it makes me so unbelievably sad for Grayson.

"Anyway," he continues, barreling on through to his story. "That night, while you guys were on your date, I snuck out and went to the gazebo. I was eighteen, so I stopped and bought a pack of cigarettes to take with me. It was the first and last time I ever tried them. It was one of the worst experiences in my life. I guess I didn't put the cigarette out all the way because before I knew it, the gazebo was burnt down, and the town was pointing fingers at me."

"Okay, so it was an accident," I say slowly. "I'm not understanding how this connects to the sermon, though, Grayson."

"Even though the town couldn't prove that I was the one to burn it down, I still get judgmental stares everywhere I go—even though I used my first big check from my company to build it back. Well—I guess they don't know that I was the one who rebuilt it either because I donated the money anonymously. They were quick to assume that I was the one to burn it down, but no one would ever guess that I was the one to build it back. And I think that sums up my life: I'm always the bad, but never the good. Lately, though, I don't feel so much like the mistake anymore, and the sermon today felt like a reminder of that. It was nice."

Tracing my fingers along his jaw, I say, "I'm sorry life has been so hard for you, Grayson, and maybe it's not any consolation—but you've always been good to me."

He drops a kiss onto my lips. It's sweet and healing and warm—all the things that Grayson can't see about himself wrapped up in a small, intimate gesture.

When he pulls back, I can tell he's done talking about it. He changes directions, and I let him because I can tell he needs it. He's not used to talking about himself, so I'm grateful for the pieces he's willing to give me.

"What about you?" he asks. "This was your task from Nate. How did you feel about the sermon?"

I consider for a moment what he's asking me.

"If you had asked me a year ago if I thought anything good would come out of the storm of losing Nate, I would have told you absolutely not, but now—I can see how God was leading me towards something I never expected."

"Oh, yeah?" Grayson asks. "What's that?"

"You, Gray. He was leading me to you."

The pelting of rain against the tin roof wakes me up. After our heart-to-heart, Grayson and I watched a movie—a rom-com to lighten the heavy mood between us. We must have fallen asleep, though, because when I look through the window, the sky is turning pink as the sun starts to set.

My head is on Grayson's leg, and his breathing is deep and rhythmic. When I roll over to look at him, he stirs for a minute before going back to sleep. He's sitting straight up on the couch with his head tilted back against the cushion—no signs of his usual grumpiness marring his face. He looks peaceful.

"I can feel you staring at me," he says, keeping his head tilted back with his eyes closed.

"I can't help it," I say, laughing. "You're just so pretty."

He pops one eye open to glare at me. "Men are not pretty."

Biting my lip to hide my smile, I can't help but tease him a little. "Oh, you're definitely pretty."

I start to jump up, but he's quicker, grabbing me and lifting me until his arms are wrapped around me like a steel cage. My back is pressed to his chest, and his lips hover over my ear.

"Tell me how handsome and manly you think I am," he teases, whispering into my ear. Turning my head, I stick my tongue out at him, refusing to give in, but when his finger starts to dig into my ribs, tickling me, I give in.

"Okay, okay," I laugh. "You win. You're the manliest man I know, and that face should be in magazines because it's so handsome."

He gives a self-satisfied smirk, loosening his arms, and I turn in them to face him.

"I've been thinking," I say, running my hand over his face that truly could be on the cover of a magazine.

"This probably doesn't bode well for me." There's a cheeky grin on his face as I pat his cheek and then put my finger over his lips, effectively quieting him.

"Shh, and listen. Don't freak out when I say this, promise?"

He nods, keeping quiet with my finger still pressed against his lips.

"I think we should host a dinner—and invite your family." That wariness in his eye turns into an all-out confrontation, but I have a plan. Grayson may think he's fooling himself and everyone around him, but he wants to get to know his family. I could see it the day that he let Avery color his tattoos, but he's too stubborn to make a move without a little push. "It doesn't have to be just your family. I would like to invite my parents and Ellie, but it would be nice to invite your family too. They want to get to know you—you should let them. You won't even have to do it on your own. I'll be there with you if anything goes wrong or you get uncomfortable."

My words are rushed, jumbling together as they come out, but I want him to hear everything before he makes up his mind because once Grayson makes up his mind, that's it. He's done.

He doesn't say anything when I'm finished—just sits and stares. Maybe this was a bad idea, but I had to offer. The silence stretches without him answering, and I begin to get uncomfortable. His fingers wrap around my wrist pulling my hand from his mouth, and heat flames into my cheeks. I hadn't even noticed.

"I was waiting—I didn't want you cutting me off again," he teases. "Let's do it. You're right. It is time that I give them the benefit of the doubt, but I make no promises that it will be permanent. I'll give it a chance, though."

"Thank you. I'll take care of everything," I say, leaning forward and kissing his cheek. "You won't regret it."

"Only because it's you," he says, reaching out and tucking a strand of hair behind my ear. "I'm glad to see you start to be happy again, Peach."

"It's because of you, you know. I would have stayed in the dark if it wasn't for you. Thanks for helping me come back to the light."

"You're wrong, Georgia. You would have found your way out on your own. It was never me."

Leaning back on the couch, I lean into his side and sigh. "It wasn't me, Gray, but I do think God's been working through you this whole time, and whether he knows it or not, Nate's had a part in it too—leading me to you, that is."

Grayson's muscles tighten beneath me, but I don't understand his reaction. Before I can think too hard about it, he says, "Yeah, maybe it was Nate's plan all along."

There's something strange in how he says it, but I don't question it too hard—even if I should.

Chapter 28

Grayson

It's the day of the dinner, and Georgia has been buzzing around my house all morning. Currently, she is standing at the stove with an apron wrapped around her waist that shows her curves, and a drying towel flipped over her shoulder. Dishes litter the countertops, and there's flour all over her face. I tried to step in and help earlier, but she shooed me out of the kitchen with a kiss and a snap of that towel to my leg. The entire scene is straight out of one of my dreams, except in my dream, she has my ring on her finger.

"How's it coming?" I ask, slipping behind her and wrapping my arms around her waist.

"Didn't I scare you out of the kitchen once already? What are you doing back?"

With my hands on her waist, I spin her until she's facing me. "I thought you would want to know that I just got a text from my brother. They are about fifteen minutes away, so I figure everyone else will show up soon, too."

A panicked look crosses her face.

"What? The food is not ready yet. I'm not ready, either. Look at me," she says, gesturing to her clothes with splotches of flour and other various foods over them. "Plus, Ellie texted this morning and asked if she could bring Harper along. I can't tell Ellie no, and you know

Harper. Everything needs to be perfect—I don't want your family to get a bad impression."

She's panicking, switching from focus to focus, unable to choose which she is most panicked about.

Taking her face in my hands, I force her to look at me. "Hey, I'm right here. We're doing this together, remember? Now, let's deal with this one problem at a time. You get changed, and I can finish up here in the kitchen. I'm not hopeless, you know. As far as Harper goes, ignore her, but if she gets to be too much, I don't mind kicking her out—this is my home, after all, and no one will make my girl feel uncomfortable in my home."

That same smile Georgia wore at church appears on her face now, and my heart nearly beats out of my chest from the sight of it.

"Your girl, huh?"

"You know it," I say, placing a quick kiss on her lips and grabbing the towel from her shoulder. "Now, shoo."

I snap the towel at her legs like she did mine earlier until she's running out of the kitchen, her hair flying behind her as she giggles.

Fifteen minutes later, she returns with her makeup done and a dress that nearly makes me swallow my tongue.

She grins when she sees me staring. The little vixen—she knew exactly what that dress would do to me.

"You look beautiful, Peach," I say, stepping towards her to kiss her and maybe run my fingers through her hair to mess it up a little, but the doorbell rings before I can make it to her.

"Showtime," she says. "Are you ready?"

"As I'll ever be," I grumble.

I follow behind her as we walk to the door, and when we are in the foyer, I stop right behind her, placing my hand on her shoulder as she opens the door. We're a united front, ready to take on the people in our lives together. It's nice having her on my side—or rather by my side because there's a difference. Even with Nate here, she was always on my side—Nate was too, but now she's standing by my side as my girl, and that's so much better. I just wish it didn't have to mean that Nate is gone, too.

Ellie and Harper stand on my front porch, waiting to come in. Ellie's smile is genuine as she looks between Georgia and me, but Harper looks like she's stepped on a rotten egg. Her nose is scrunched up in disgust, and not for the first time, I'd like to knock that look off her face, but instead, I paste on a smile as I wave Ellie into the house. When Harper passes by, I let it drop into a sneer.

"Your home is so nice, Grayson," Ellie says, looking around the foyer.

"Thank you. Georgia decorated it," I say, pulling Georgia to my side.

"Of course she did," Harper mutters under her breath.

"What was that, Harper? I don't think I heard you correctly. Were you telling Georgia how great of a job she did?" There's none of the niceness I had for Ellie in my voice. Instead, it's ice cold. This is one time I will let my anger show. Ellie allows Harper to get away with a lot of things because she feels sorry for her. She hated that she couldn't make her husband stay around for her kids, but I don't care what Harper's excuse is. She's not going to talk to Georgia like that in my house.

Harper sends me a glare but otherwise remains silent.

Georgia clears her throat and steps forward to Ellie. "Here," she says, taking the dish that's in Ellie's arm. "I'll take that and show you to the kitchen."

Ellie follows her, chattering about the house as they go. I stay where I am, crossing my arms as Harper watches them go. It's time this little problem Harper has is taken care of once and for all. When Georgia and Ellie disappear into the kitchen, Harper turns her attention back to me, glaring.

Lowering my voice, I say, "This is how this evening—and really any other interaction you have with Georgia—is going to go, so listen to me closely because I won't repeat myself. From now on, you're going to treat Georgia with respect. You're going to drop this attitude that everyone owes you something because they don't—especially Georgia. It's not her fault Nate loved her, and it's not her fault that Nate died. So grow up and get over it because if you don't, you will see a side of me you haven't. I've let you be a brat because you're Nate's little sister, but that good grace is gone. Test me if you want to, but you won't like it."

Her eyes are angry, and her nostrils flare as she steps right up to me. She's significantly shorter than I am, so she has to look up to talk to me, ruining any power she thought she held.

"You better watch yourself, Grayson. I know more than you think I do." She twirls on her heel and stomps away from me.

There's another knock at the door, and this time, it's Georgia's parents, with Brooks, Kip, Emryn, and Avery standing behind them. I didn't think I'd ever see the day I'd welcome the presence of my brother and father, but here it is. Hopefully, they will serve as a barrier to Harper's attitude. Stepping aside, I motion for the group to file in.

"Georgia is in the kitchen," I say to her parents. Her dad claps me on the back as he walks by, but her mom stops right in front of me.

"It's nice to see you, Mrs. Williams."

"Oh, hush," she says, wrapping her arms around me and holding me tight. My body stiffens involuntarily, but I didn't expect this from her. She's not typically an affectionate woman. She loves Georgia, but the woman knows how to wear a stern face. "Thank you for bringing my daughter back to me."

It's a whisper in my ear, but I can feel those words through my whole body. A knot sticks in my throat, so instead of responding, I nod. She gives one short jerk of her head before stepping back and following her husband to the kitchen.

Brooks is next through the door, making smooching noises as he passes. I stick my foot out again to trip him, but he notices this time, jumping over it and laughing. Avery follows her daddy and shakes her head, scolding me with a, "That wasn't very nice," and a wag of her finger. Emryn follows the pair, laughing at their antics and kissing me as she passes.

Kip is the last person to enter, and he waits inside the foyer as I close the door. His hands are shoved in his pockets as he stares at the floor. When he raises his eyes to me, there are tears in them.

"Thank you for the invite, Son," he says, emotion clogging his voice, and oddly, it doesn't make me want to rage against him.

Voices and laughter surround me at my dining room table. When I bought it, Georgia advised me to buy a big one so it could be filled with friends and family. At the time, I didn't have the heart to tell her that I didn't think there would be a day when more than three seats would be filled, but as I look around, I'm glad I took her advice.

Georgia stands and starts to clear the table, and I stand with her, moving to help.

"You cooked. I'll clear the table. Sit," I demand, taking the plates from her hand. Out of the corner of my eye, I see Brooks make eye contact with Kip and dip his head towards me.

"I'll help," Kip says, standing from his seat and gathering plates in his arms.

He follows me into the kitchen, the swinging door closing behind us, and we are alone for the first time all day.

"Do you have a minute to talk?" he asks, placing the dishes in the sink.

"Go for it," I say, rolling up my sleeves and turning the water on. My answer comes off gruff, but it's my defense mechanism. I've spent a lot of years creating it, and it's hard to switch off.

He grabs the drying towel from the top of the counter, and as I wash, he dries.

"I want you to know my story, and if you don't want anything to do with me after you hear what I have to say, I will respect your decision. I can't do that until you hear my side, though."

Nodding, I continue to wash the dishes, waiting to hear what he has to say. I've been hard on him. It's not his fault that my mom didn't tell him about me, but at the same time, I know she did it to protect me because she didn't think he would have been good for me. He was a drunk, and she didn't want to raise a kid around that. Getting to know him now, though, feels like a betrayal to her—and the hard life she lived so that she could protect me.

"When I was a kid, my dad, well—let's just say he wasn't the best man. I was an angry kid with a bad home life that I hated coming home to, so I started acting out. But I didn't realize that it would lead to a life of addiction. Eventually, I guess I got to be too much for my parents to handle—or they just didn't want to deal with me in the first place." He stops, studying the plate in his hands before continuing, "They sent me to live with my grandfather. I was sixteen at the time and drinking entirely too much. I lived there for six months before he passed away. Somehow, the system wasn't notified that I was living with him, so I was alone for the first time in my life. I had to face the decision of either going back to my dad or making it on my own—I chose to do it on my own. But a sixteen year old kid should never have to make the decisions I did. I was lucky that alcohol was all I became addicted to."

"What happened then?" I ask, scrubbing the plate in my hand harder than it needs. "Where did my mom fit into that timeline?"

He takes a deep breath and lays the towel on the counter.

"I met her when I was twenty-five. By that time, I'd moved around a lot, never really settling anywhere, but your mom—she was something special. I knew it the first time I laid eyes on her. But it's not easy to change. I was past the point of being an alcoholic—I just hid it well at first. When she found out, she tried to get me to quit, but I made the wrong decision. Eventually, she left and took you with her, but I didn't even know about you. Grayson, look at me when I tell you this." He pauses and waits for me to turn my head to him. I take my time, washing the dish in my hand and drying it before I lift my eyes to him. "I want you to know that I would have been there if I had known about you. I wasn't the best dad to Brooks, but I'll tell you like I told him—you two are the best things about my life. Don't you forget that."

Clearing my throat, I turn my head away from him and wipe my cheek on my shoulder, pretending to myself that the water there is dishwater and not tears.

"I'll uh—" I say, swallowing hard before I continue, "I'll think about what you said."

"Thank you." He picks the drying towel back up. We go back to work, letting the silence wrap around us until the swinging door bursts open, and Brooks walks in.

"Are you guys done crying yet? Because that little firecracker of yours said she made pie, Grayson, and I'm not missing out on pie."

He rubs his stomach, acting like he didn't just eat a full meal five minutes ago.

Beside me, Kip chuckles, "Brooks, there really isn't any wonder that your daughter acts the way she does."

Brooks shrugs, "She gets it honest."

Then he turns and heads back out the door he came from. When it's about to swing closed, he sticks his head in again and says, "Hurry up. I'm hungry."

And that's why I spend the next ten minutes washing the dishes until they shine. Usually, I would leave them to put up later, but just to spite him, I do that too. By the time I walk back into the dining room, he's glaring at me like he might give me a black eye, and I smile at him, daring him to try.

Maybe having a little brother won't be so bad after all.

Chapter 29

Georgia

"The pies are warming over in my apartment," I say when Grayson returns. "I ran out of room over here while I was cooking. I'll go grab them and be right back."

Standing, I turn my back so it's to the rest of the room, and only Grayson can see my face. "Are you okay?" I mouth.

He gives me a subtle nod and winks at me, and that's good enough for me right now. I'll ask him more about his talk with Kip later after everyone has gone.

"I'll help you," Harper says.

I whip my head towards her, suspicious of why she's being so nice all of a sudden, but she's looking around the room, smiling at everyone until she gets to Grayson. Then that smile turns a little scary.

I'll be asking Grayson about that later, too.

"Thanks," I say, having no choice really but to accept.

When we get out into the hallway, Harper's smile drops from her face, and she stomps in front of me and out the door. She's waiting for me by my apartment door when I get outside. Hurrying across the driveway, I pull the key out of my pocket and unlock the door. She steps through without a word.

The scene is a strange déjà vu of the night of the anniversary of Nate's death. Harper walks around the apartment, making herself at home as she picks stuff up and turns it over.

"It looks oddly clean in here," she comments.

"Yeah, Harper. That's what happens when you clean."

"Or don't stay here," she mumbles under her breath.

I'd been pulling the pies out of the oven, but at her words, I set them on the counter and spin around to face her. "You know what, Harper. I've let a lot go with you because I've felt sorry for you, but I'm done. You and I are going to settle this right now."

"I don't know what you mean." Her voice is sickly sweet. It sounds like a warning, but I ignore it.

"You know exactly what I mean. You're mean—actually, you're more than mean. Sometimes, you're just nasty to me, and I've never figured out why. So let's get it out now and put it past us so we both feel better because I'm tired."

She scoffs and rolls her eyes. "Oh, little Miss Perfect, who everyone loves, is tired because one person chooses not to like her. That must be so rough for you. Let me see if I can cry you a river, or better yet, let me see if I can burst that bubble of yours—Grayson's dating you because my brother asked him to. You're right. I do feel better."

She drops that bomb in my lap and walks away like she didn't just turn my whole world upside down in a matter of seconds, but she doesn't get far before I'm running after her and grabbing her arm.

"Stop. You aren't going anywhere. Explain what you mean by that because, from where I'm standing, you just look jealous. Where's your husband, Harper? Oh, that's right, he's out of town with 'friends' again." I throw air quotes around the word friend because she's used that excuse for Cole a couple of times now, and each time she does, it gets thinner and thinner.

"Oh, honey. I am not jealous of you. If you don't believe me, ask Grayson about the letter from my brother."

My face visibly pales at the mention of a letter from Nate. My grip on her arm loosens, and my stomach roils, threatening to send back up the food I just ate. Harper must see that she struck a nerve because a slow, sarcastic smile spreads across her lips. The letters are Nate's MO I've been receiving my own for months, but when did Grayson get one? And why didn't he tell me about it? The sick feeling in my stomach continues to build.

"Are we done with our little talk now?" Harper asks, pure glee filling her voice as she watches me.

I refuse to cry in front of her, so I nod, swallowing hard as she gathers the pies in her hands and leaves.

"Good chat," she calls over her shoulder while I'm left wondering how my life just got flipped upside down once again.

I'm cleaning up the rest of the kitchen and putting away leftovers when Grayson walks in.

After dessert, my mom and dad left first, followed by Harper and Ellie. Harper gave me a self-satisfied, smug smile as she got up from the table to leave. After a while, Grayson's family followed suit.

I remained quiet all through the rest of the dinner. I could feel Grayson's eyes on me while we ate, but I couldn't bring myself to look at him. No—I need to be calm and collected so I can talk to him.

There's an explanation for what Harper said. There has to be. If Nate sent him a letter, there's no way it told Grayson to date me. Maybe Nate had asked Grayson to take care of me once he was gone, and Harper saw it somehow and misconstrued it. But, then, why did he hide it? When Grayson admitted to having feelings for me, he'd said he had loved me his whole life, but what if he was just saying that? What if his obligation to Nate meant he felt he had to lie to me?

My knees nearly buckle at the thought, and I tighten my grip on the countertop to keep from falling over.

Counting, I find five things I can see, four things I can touch, three things I can hear, two things I can smell, and one thing I can taste. When I'm done with the exercise, my nerves are only marginally calmer, but it's enough that I can think.

Harper is bitter. That's a fact that I've never questioned, and it also goes to say that she likes hurting me. So—maybe she twisted whatever she saw to hurt me. It's a reasonable thought. Grayson has never given me a reason to question him, and I owe it to him to let him explain.

"You okay?" he asks, taking the food from my hand and putting it in the refrigerator.

"Not really. Can we sit?" I ask.

His brows dip and concern as he studies my face, looking for any signs of the problem, but when he doesn't find anything, he nods and leads me over to the bar—a place where we seem to have all our important conversations lately. What's one more to add to the mix?

"What is it, Georgia? You're starting to scare me. What happened with Harper? You started acting differently once you came back with her."

I cross my legs and then uncross them, trying to get comfortable so that I can just ask him, but I realize that this whole situation is uncomfortable. I'm just going to have to spit it out.

"Did Nate write you a letter?"

The question hangs between us, and I hold my breath, waiting for his answer. But when it doesn't come in one…two…three seconds, I know.

It's okay, though. Just because Nate wrote Grayson a letter doesn't mean it says what Harper thinks. Although—why would he hide it from me if it wasn't bad?

Maybe he was embarrassed by it.

This back-and-forth argument in my head isn't getting me anywhere, and the longer Grayson waits to answer, the sicker I get to my stomach.

"Yes," Grayson says at last, but he doesn't expound. Why doesn't he explain?

"Why didn't you tell me that? I mean, I've shown you every letter I've received."

"Because you needed my help to complete Nate's tasks for you—or at least, you thought you did. I didn't need your help with mine."

So Nate did ask him to do something. My stomach twists even more. I'm going to puke by the end of this.

"Can I um—Can I see the letter?" I ask.

Grayson's fist tighten in his lap, causing the orchid to move on his wrist. My eyes are drawn to it. "It's a promise to his best friend," he'd said when Avery had asked him. He used my favorite flower to represent a promise to his best friend—a promise to Nate. He doesn't move to get the letter, but somehow, I already know that Harper was telling me the truth.

"Get the letter, Grayson," I demand, my voice turning hard and cold.

He nods and rises from his chair without saying a word. I want to yell at him to say something—anything—but I remain quiet as he walks into the living room and rustles through a box on his bookshelf. His movement becomes frantic as he searches through the box. When he turns back to me without the letter in hand, anger hits me like a freight train.

This is a game to him. I'm a game to him. He doesn't want me to see that stupid letter because he's afraid he'll have to admit what this really has been over the past year. It would mean he has to admit that he's just another person in my life who thought they knew what was best for me. I thought I was finally making my own decisions—being selfish—but it turns out I was only being played.

Betrayal causes my eyes to sting, and once again, I find it hard to breathe. I thought death hurt, and it does, but it's a different kind of pain when the person you thought you knew—the one standing right in front of you—isn't that person. It's like facing a different kind of death, and I hate it.

"I—I can't find it. I swore I put it there, but it's not there. I promise, Georgia," Grayson pleads as he walks towards me. Those icy blue eyes I love so much are flat, devoid of emotion, and it's more telling than anything.

"When did you get it, Grayson?" I ask, my voice is cold, but I can't seem to change it. Every part of me is numb right now. It's my body's way of protecting me from the pain I know is coming.

He dips his head, staring at the floor.

"A year ago," he mumbles.

An icy pain laces through me, stabbing through the numbness.

"A year," I say quietly. I'm so stupid. "A year?" This time, it comes out as a yell as I leap to my feet. I can't take sitting here any longer. Pacing back and forth, I let the betrayal slice through me, opening each vein and causing me to bleed.

Every piece of anger I've been holding in since Nate died bubbles out of me.

I'm angry—so angry that I don't know what to do with all of it that's burning through my body. I'm not just mad at Grayson either. I'm angry at Nate, too—and myself. But the problem is, Grayson is the only one here for me to unleash that anger on.

Fair or not, he gets it all.

Grayson tucks his hand behind his back and has the nerve to look sheepish. He still hasn't bothered telling me what the letter said. Maybe he can't find it, but if he weren't ashamed, he would have already fessed up about what it said. That only leaves one logical conclusion—Harper was right.

Tears clog my throat, but I refuse to let them drip down my face—not in front of him.

Slowly, I approach him until I'm standing right in front of him. He looks up, his eyes roaming my face as he studies me, waiting for what

I have to say.

"I'm leaving," I say, slowly so he catches every ounce of hurt I'm throwing at him. "I'm going to get my stuff from my apartment and go back home—my home. You've done your due diligence. You kept your promise to Nate. Now you're going to make a promise to me. Don't follow me. I need space. You're always telling me to be selfish—well, here it is, I'm being selfish. Every letter I got from Nate felt like being run over by a train. Right now, I have too many feelings to sift through. I can't do that here with you. I don't want you to hurt, but at the same time, I'm hurting because you kept this from me. You kept it from me, Gray."

I want him to understand—no, I need him to understand why this hurts so bad. It has nothing to do with what the letter says. I'm sure that will hurt too, but this pain running through me has everything to do with the fact that he intentionally withheld something from me. It feels like every time the town tried to help me heal. They did so with good intentions, but ultimately, it was because they thought they knew better than I did about what I needed.

"I'm sorry," he whispers, and it's the final stab that sends me over the edge.

"The day Nate died, I learned that love isn't always sunshine and rainbows. Love is the single most painful thing I've ever experienced, and here you are proving that again because I did, Grayson—love you, that is."

His face melts into shock as the words hit him. My heart aches to wrap my arms around him and soak up the presence of his strength, but not this time. He can't save me this time, because this time, he was the one to break me.

Chapter 30

Grayson

Georgia loves me—but she left.

She *loves* me, *but* she left.

The words infiltrate my brain, but they won't sink in. Her car rumbled out of the driveway fifteen minutes ago, but I can't move from where I was when she left.

I should have told her about the stupid letter—I meant to. I was going to, even, but I was afraid of this—of her walking away. Now she's gone, and I don't know what to do. She asked for time, but I don't want to give her time. I want to drive to her house and make her talk to me, but that would contradict every time I've told her to be selfish—to find what she needs and take it. Pushing her won't help, so I'm stuck here, staring at the door, silently praying she comes back.

The silence rings in my ears, and I can't take it anymore. I pull my phone out of my pocket, dialing a number I never thought I would.

It rings several times. I'm about to hang up when my brother's voice comes from the other side. "Hello."

I can hear the confusion in his voice. He hasn't even been gone an hour yet. I struggle to put words to why I'm calling, but the truth is I don't know. It's not like Brooks can call Georgia and make her change her mind, but I just needed—someone. Georgia is usually my someone—so Brooks will have to do for now, at least until I can think of a way to get Georgia to talk to me.

"It's Grayson," I say, stating the obvious.

"No, really? I never would have guessed from my caller ID."

I don't have time for sarcasm.

"Why did you get your tattoo?" I ask, ignoring his attempt to be funny. I don't think he can handle the switch in conversation because silence follows my question.

Pulling the phone away from my ear, I check to make sure he's still there. It still shows connected, so I place it back to my ear and wait.

"It means—"

"I know what it means," I interrupt. "I want to know why you got it."

There are muffled whispers on the other side of the phone, and heat creeps up my neck as I think about Emryn on the other side, listening to the conversation.

"You know what? Never mind. I'll talk to you later."

My thumb hovers over the screen, ready to hang up, when Brooks calls my name. I don't answer, but I don't hang up. He must think that's good enough because he continues, "I got it as a reminder."

"Of what?"

My entire body aches with the pain of all the choices I've made in my life—all of them leading me to places of heartbreak. So, I have to wonder what Brooks knows that I don't because from where I'm standing, it doesn't seem like he knows heartbreak.

"Do you know that night I came to your office for an interview?" he asks.

"Yes. What about it?"

"That night almost led to my divorce."

Shock hits me in the chest. That night, I had been the worst version of myself. I thought Brooks was a deadbeat who'd come out of the woodwork, trying to take advantage of me and the success of my business. I'd been cruel at best, and when Brooks realized he wasn't going to get anywhere with me, he'd said he was only trying to save his family. He'd left after that, not looking back, and I'd chalked it up to him trying another angle to get the job. But then he'd gotten a different job and started reaching out without the position hanging over our heads, and ever since then, he's kept calling and showing up. Now we are here, and I realize I've been the worst kind of brother. If I were him, I'd hang up the phone and never speak to me again.

"I didn't know."

"Of course, you didn't know," he scoffs. "How could you have? I didn't either. I thought I was just walking into a job interview, only to meet my big brother, but I guess that's part of why I got the tattoo. We don't know God's plans for us, but we can guarantee they are meant for our good. It took me a long time to realize that."

"What about you and Emryn? How did you fix that?"

He chuckles—actually chuckles—like the thought of his almost divorce is funny to him. "With a lot of communication and work. We're still working on it, but I've found that God knew what he was doing there, too. He knew the woman he was placing in my life—someone who is kind and patient, and when I can't see who I am, she's there to remind me. But she also doesn't mind giving me a swift kick in the pants if I mess up, either. The biggest thing, though, is that we are a team. We work together and talk about things, even if they scare us."

I make a non-committal sound in the back of my throat, thinking about what he's said. I've held onto the strings of my life pretty tightly, never trusting that God had good things for me because I'd never gotten them in the past. Georgia was the first good thing in my life, and I screwed that up. Look at me go.

"Are you okay, Grayson?" Brooks asks, his voice serious for once.

"I'll be fine," I say, hanging up the phone, but it's a lie. My whole life, I've been good at running people off, pushing them out the door. It didn't bother me when they left, but this time, I pushed out the one girl I wanted to keep.

It's an hour after Georgia left, and I'm sitting in the middle of my living room, the contents of my whole house surrounding me. I've searched high and low for the letter, but I can't find it.

After talking to Brooks, I realized the letter is my saving grace. If I can get Georgia to read it, maybe she'll understand why I did what I did. Maybe she'll finally get that I've been in love with her my entire life. She questions that, and I don't blame her. It's not like I gave her any inclination before this year. I couldn't, not when she was in love with Nate, but despite that, I want her to know that I'm telling the truth.

The front door creaks open, and for a minute, my heart leaps to my throat, thinking Georgia's come back, but when I see Brooks's dark hair and shocked face as he takes in the drawers surrounding me, it slows to an unnatural rhythm—hammering to the beat of my heartbreak.

"What—uh—-what is all this?" Brooks asks, wincing as he looks around the house. Everything I own has been torn apart—couch cushions are lying on the floor, drawers are pulled out and turned upside down, and papers litter the floor. I can't find the energy to care, let alone clean it up.

"I was looking for something."

"I can see that," Brooks says, cautiously approaching me.

"What are you doing here?" Usually, I would give him some snarky comment, keeping up the brother banter, but I can't be bothered right now. My life is in shambles, and he's here to witness it.

Figures—feels like payback from the first time I met him.

"You called." He says it like it should explain everything, but it doesn't. Yeah, I called, but I never asked him to come back.

"And?" I ask.

"You called, and we're family. The Grayson that called me is not the same Grayson I left here an hour ago. I could hear the pain in your voice, Gray, and the Montgomery brothers don't let each other face pain alone—not anymore. I sent Emryn and Avery with Kip and turned around. You needed someone. It's as simple as that."

"My name's not Montgomery," I mumble, leaning against the bottom of the couch because I don't know what to do with his admission. I don't know how to let people in.

Brooks shoots me a look, pursing his lips and narrowing his eyes, but he doesn't address what I've said.

"Where's Georgia?" he asks, looking around like she might pop out of the disaster surrounding me.

Pain, unlike anything I've ever known, lances through my chest. It takes me a minute before I can breathe again.

"She left."

"Like left to go home or left, left?" he asks.

Cocking an eyebrow, I glare at him and spread my arms wide for him to look at the mess around me. "What do you think?" I ask.

"Okay, okay," he says, holding his hands up. Walking over, he pushes the papers off the recliner across from me and sits down. "Tell me what happened so I can help you fix this. I'm the master of communication now. Just ask, Emryn. I can help."

Sighing, I tell him everything—starting with the first time I saw Georgia and ending with her walking out. When I'm finished, he whistles between his teeth, shaking his head.

"That's a lot, Gray."

"Thank you, Brooks. That was very helpful," I say sarcastically.

"Sorry. So what's the plan? How are we getting her back?"

Smirking, I ask, "We?"

"Yeah, Grayson—we. I told you, you're a Montgomery now. You

don't do things alone. So where do *we* start?"

When Kip and Brooks came into my life, I never thought we would end up here—in a place where my relationship is starting to heal with my dad, and my brother is becoming one of my best friends. But here we are, and I don't regret it, despite how much I thought I would.

"I have to find the letter. It's my only chance of getting her to believe me."

A wide grin spreads across his face as he stands. "So let's find that letter."

And for a minute, despite the heartbreak of not having Georgia here by my side, a sense of peace overcomes me because I have my brother on my side—something I never realized I needed.

Chapter 31

Georgia

My hands tremble on my steering wheel as I take the last turn that leads to my house. My real home—the one that I've avoided for a year because going back meant having to relive the day Nate died again, and I wasn't ready for that.

Now, I need to be close to him—to find closure in the place he left me because maybe then I will understand what he was thinking when he sent that letter to Grayson.

Betrayal sits hot in my stomach. It was easy to accept that he thought I couldn't take care of myself when I was the only one getting the letters, but now that I know he trusted me so little that he had to ask Grayson to take care of me, too—it stings.

Memories run through my head as the house looms in front of me.

The day Nate and I bought the house. He'd swept me up in his arms and carried me across the threshold with a big smile.

The time he nearly fell off the ladder trying to hang Christmas lights for me. My heart had dropped to my toes, but he'd merely laughed it off.

Every time we sat on the porch, rocking in the rocking chairs and discussing the plans for the future.

Sometimes, I still think about what we would be doing now if he was still here, but those thoughts happened less and less when I was with Grayson.

Instead, I had started to imagine a future with him, and that's part of the problem—despite the letter, I'm still imagining a future with Grayson, but how can I have a future with someone who didn't trust me? How can I trust that he's not with me because of a sense of duty to Nate?

The cold starts to sink into my bones as I sit in the car, staring at a house I no longer have a future in. This place is full of ghosts now, and I've let the ghosts of what could have been haunt me long enough.

A knock at my window startles me, and I turn to find my neighbor standing beside my car. She's a frail, elderly woman but one of the sweetest people I've ever met. After Nate and I moved in, she made us a dessert every Friday and brought it over. I think she was lonely. Her husband had passed a few years before, and none of her kids ever came around. Guilt pricks at me because now I'm that person for her, too. I didn't check on her after Nate died, and I should have. It's one more place that I failed. The list is getting long.

Opening my door, I step out of the car to stand in front of her.

"Hello, Clara."

"Oh, Georgia, don't you be shy. Get over here and give me a hug."

She's shorter than me, so when her arms wrap around me, I have to bend so she can reach me. She smells like apples and cinnamon, and that smell is my undoing. Tears slide down my face as she holds me.

"I'm sorry I didn't come back to check on you after Nate died," I whisper as I press a kiss to her weathered cheek.

"Honey, don't you apologize. I know what it feels like to lose the other half of you. It's hard to see past that grief. I'm just glad you're back now. Besides, I've been getting updates on you from that nice young man who comes around every once in a while."

Pulling back to look at her, I ask, "What young man?"

"You know, that handsome one with all the tattoos."

"Grayson?" I ask, my heart picking up speed inside my chest.

"Yes—that's his name. I'm not great with names. I'm getting old, you know."

My brows dip as I consider what she's telling me. "Why was Grayson here?"

When she sees the confusion on my face, she chuckles. "Well, I guess that boy has it worse than I thought. I assumed he was coming around because you asked him to keep up with the place, but now I can see it was something else entirely. Look around you, Sweets. A house doesn't stay this organized when you don't come around for a year."

There's no judgment in her voice, but it hits me anyway. The truth is, I didn't even think about keeping the house up while I was away. I should have, but I didn't.

Looking at it with fresh eyes, I can see all the places Grayson has touched.

The grass is short, having been cut right before winter hit, and the posts that had been chipping with paint before I left gleam white with a fresh coat.

I was stupid—so, so stupid. Grayson has shown me a million little ways that he loves me, yet I ran the first time that Harper made me question that. I became another person in his life who didn't stay because I was afraid of losing him and having no control over it like I did with Nate, so I left before he could. My throat aches at the realization that I've created my own heartbreak here—not only my own, but Grayson's, too.

"I'll—uh—see you later, Clara. I'm going to go in now."

She pats my arm, a look of understanding passing through her eyes. "Of course, dear. Don't be a stranger, okay?"

I nod, the lump in my throat preventing me from answering, then walk up the steps of my front porch. With each step I take, I notice a new place that Grayson has been—there's no longer a creak in the bottom step, and a salt bag sits beside the front door where he must have come over and salted the sidewalk when it snowed.

The dread of how badly I've messed up sinks deeper into my stomach as I step through the front door into the house. Everything looks just like I left it, but instead of the layer of dust I was expecting, everything is clean—waiting for me to return to it.

Nate's jacket lies across the back of the couch, and I pick it up, putting it to my nose and breathing it in. If I concentrate hard enough, the faint smell of my husband's cologne still lingers, but it no longer comforts me as it once did. That comfort smell is how Grayson smells when he pulls me close. He smells like home to me now, and instead of being there with him, I'm sitting alone in a house that no longer holds anything for me.

There's only one thing that's keeping me from dropping everything and running back to him, and that's the realization that I've used him as a crutch for my healing. He's been by my side every step of the way, and my heart doesn't ache anymore because of him. But if I continue on that path, maybe one day he'll question if I'm with him because I love him or if I'm with him because he makes the pain disappear. I don't want him to ever question that, so before I go back, I have to find a way to heal myself.

Pulling my phone out of my pocket, I send him a text.

Georgia: *Give me time, okay?*

But when he doesn't respond, I wonder if my time is already up.

After realizing that I'd been relying on Grayson to heal, I scheduled an appointment with the therapist I started seeing after Nate died. Now I'm sitting in the waiting room, my hands in my lap and my knee bouncing to an unnatural rhythm.

It's been two days since I texted Grayson, but I still haven't heard anything, not that I blame him. I shouldn't have walked out the way I did. He didn't deserve that.

"Georgia." Dr. Burkes calls my name, and I stand to face her. She's not much older than me, and I initially hesitated to see her. I wasn't sure what she would know about grief besides what she found in a textbook, but the first time I met with her, she was kind, listening to all the things I was angry about without judgment. She didn't tell me that I shouldn't be angry or that everything would be okay. I hated that the most after Nate died. Everyone kept saying that someday I would be okay. Instead, she had sat and listened. When I was done spouting my anger, she told me my feelings were valid.

I'd needed that.

"How are you?" I ask as I walk past her into her office.

She gently smiles and says, "I'm doing well. It's nice to see you again."

Giving her a polite nod, I say nothing. It's been a while since I've been to her office. It wasn't that I thought I was healed, but I was getting out of bed. I figured that was as good as it was ever going to get.

I should have kept coming. Maybe if I had, I wouldn't be sitting here with a broken heart of my own doing.

We take our seats, me on the couch and her in a chair across from me.

Then, when we are seated, she asks, "So—what's new in your life?"

Scoffing, I think about the letters and everything that has happened since the first one, then say, "Well, you know—a lot."

It's the best summary of my life in the last few months.

Laughing, Dr. Burkes says, "How about we unpack it then? Tell me one big thing that's happened to you since I last saw you."

"I fell in love with my husband's best friend."

A shocked silence falls between us. Dr. Burkes blinks several times, trying to determine if she heard me right, and then a big grin spreads across her face. That was—not what I expected.

"I'm so proud of you," she says, her smile still covering most of her face.

"Maybe you should wait for the rest of the story before you make proclamations like that," I mumble.

Sitting back in her chair, clipboard in hand, she says, "So tell me."

A sigh slips past my lips. I haven't told anyone besides Grayson about the letters, and telling her feels like letting someone in on a secret only meant for him and me. But if I don't tell her, I'll be stuck in this in-between stage of grief and healing forever, and I don't want to be there anymore.

"I've been receiving letters from my husband for about three months."

Another shocked silence, then, "What–uh—okay? I have to say this is a new one. I haven't ever had this before. I'm going to need you to help me understand."

Nodding, I swallow hard before saying, "The letters have been coming in the mail. The first one was just—Nate's way of gaining control after he found out he had cancer—I think, but then they kept coming. Those were different. Nate wrote them after he found out he was terminal. Each letter had a new task for me to complete. He wanted to help me heal—even though he wasn't here."

"Did you complete the tasks?" she asks, carefully considering me.

"I did, but not alone. I asked Grayson to help me. Do you remember me talking about him at my last session? He was my husband's best friend—mine too, in a way." She nods but doesn't say anything, so I continue, "Anyway, at first, it was fine because the first task was simple, but then I got the second letter. Nate told me I had to go on a date. So, I asked Grayson to go with me because I realized that over the course of the year since Nate died, my feelings for Grayson had started to change. I thought the date was the best way to explore that—and it was, but I didn't anticipate Grayson receiving his own letter from Nate."

"And what did his letter say?"

I shrug, not wanting to tell her the rest of the story.

"You don't know, or you don't want to tell me?" she asks, leaning forward and resting her arms on the armrest of her chair.

"A little of both—I guess. Nate's sister is the one who told me about Grayson's letter. She said Nate asked Grayson to date me—or maybe it was take care of me. It is Harper we are talking about, after all. She practically hates me. Anyway, I don't know what it said because when I asked Grayson about it, he couldn't find the letter. I left after that."

She hums at this point and taps her finger against her lips.

I remain silent, waiting for her to drag the rest of the story out of me.

"There's a lot I want to discuss here, but let's start with what Nate's sister said. Did you ask Grayson what the letter said?"

"No." Heat blooms across my face.

"Why not?"

"Because he got it a year ago, and even after I told him I was receiving letters from Nate—letting him read them even—he never once mentioned that he had gotten his own. It felt like I couldn't trust him to tell me the truth about what it said."

"I think that's valid," she says, her eyes zeroing in on mine.

Her answer surprises me. "You do?" I ask.

She nods, keeping eye contact with me, and I try not to squirm under her gaze. "I do, but I also think that communication is important. Would it have made a difference whether Nate asked Grayson to date you or take care of you?"

I shake my head.

"Why not?"

"Before Harper told me about the letter, Grayson told me he'd been in love with me most of his life. I thought he was exaggerating that at first, but I think—I think that Nate knew about how Grayson felt. I don't know that, but it feels like something Nate would know, especially considering my other letters—and something he said before he died."

Her brows dip. "What did he say?"

"The day we found out he was terminal, I had a panic attack. I didn't want Nate to see, so I left his room and went for a walk. When I returned to his room, he was on the phone with Grayson. I remember they were talking about me, and Nate wanted to tell Grayson something. Then I came back into the room, and Nate got off the phone. I didn't think about asking about it. I was too lost in my grief. Then, later that day, Nate was being bossy and making demands, and I asked him if he had any others. He'd said maybe. I told him they had to be easy if he had any more. He'd said that love is always easy. I think maybe he was talking about Grayson then. I think that was his plan the whole time."

I'd forgotten about the conversation until last night as I was alone in our home. Then it'd come rushing back, along with the realization that I think Nate's been leading me to Grayson this whole time.

"You say that like it makes you sad."

I shrug. "Because it does. Nate and Grayson—they've both been doing the healing for me. I haven't done any of it on my own. I just—I need to heal on my own before I can think about being with Grayson."

"Are you thinking about being with Grayson?

"Yeah, I am because I realized there was never a question about whether he loved me. It was always a question of whether I would let myself be with him, and right now, the answer is no until I can prove to myself that I'm healed all on my own. He deserves that."

Dr. Burkes purses her lips. "How do you plan on doing that?"

Another shrug from me. "I guess that's why I'm here. I was hoping you would advise me on where I should start."

She sits and considers for a moment, and I worry my whole body might explode from anticipation.

"My advice," she says at last, "would be to talk to Nate. A year ago, you were in a different place. I advised you to talk to him—tell him about your life and day—now I think it's time you tell him about all your anger and sadness, along with the happiness that you've found. Then, and only then, do I think you'll be able to move forward."

"That's it? You think it's that simple?"

She laughs. It's light and merry, contrasting everything running through me right now.

"No, Georgia. Healing is never that simple, but I think it's the step you need to move forward with Grayson. When you do move on, you will have days that you miss Nate, and that's okay. You just have to continue to find pieces of yourself again. Find what makes you happy—not anyone else—and give yourself permission to feel it."

"What if I'm scared of finally accepting the reality of Nate being gone?"

Her face sobers as she looks at me. "Your options are—either accept that reality or let Grayson go. It's up to you."

Chapter 32

Georgia

It's Saturday morning, the day I always visit Nate. I'm getting ready and dressing up because I know this time is different than all the rest.

A knock at my front door has me putting down my curling iron and praying it's Grayson.

My entire body freezes when I get to the door and look through the peephole. Harper stands on the other side of the door along with Ellie. A rage I've never known before burns through me as I sling open the door and place my hands on my hips, glaring at Harper.

"What are you doing here?" I ask through clenched teeth. My tone is calm and controlled, but inside, I'm one comment away from exploding.

From beside Harper, Ellie asks, "May we come in?"

I take a deep breath through my nose and exhale slowly, trying to gain control of myself, but it doesn't help.

"You can," I say, turning my gaze to Ellie, "but she can't."

"Georgia—" Ellie starts.

"No, Ellie. I'm sure Harper hasn't told you what she said to me, but I'm done playing nice. I love you, but you have a habit of defending her because you feel sorry for her. I can no longer do that—not until she gets over her problem with me. I will not invite her into a home that already holds the worst possible memory for me."

Ellie nods, tears shining in her eyes but acceptance written on her face.

"I'm sorry." The words are whispered, and shock resonates through me as I turn to Harper.

"What did you just say?" I ask, my ears unable to believe what I just heard.

"I said that I'm sorry," she says, more confident this time.

She avoids making eye contact with me, her face flushed beat red, and in shock, I step back, opening the door wider for the pair to step through.

When they are inside, and I've closed the door behind me, Ellie nudges Harper with her elbow, prompting her to continue.

"Look," she says, finally making eye contact with me. "I should not have said what I did. It wasn't my place. I was having a bad day and took it out on you."

Crossing my arms over my chest, I glance to the side, refusing to look at her because my blood still boils when I do. "Every time you see me is a bad day, Harper. That's not the first hateful thing you've done to me, and I'm tired of just letting it roll off my back. I don't understand what I've ever done to make you hate me so much."

She lets out a long sigh, and I can hear the weariness in it. She's tired—maybe more than I have ever been—and that makes me sad for her despite all the hatefulness she's thrown my way.

"It's never been you, Georgia—at least, not really. When my dad left, Nate was the only good man I had left, and I was jealous that you got his attention. I was a young kid who was missing my dad and brother, and I blamed you for that. I let that blame fester until I hated you, but—I realize it was never your fault. I just needed a place for all my anger, and you got the brunt of it. Mom and I," she says, glancing at Ellie beside her, "we've had a long talk, and I'm working on it."

"How did you know about the letter?" I ask, not willing to accept the apology just yet.

Her face blooms redder than before, and I lean against the wall, waiting for her answer.

"That's—um, that's kind of why Mom's here. She needs to tell you her story first before I can tell you mine."

My gaze slices to Ellie, a slow panic building in my chest.

There's a tired smile on Ellie's face as she studies me.

"Can we sit?" she asks, and I nod, all my energy seeping out of my body.

The three of us walk over to the living room couch, and I sit in the chair beside the window while Harper and Ellie sit next to each other on the sofa.

Over the last couple of days, I've slowly started boxing up some of Nate's things, and tears swim in Ellie's eyes as she sees the boxes sitting in the corner.

"I was going to ask you if you wanted anything before I donated them," I say quickly, afraid she will be angry at me for getting rid of some of the memories of her son.

She must realize that because she shakes her head and says, "It's time, Georgia."

I nod and sit back in my seat, an ache deep in my chest. It is time, but it doesn't make it easy.

"What I'm about to say—-well, I just need you to promise to listen to me before you say anything, okay?" Ellie asks.

I bob my head, afraid to speak.

"Before Nate—passed," she says, pausing and stumbling over her words, "he—uh—he asked me to do something for him. He had found out he was terminal, and his time was limited. There was a day you needed to run some errands, so you asked me to sit with him. I did so willingly, wanting as many days with my son as possible. While I was here, he asked me to bring him a pen and paper. I'd argued, telling him he needed to rest, but he'd insisted. He said it was important, so I gave in. He sat up in bed with his hands trembling and wrote a letter. After he was finished, he asked me for a favor—one that I could tell meant everything to him."

She stops here, letting the puzzle pieces click together in my mind. My whole body is shaking, and I have to wrap my arms around myself to keep from falling apart.

"You are the one who has been sending the letters," I say, my voice quivering.

She nods and continues, "Nate was so scared you wouldn't be okay without him. He could see you floundering already, and he just wanted you to be okay. That boy loved you so much that he was willing to put himself aside to help you move on. I could see how much each letter caused him pain—both physically and mentally—but even when I insisted that he stop, he refused. He kept writing, and I was so proud of him for loving you like that. He was the man that his father could never be."

"Why did you wait a year to send them?"

A vice grip around my lungs makes it hard to get the words out.

"When Nate asked me to send the letters, he made it clear that I was to send them at my own discretion. He wanted me to send them when he knew you would be willing to listen to what he had to say. After he passed, I worried that time would never come, but then I saw how Grayson took care of you and how you let him take care of you. I knew that eventually, that time would come."

"Did you send Grayson's letter, too?"

A sheepish look crosses her face, and she dips her head, nodding.

"Did you—uh—did you ever read any of the letters?" I ask.

"No, Georgia, no," she says, shaking her head vehemently. "Those letters were meant for you and Grayson—never for me."

A flash of disappointment runs through me. It's not that I wanted her to read the letters. I'm glad she didn't, but at the same time, part of me still wants to know what Grayson's said—not because I don't trust him, but because I'm curious to know what Nate said to him. I turn my head to Harper, who is squirming in her seat.

"Your mom didn't read them, but you did, didn't you?" I ask, anger creeping back in.

She swallows hard and nods. "But only Grayson's, and not even all of it. It wasn't finished when I read it. I should have never told you what I did about the letter because it's not technically true. I mean, kind of it is, but I dishonored my brother's memory by twisting his words, and I'm sorry."

"What exactly did it say, Harper?" There's ice in my voice as I stare at her. She apologized, and eventually, I'll accept it. Not today, though. It's going to take some time.

"I—I can't remember."

"Convenient," I scoff.

"I promise, Georgia. I can't remember exactly what it says, and I won't get it wrong and twist Nate's words again. I'm sorry."

Huffing, I stand, and Ellie and Harper follow suit. Looking at Ellie, I say, "Thank you for telling me about the letters, and I should probably thank you for sending them too because they've saved my life—truly. I know it must have been hard for you, but I appreciate it."

She steps forward, wrapping her arms around me, and whispers into my hair, repeating the same question she asked me the day the first letter arrived. "Have you found happiness yet, Georgia?"

"Yeah, Ellie, I have. Now I just have to work on getting it back."

Pulling back, she smiles at me—it's genuine and loving. "I don't think you'll have to worry too much about that," she says with a wink as if she's in on something I'm not. "I have one more thing for you."

She reaches into her pocket and pulls out an envelope. The writing is that same elegant slope I've seen on every other letter, and I know in my gut that this one is the last.

"Thank you," I whisper.

Patting my cheek, she steps back, and I turn to Harper.

"I'm not ready yet, Harper, but I heard your apology. I appreciate it, and I hope that when I am ready, maybe we can find a new path and be friends."

A lone tear slips down her cheek, and I fight to hold back my own.

"I think I'd like that," she says.

"Me too." I offer her a small smile—a white flag for the feud I never wanted to have.

"We're going to go," Ellie says, giving me one last hug. "If you need anything, I'm only a phone call away."

When they walk out the door and I'm left alone, I squeeze the letter to my chest, aching at the thought that these are the last words I'll ever receive from Nate.

With one deep breath, I rip the top of the envelope and pull the letter out.

My name is written at the top, just like every other letter, and I have to sit back down to keep from falling. My heart beats in my ears as I begin to read.

Georgia,

This has to be my goodbye letter.

My body is shutting down quicker than I planned, and I'm running out of time. I can only hope my words have helped you so far. I want you to heal, baby. Don't be sad for me anymore—live your life and love. If this has all worked out the way I planned, that last one won't be too hard. Grayson loves you. He has since we were kids. Now that I'm gone, I hope you let him love you. He's the kind of man I want for you.

I'm sorry this letter is shorter, but I hope it has the most impact. I hope you can give Grayson some of the love you've given me, Georgia. You have a way of making a person feel seen, and he could use that.

Together, love each other and build a relationship in Christ. Those are the things I hope for the most.

I'll see you again.

Love,

Nate.

Sobs wrack my body, tears slipping down my face and dripping onto the letter as I read his last words to me. And as I fight for control, I place a kiss over Nate's name right where my teardrops have fallen.

It's time for one last goodbye.

Chapter 33

Georgia

The walk to Nate's grave is different today—the cold air is less frigid than it usually is this time of year. It's like the world is setting the stage for my goodbye.

When I reach his headstone, I kneel on the ground in front of him, tracing my fingers over his name in a loving caress.

"Hi, Nate," I whisper into the air.

For a moment, I let the noises of the world surround us, enjoying my time with my husband before everything changes.

"Listen, I got your letter—the last one, I mean. You're sneaky, you know that? All this time, you've been pushing me towards the man that's been there all along."

I sigh, turning so I'm no longer on my knees and sitting so my back rests against his headstone. The breeze blows my hair, and I imagine it's his way of wrapping his arms around me.

"I've been angry, Nate—so very angry—and I was mad at myself because I promised you I wouldn't be. But you were my best friend, and I didn't know how not to be. This whole situation hasn't been fair, and I hate that. None of us deserved losing you, but it was the hands that life dealt us. Grayson and I had to learn to deal with it. I didn't, though. Rather—I couldn't. I was lost in the dark, searching for a way out, but there was no light to lead me home, Nate—not until Grayson.

He led me home. He is home, and I think it's a relief knowing that you're okay with that—that you expected it even."

The words clog in my throat as I think about all the ways I've messed up with Grayson.

"I have to admit something to you, though, Nate. I messed up. I really messed up. Grayson—he's fragile, and I think I might have shattered him. We haven't talked in a while. I was a coward, and that's on me. I'm going to fix it, though. I have to fix it because I love him, Nate."

That confession burns. I never thought I'd be telling my husband that I love another man, but I know he'd be okay with this one. When the words are out, floating up to where Nate watches over me, the weight I've held on my shoulders since the day we found out Nate had cancer finally lifts.

I asked Dr. Burkes what it meant to heal on my own, and she said to talk to Nate. But I think the healing came when I finally gave myself permission to live without Nate. I've held back a piece of myself, even while I was doing what the letters asked me to, because there was still this sense of guilt on my shoulders because I was here to live and Nate was not. I get it now, though—the idea that I can live the life Nate never got to. By falling in love again and choosing to live my life, I'm honoring his memory, which gives me the peace I've been so desperately searching for.

Slowly, I stand to leave. This goodbye feels different than the others—like nothing will be the same after I leave—and I guess that's true because, with each letter, I've changed. I'm no longer Nate's wife—the girl he married after high school. I'm someone new—a girl he'll never get a chance to know. That no longer scares me like it used to.

"I'll see you next time, Nate."

Chapter 34

Grayson

It's been a week since I've seen Georgia. I'm miserable. She asked me to give her time, and I'm respecting that. She contacted HR and asked to use her vacation time this week, so I haven't seen her at work either.

"Uncle Grayson, Uncle Grayson," Avery yells in my ear from beside me.

"Avery, you're on a level ten. Maybe you can drop it down to a five, huh?" I say, rubbing my finger in my ear that she just pierced.

"You're so funny, Uncle Grayson. I'm not ten or five. Remember, I'm four," she says, pointing at a banner that reads "Happy Fourth Birthday, Avery."

Despite the ringing in my ear and the weight on my chest, I have to bite my cheek to keep from laughing. The kid is something else.

"You got me there, Avery. Now, what did you need?"

A sneaky grin slips onto her lips, contrasting her angelic face. Wariness overcomes me as I squint at her, trying to decipher where this is going.

"I told my friends how you let me color, and since it's my birthday, I thought we could color again," she says, hitching her finger over her shoulder and pointing at three little girls behind her—all armed with an array of highlighters and markers.

A groan slips past my lips, and Brooks chooses this moment to appear. He's wearing the same sneaky grin his daughter had on her face moments ago—now I know where the markers came from.

"Please, Uncle Grayson," Avery pleads from beside me, sticking her lip out and widening her eyes into puppy dog eyes until there's only one answer for me to give.

Sighing, I roll up my sleeves. "Fine," I say, as a gaggle of four year olds attack me.

Brooks's laugh is sinister, and I glare at him over the top of the girls' heads.

"Payback," I mouth, but he continues to laugh, walking away and leaving me to fend for myself.

Thirty minutes later, when every inch of my arms has been colored on, the girls finally release their grip on me, and I make a beeline to the kitchen, hoping to hide away. But first—my present to Avery.

Brooks stands in the kitchen beside his wife, dipping his finger into the icing as she swats him away. When he sees me, his face lights up, taking in the colors adorning my arms.

"Nice tattoos, Gray," he says, pure glee filling his voice.

I smirk and turn my head, calling Avery's name until she appears in the doorway.

"Yes?" she asks.

"Would you like to open your present from me now?"

Bouncing up and down on her toes, she squeals and rushes towards me. I pick her up and sit her in front of the counter.

Pulling a small box out of my pocket, I hold it and look at Brooks before offering it to Avery. As she rips into the paper, I say, "Now this is a gift—no takebacks."

The same wariness I felt earlier creeps into Brooks's eyes, and I can't lie—that look causes pure satisfaction to course through my veins.

Avery tears through the wrapping paper and then the box, and even though I prep myself for it, I'm not ready for the squeal she lets loose, piercing my ear drum when she sees her gift.

"Thank you, Uncle Grayson. Thank you."

"What did you get?" Brooks asks his daughter.

She turns her present towards her mom and dad and, with a look of pure delight, says, "Tattoos."

There's a stack of temporary tattoos in her hand that are a replica of every tattoo I have. The one on top is my favorite, though. It's the orchid I have on my wrist.

"Yeah, Uncle Grayson. Thanks a lot," Brooks says dryly.

I pretend not to notice his sarcasm as I say, "You're welcome."

Avery takes off to show her friends, and Brooks stays behind with me. I wait for him to chastise me, but he just rolls his eyes and stays silent. My form of punishment comes in a different way, though.

"Have you talked to Georgia?" Emryn asks, sending a dagger straight to my heart at the mention of her name.

Shaking my head, I remain silent, refusing to engage, but I'm learning that my sister-in-law doesn't back down easily.

"Why not?" she asks. "Brooks helped you find the letter, right? That was the plan: find the letter and show Georgia. So why haven't you shown her?"

Narrowing my eyes, I look at Brooks and say, "Your wife should have been a lawyer." Then I turn my attention back to Emryn to answer her question. "She asked me to give her some time, and that's what I'm doing. She has to come to me this time because she needs to know she's strong. I want her to make the decisions that are best for her because she knows they are—not because I've pressed her into making them. And that's what I did when I didn't tell her about my letter before I agreed to help her with hers."

Emryn nods and chews on her lip, looking suspicious, but she turns her back to me before I can examine it further. I'm about to ask her what that look means when the doorbell rings.

"Brooks, I need you to help me with the cake. Grayson, can you grab the door, please?"

"But I—" Brooks starts, but Emryn turns her head and sends him a withering glare, so he closes his mouth and nods.

Suspicion prickles up my neck, but I don't question it. Spinning out of the kitchen, I walk to the front door—my heart racing a mile a minute.

Through the glass, I catch a glimpse of raven hair, and the racing stops, slowing until I can count each beat.

Wrapping my hand around the knob, I wrench open the door.

"Hi, Grayson," Georgia whispers, and I feel that greeting all the way to my toes.

My girl has finally come back to me.

"Can we talk?" Georgia asks, jerking her head towards the steps on the front porch.

"Of course," I say, a mix of joy and trepidation running through me as I step outside and follow her to the steps.

This past week without her has been miserable. Having her beside me now is like stepping into the sunlight for the first time after a long winter. She's my sunlight—the part of me that makes every good piece of my life brighter.

She lowers herself to the top step, and I sit beside her. I want to reach out and rub my knuckles along the skin of her jaw, but I keep my hands in my lap instead, letting her come to me.

"How did you know I was here?" I ask, careful to keep any emotion out of my voice.

A blush creeps into her cheeks as she looks down at her lap. "Emryn."

"Of course," I grumble. It comes out harsher than I mean it to, and Georgia must take it the wrong way because her shoulders sink in defeat.

"We sort of started to become friends after the first time they visited your house. We exchanged numbers, and she started texting me. I hope you're not mad. I'm sorry I didn't ask you how you would feel about that. I should have," she says in a rush.

"Georgia," I say, placing my hand on hers, unable to hold myself back any longer. I need to feel her skin against mine like I need to breathe. "It's okay. That's not what I meant. I meant she was acting suspicious—like she was up to something. I wasn't trying to hide from you. I forever want you to know where I am."

Her eyes meet mine, a flicker of hope lying in those green irises.

"Really?" she asks, and I can't help the disappointment that stabs at my heart. I'd hoped she understood how important she is to me since she is here, but she still doesn't get it. As much as I don't want it to, that hurts. My whole life, I've been trying to prove myself to someone, and I'd just hoped that Georgia was the person that could see me. Despite that, though, if she needs reassurance, I'll offer it to her every day of my life as long as it means I get to keep her.

"Really, Georgia," I say, reaching into my pocket and pulling out my wallet.

Curious, she tracks my movements, causing her brows to dip as she watches me.

With my wallet in hand, I pull a slip of paper out, holding it between my middle finger and forefinger. I extend my hand to her, and realization dawns on her.

"Is that Nate's letter?"

"Yes."

"You found it?"

"Brooks helped me," I say, and a look of surprise crosses her features. "It's a long story. Take it. Read it."

She shakes her head, her hair falling across her face as she does.

"I want you to, Georgia."

The set of her face becomes more determined, and she gives one more stiff shake of her head.

"No, Grayson. Listen to me." She takes my hand and holds it between hers, trapping the letter in between us. "I had no right to demand to see that letter. I should have trusted you—I do trust you. I was just—scared."

"Of me?" I ask. The thought sits like a lead balloon in my stomach.

"No," Georgia says vehemently, shaking her head and hair spilling around her. "Never you, Gray.

"Then what?"

Her teeth sink into her bottom lip, and I hold my breath, waiting for her answer.

"Of myself, mostly. You're right—I tend to make decisions because other people want me to, but you—you're the first decision I've made in a really long time because it was something I wanted. You are something I want, and when Harper told me about the letter—I was just afraid of losing you. If you were only with me because Nate asked you to—well, it was only a matter of time until you realized we couldn't live our life like that. But here's the thing, Grayson—if I had been listening to you, really listening to you, I would have already known that you weren't going anywhere. You've shown me that you love me in a million little ways, and I ignored those signs because I was too busy being eaten alive with my own guilt."

"Guilt?"

Her sigh is heavy. "At first, it was guilt because I felt things for you that felt like a betrayal to Nate, but then I started getting his letters. I realized that he didn't want me to spend the rest of my life being lonely, but I still felt guilty because I didn't think he meant to move on with his best friend—when I found out that was exactly what he meant—well, I was upset with myself because I wasted so much time holding myself back from you. You deserve everything, and instead, you've given me everything."

A lightness I've never felt before in my life feels my soul. It's like coming home.

"Oh, Georgia," I say, pulling my hand from hers and dragging her towards me. She comes willingly as I lift her and place her on my lap. "You've given me more than you'll ever realize. You've been the light guiding me home my whole life. This last week has been dark without you."

She dips her head to my shoulder, and tears fall onto my shirt. "I'm sorry I left, Grayson."

"Read the letter, sweetheart. Not because I think you need it to trust me, but because I want you to have that final closure—leaving no other secrets between us. But fair warning, once that happens, you're mine forever. I won't let you go again."

Lifting her head from my shoulder, she smiles at me. "Do you promise?"

"Always, Peach. Always," I say, placing a kiss on her temple.

With her still on my lap, I wrap my arms around her waist and stand, handing her the letter when we are both on our feet. She takes it from me, her hands trembling.

"Are you sure?" she asks.

"Yes, because I have nothing to hide, and I want forever with you. Take your time, and when you're ready, I'll be inside waiting for you."

She nods, and I give her one more kiss on her cheek before turning and walking back inside.

Only a few minutes separate me from the rest of my life with the girl of my dreams.

Chapter 35

Georgia

I watch through the glass door as Grayson retreats down the hallway, the letter clenched tightly between my fingers. Coming here today, I wasn't sure how Grayson would feel. Once again, though, he's proven that he's a better man than he's ever given himself credit for.

Once he's out of sight, I sit back on the steps and hold the letter in my hand, folding and unfolding the corner until I gather the courage to open it up.

The folded lines are worn, and I'm careful as I unfold it so I don't rip it.

Grayson's name is written at the top in Nate's neat handwriting, but seeing it doesn't hurt nearly as much as it did the first time I saw it in my letters

I've come a long way since that day, and I think Nate would be proud. I'm proud—and that means a lot on its own.

Gray,

If you're getting this letter, it means I'm gone. I'm sorry I couldn't be the one that stayed around for you, man. I want you to know I would have if I could, but if everything goes as planned, you will have something better.

You're one of my best friends, and because of that, there is something I need you to know.

You're a good man, Grayson Lewis.

I know the town continuously reminds you of your past, but you are more than that angry kid with a chip on his shoulder. That's hard for you to believe—I get it—but it's true. Keep that part in mind when you read this next part, okay?

I need you to do something for me, and it's big—probably the most important thing I've ever asked of you. But I need to start with a story, something you've never heard from my side.

When my dad left, I was a sixteen year old kid. I could have been angry—heck, I should have been angry, Harper was, but for me, I was just numb. The man I looked up to my entire life up and left. I finally understood what it felt like to be you, and even though I know how you felt about her, Georgia made me feel something. She was this bright star, shining through all the black spots that were happening. I can't say I regret loving her—it would be a lie—but I regret that it put out some of your light because I did.

Yes, Grayson—I knew. I've always known you loved her, too, but I needed her light, and I may not be sorry for loving her, but I am sorry that it made you feel unworthy because I did.

This is where the favor comes in, and it's the second selfish thing I will ever do. I need you to take care of Georgia—not just take care of her, but take a chance at love with her. You deserve to date her. And marry her. Have lots of babies together. But most of all, make her happy. This isn't just for her. It's for you, too. Don't just take care of her. Let her take care of you. You've stood on the sideline while Georgia and I had our happy ever after. Now it's time for you to have yours. You are her friend, and I think she could love you one day. All you have to do is show her the side of yourself that you never show anyone else.

You're a good man, Grayson Lewis. Don't forget that.

Love,

Nate

When I reach Nate's name, I wipe my sleeve against the back of my cheek. It comes away with black smudges across the fabric from the mascara running down my face. The day Nate's dad left is the only day I ever remember him without a smile. The next day, it was like nothing had happened. He went about his life smiling at everyone and taking care of Ellie and Harper. I was too young to recognize the pain he was hiding then, but I loved him the best way I knew how.

And as far as Grayson goes, I guess I was too naive there. I never recognized the feelings he had, but looking back, I can see it now. He loved me in all the ways his brokenness would allow, and when Nate stepped up and we started dating, Grayson stepped aside because he thought Nate was the better man.

Honestly, I'm not sure how to feel about all this because to say that I wish things had been different for Grayson—that he had felt loved during that time—means that Nate and I may have never had our life together, but I want good things for Grayson—I always have.

The thing is, I may be confused about the past, but I'm not about the future. I want all the things that Nate mentioned in the letter. I want the dates, and the ring, and the babies—and I want them all with Grayson.

When Nate died, I gave up. I didn't want to dream anymore, but he's healed me through his letters, and Grayson has helped—but mostly, I've finally healed myself enough to let love in again.

Chapter 36

Grayson

My family is gathered around me, singing Happy Birthday to my niece.

Kip is to the left of me, his hand on my shoulder like a proud father, and I've finally accepted that it's exactly what he is. When I first met him, I cast him as the bad guy. I was willing to let him be the villain in my mother's story, and the truth is, he probably was—but that doesn't mean he has to be the villain in mine. I want to get to know him and let him get to know me.

Brooks and Emryn are on either side of Avery, smiling at their daughter with pure love on their faces as they look at each other. There's a tightness in my chest as I watch them. I hope my life looks just like that with Georgia by my side one day. It's the future I want for us—the one I pray we can find.

The door to the front door squeaks open down the hall, and I watch, holding my breath with my heart beating so hard that I'm afraid if anyone were to pay attention, they would see it through my shirt. Just when I'm worried I may pass out from the anticipation, Georgia appears in the doorway, and it's like my heart whispers, "There she is" at the sight of her.

There are streaks of black under her eyes where she's been crying, but my eyes are drawn to the smile on her face. It's watery and a little sad, but when she sees me, all that sadness disappears.

Kip claps me on the shoulder and moves aside as the singing ends. Georgia walks towards me, slipping in beside me and wrapping her arms around my waist, and as Avery blows out her candles, I make a wish too—or maybe it's a prayer because I've come to realize that while a lot of things have been hard in my life, God made sure I had good things too. He gave me Nate and Georgia, and when I lost Nate, he left me the girl standing beside me—so I pray that he keeps giving me the good things with the bad, and I'll take it all in stride with the sweetest peach I've ever known.

Georgia pushes up so that she's standing on her toes. Leaning in, she whispers, "I want forever, too."

Then she kisses my cheek, and I know I've made it.

"I love you, Georgia," I say, turning my head to capture her lips with mine.

Her words are mumbled against my lips when she says, "I love you, too."

"Ewww," Avery says, turning away from her birthday cake and catching me kissing Georgia.

"Yeah, ewww," Brooks adds, placing his hand over his daughter's eyes.

Lifting my head from Georgia's, I glare at Brooks. "Is there a return policy on little brothers?"

"Not on your life, Gray. Not on your life," he says, punching me on the shoulder and making a run for it.

With Georgia still in my arms, I watch him run away, my narrowed eyes tracking his movements. Georgia laughs, jarring my attention back to her.

"Go on," she says, dipping her head towards where Brooks just disappeared through the door.

Laughing, I press a kiss on her forehead and take off running after the brother I never realized I wanted.

Epilogue

Grayson
6 months later

"Are you sure you know what you're doing?" I ask again.

Avery rolls her eyes, "You've said it a hundred times, Uncle Grayson. I know what I'm doing."

Sweat gathers in my hairline, and I don't know if it's from the heat or my nerves.

Georgia will be here any minute, and I have to get myself together. Brooks dropped Avery off this morning, and I didn't mention my plans to him when he left. If I had, he would have stuck around for sure.

A car door closes on the other side of the house, and now there's no question—it's the nerves.

Taking a deep breath, I bend down so I'm face-to-face with Avery. "It's show time, kid. You ready?"

"Duh," she says, and I almost laugh. Brooks is going to have fun with her when she's a teenager.

The back door slides open, and Georgia steps out onto the deck. She's radiant in the summer sun. Her dark hair hangs loose around her shoulders. She's wearing cut-off shorts that show off her summer tan and a tank top. Even dressed down, she is beautiful.

"Georgia, Georgia," Avery yells and waves her arms like a mad woman, as if Georgia can't see us standing right in front of her.

This is going spectacularly already.

"Cool it," I say out of the side of my mouth to Avery. "You're making us look suspicious."

Avery turns her head and raises one eyebrow. "I don't know what that means, Uncle Grayson."

"Nothing," I say, nerves building by the second. "Just follow the plan."

"You got it," she says, giving me a thumbs up and bringing more attention to the fact that we are up to something.

Georgia approaches, a grin on her mouth and suspicion in her eyes.

"What's going on, guys?" Georgia asks.

"Avery has something to show you," I say, putting my hand on Avery's shoulder and guiding her forward so she's standing in front of Georgia.

"You do?" Georgia asks, kneeling so she's eye to eye with Avery.

"Yup. Uncle Grayson says it's something important, but I can't tell momma because she will yell because he gave me another tattoo—and the last ones took forever to come off."

Standing behind Avery, I groan—trying again to remember why I let Avery in on this secret. I think she has some kind of cute magic because when she saw my new tattoo and begged me to tell her the story, I couldn't resist those puppy dog eyes. When I told her the story, she insisted on being a part of this, and here we are.

"Well, don't wait," Georgia urges. "Let me see it."

Avery flips her arm over, showing Georgia the tattoo.

There's the orchid that matches mine, and underneath it, in cursive letters, it says, "Aunt Georgia."

"Will you be my Aunt Georgia?" Avery asks, and I step up so I'm standing beside them.

Dropping to one knee, I pull a box out of my pocket and take Georgia's hand. Tears are shimmering in her eyes as she watches me push up my sleeve to reveal a small peach beside the orchid on my wrist.

"Avery wants you to be her aunt, but I want you to be my wife. You promised me a favor when I let you drive my truck, and I'm calling it in. Peach, will you do me the favor of spending the rest of your life with me?"

She bends down, taking my face in her hands. "Forever, Gray. Forever.

Avery cheers beside us, clapping her hands and giggling.

Standing, I take Georgia in my arms and thank God for best friends and second chances.

About the Author

T. Bell writes real and relatable romance novels with all of the swoon but none of the spice.

You can connect with me on:

- https://www.facebook.com/profile.php?id=100091232274801
- https://www.tiktok.com/@authort.bell?_=8fvlXcapeBu&_r=1
- https://instagram.com/authort.bell?igshid=YTQwZjQ0NmI0OA==

Also by T Bell

Letters of Grace

Redemption

Printed in Great Britain
by Amazon

58644407R00145